The Case of a Night Detective
(Death Shall Follow Night)

By Jay A. Harris

The Case of a Night Detective

(Death Shall Follow Night)

A Novel by Jay A. Harris

Markata Publishing

Cover: Licensed Stock

First Edition

Second Printing

ISBN 979-8-9863556-1-0

Chapter 1

Body of Evidence

Narrated by Trémeur "Tray" DuChaine

I watched Veleta Robbins squatting in near darkness, her rear close to scraping ground as she circled the crime scene. The feathered beams from our sedan's headlights gave her little help on this night. With her flashlight at eye level, she was still an inspiration, but one I didn't always care to follow, especially while wearing a clean pair of shoes. She, on the other hand, I had a feeling was never embarrassed about getting dirty. An attractive sister, the typical man couldn't see beyond her loose two-piece men's suits, short hairstyle, and neckties, hers now dangling through the weeds. As impressive as she was, I stayed propped against the sedan parked on a gravel road while she did her thing. Almost twenty yards away I saw the entire scene just as clearly from where I stood. Sprayed chalk lines and police tape wrapped around leaning pine trees were as bright as day to me. Even traces of luminol stood out, but to *my eyes* only. By the outlines, you'd think a hiker and her dog had been "smoked," gunned down, but this was far from the truth. Well, half as far.

The bodies had been removed two nights before; we'd already seen all the crime scene photos—gruesome, every last one of them. A seventeen-year-old girl's body had been found after being mauled by a crazed dog—more like mutilated according to the photos. Bloody gashes ripped across both her neck and chest, a bear attack seemed more likely. But two local boys, each in their upper teens, who'd taken claim to the rescue attempt, both had reported they'd caught the dog in the act, followed by blasting its brains across the trees. The question now was why Veleta and I, two Louisiana Bureau of Investigation agents, had been sent out to investigate an animal attack in Livingston Parish? And why after-the-fact in the middle of the night? The answer was complicated.

Two days earlier, the night after the attack, I went to the coroner's lab to view the girl's post-mauled body. Due to the unusual nature of the crime, she'd been taken to a medical specialist at the Baton Rouge coroner's office. The lab's acrid fumes consumed me as soon as I entered, and remained in my senses for hours afterwards. On the stainless-steel table lay her cadaver, still shredded, now a pale blue. Whether by dog or bear, it was all pretty difficult to believe.

"I know what you're thinking, Mr. DuChaine," the medical specialist, a doctor, said to me. "You're thinking not even a wild dog could have done this."

That was weird. Were my thoughts *that* transparent? "Something like that," I said.

"And you'd be correct in thinking so. The depth of bite indicates the jaw pressure of a wolf, but the spacing, the vast number of canines... more like... something not of the animal kingdom at all." He dipped his head, where he rolled his eyes and a smirk in my direction. "If you catch my drift?" Much like his dramatic cadence, his stare lingered as if I had the answer.

"Hmph." I didn't have much to say, because I *didn't* have an answer. Interestingly enough I'd seen a lot of bite wounds over the years, but never one like this. "Could it have been from a rabid domestic dog?"

"Unlikely. However, we *did* test for rabies right away, but found no signs. And there was something else unusual."

"What's that, Doc?"

He pulled out the original photos of the dead German Shepherd mix and handed it to me. "Lots of blood on the dog's muzzle... very little on its teeth."

I glanced it over a few seconds, but I didn't get it; I even wondered: *Dog takes a chomp, dog licks its chops—what's so unexpected about that?*

"There's more," the specialist said. "There were absolutely no dog hairs on the girl's body—not one strand. And the saliva samples— totally inconclusive."

I felt my brow flex. "That—is pretty interesting."

Now here in a wooded Livingston neighborhood, a place almost forgotten by modern times, the reason for Veleta's presence and mine was clear: something of unknown origin had emerged and needed to be stopped. I remained against the car with my arms now folded. Still squatting and swaying side-to-side around the site, Veleta continued inspecting with her flashlight now as far out as her arm could stretch.

"I guess someone like you doesn't need much illumination here, h'unh?" she asked without looking back.

"Just go on," I said, "pretend I'm not here."

I didn't need to say it; she was already too deep into corralling the scene to expect any response. Soon, continuing like I was nowhere around, she mumbled towards the contorted outline as if the young victim were still twisted in it, "Sad. Didn't your Uncle Jimmy teach you not to walk alone in the woods at night, 'Little Red Riding Hood'?" Veleta may have been mumbling, but I'd heard her clearly. She aimed her light closer and brushed a few leaves aside before snapping a phone-photo. "Did anyone notice—"

"The brushed-over footprints?"

"Yeah..." She took another photo.

"Yep. They sure did."

"Hmph. Then did they notice—"

"That they're barefooted?"

"Wow, what's it been? Two whole weeks and already we're finishing each other's sentences?"

"I'm finishing yours, actually."

She rose up with her sights glued to the ground. "Yeah... So, why hasn't this been mentioned?"

I huffed, having already wondered the same. "Well, our local predecessors seem to think: due to the severity of the *bear's* attack, all human involvement has been ruled-out of the equation. That's pretty much how they put it."

"And did these *predecessors* happen to find *bear*-prints anywhere?"

I tightened my forearms and squinched. "You do know where we are and who we're dealing with, don't you?"

"Granted, but—" She threw up her hands. "Well, was either of the boys barefooted when they found her? Like, did they match either of their shoe sizes?" Only a mild pause came between us before she went absolutely ballistic. "Jesus, man, help me out here!"

By then, I was too busy looking at the old porch-house where the road dead-ended. "You know what? I believe all our questions will be answered after we take a short ride up this road right here."

After our short ride, that old house didn't yield the "golden egg" I had expected. Per reports, it was where the two teenage boys who'd found the body lived—there with their aunt, Mary McCullup. Unfortunately, no one was home, not even a light was on. Two strangers knocking on the front door at night may have been a good reason for anyone to take cover. Yet even if a mouse was sleeping inside, I would have heard it.

Coming up empty didn't sit too well with Veleta either, at first exasperated, and now asleep in the passenger's seat as I drove us back to Baton Rouge. Her snoring was the only activity on I-12 that late at night, but faint enough for me to reflect on the backstory behind this entire evening, and before.

The victim was Lolly Baker, the niece of Livingston's Council-President Jimmy "Slim" Baker. Slim, a man who bore no resemblance to his nickname, had also been skeptical of the rabid dog attack theory, but for other reasons. In turn he had called in the L.B.I. over his own sheriff, but never did Slim expect any of it to lure in the State's new V-Unit, and the "V" didn't stand for "victims."

Next to the medical specialist, both Veleta and I were Louisiana's masters of bite-wounds, also for different reasons. We'd known one another in passing for a few months and had only been partners a couple of weeks. Throughout, her composure had been commendable, downright incredible if you ask me, considering she had been riding one seat away from the L.B.I.'s first Vampyrian agent. A "V" was what I was called for short, and my kind's presence was no longer a myth. Together, Veleta and I formed the first ever Vampyrian-Unit, V-Unit for short, another initiative to desegregate humans and Vs since the Vampyrian-Human Treaty had been signed years ago. It had all come in the wake of Ichorstim, a nutritious additive that kept drawn-plasma stimulated—virtually alive—and the key factor in restoring our citizenship since the nineties. We were now post 2015, and although the resulting relations had been tolerable, they didn't come without a twinge of discomfort, especially for humans. Nonetheless, combined with support groups and therapy, Ichorstim had proven to be the perfect appetite-killer for us Vs. As a new-age V, I never needed much therapy; that was saved for the older ones, the geezers.

On the other hand, Veleta's steely nerves were a mystery to me, and she was never forthright about her process. Assignment to the Unit was meant to be a shit-job for her, a new female agent to the L.B.I. And with Vs' activities being less controversial these days, it was also a job that had seen little-to-no action until now—making it an easy decision for her male-dominated higher ups in Baton Rouge. "No biggie. Stick the butch-dyke with the fucking bloodsucker for a while," was what I'd heard them say behind closed doors. *Assholes,* was what I'd felt like saying to them. "Butch-dyke"

was something I would have never thought or repeated to Veleta. But all-in-all, she'd been taking the entire experience like
a trooper, a well-versed one. Sometimes it was like riding
around with a fanatic. This woman knew things about V-
history I didn't even know.

Veleta was a rookie only to the bureau, but having
served a brief prior stint as a Baton Rouge police investigator,
detective work wasn't new to her at all. Me, I was an army-
vet, eventually police-trained once the local chapter of the
Vampyrian Council had approved the union. The V-Council
saw me as one of very few Vs still connected to humanity—
making me their first recommendation to serve the L.B.I. But
not everyone saw my connection as favorable.

The next day after our night in Livingston, I returned to the
coroner's lab where I stood over Lolly's corpse for our last
viewing. This time Veleta was beside me, her nose stirring
around the table just like at the crime-scene back in the woods.
Whatever was trickling through her probing mind, I was con-
ducting my own type of study from one spot. Lightly touching
Lolly's wrist, I closed my eyes and inhaled deeply; my senses
were searching for a memory, but not my own. Several empty
seconds passed before my thoughts were broken by a man's
voice.

"Agent DuChaine?" the medical specialist, the same
one, asked while entering the lab.

"Wha'?" I withdrew my hands like a thief.

"Can I help you all with anything else?"

"No, Doc," I said. "It's still a mystery."

Veleta and I were back in the sedan heading to the Bureau
soon after, and it was late afternoon. If there was any wonder
about the daylight thing, this wasn't a vampire flick. The true
virus left behind as many varying traits in its carriers as the
DNA it attacked. The sun was torturing, blistering, even instantly boiling to some, but to others, only mildly irritating. I
was one of those others. But to even things out, Coppertone
was making a fortune off its new niche clientele, some who
walked around coated and shimmering like "Goldfinger" just
to taste sunlight. *My* sheen was only lightly applied. Now, the
ageless thing, that wasn't a myth. That was totally real.

    "What was that back there?" Veleta was peering at me
from the passenger's seat.

    I glanced in my rearview mirror. "Where?"

    "No, not behind us. Back in the lab."

    "What exactly?"

    "That thing, that thing… with the meditation."

    "Oh. Nothing. Just profiling. Collecting thoughts," I
said flatly, which wasn't a complete lie.

    "Well, did anything come to mind?"

    "Mmm, nope."

    But if her stare were an ancient-forged sword, I would
have been stabbed in the brain. "I heard about your type," she
said, wagging her finger like a switch.

    "My *type*? What are you talking about?"

    "Detection of the residual spirit. I read about it. You
have it, don't you?"

    "I don't have a clue what you're talking about."

    She had me. Beyond physical traits, some of us were
left with other gifts, the most popular being hypnosis, but still
rare. Mine happened to be catching a glimpse of the residual

soul, imprinted memories left behind by a spirit frightened shitless. It was a rare ability too, one that yielded nothing this time, far too long after Lolly's soul had left the stratosphere. It was something I rarely, if ever, had discussed with any human, and I wasn't going to start here, not even with my partner.

But Veleta wasn't the type to give in easily; she recovered like Ali against the ropes. "I bet you can hypnotize folks too, can't you?"

"Wrong."

"Yeah, right. Go ahead. Try me. I'm ready," she said while twisting in her seat, her eyes wide and battle-ready like fiending for a fix.

"Got-damn, Woman! What is this, a *fetish*?"

"Hell no! Don't be ridiculous! I just need to be prepared in case we come up on one of your *friends* out there in the dark. So, come on, try me. I've trained for this."

"Well, if we're after *anyone*, it won't be one of *my* friends. Plus, if you've really been studying, you'd know that that trait is more common among Old World Vs. And even if I could, which I can't, I'm driving right now. But I'm sure someone with as *trained* a brain as yours wouldn't feel a damn thing."

Veleta shifted back straight into her seat and looked out her window. "Wuss. And you bet your sweet ass I wouldn't," she mumbled. Several minutes passed before she spoke again. "So, you think we oughta head back out to the woods tonight?"

Having had more time to mull things over, I tucked my lip; my fingers danced atop the steering wheel. With the nature of those bitemarks and footprints, we may have been dealing with a V hyped-up on some damn drug no one's ever heard of—maybe a son-of-a-bitch I wouldn't have been able to even handle. Whatever it was, I wasn't going to let Veleta get mixed up in this any further. *Hell, we could be dealing with something monstr—*

"Tray!" she blurted.

I flinched. "What?"

"Damnit! How many times do I have to call your name? I thought you guys could hear *everything*! Were you even listening to me?"

Apparently not. "What?"

"I said, 'Are we going back out to the woods tonight?'"

I stroked my chin with only one solution: "Yeah… about that…"

Later that evening was one I had to travel alone, leaving Veleta behind and unaware I was back on that same backroad in Livingston Parish. As much as I respected the kid's spunk, instincts just short of a big brother's had overtaken me—or a *father's*, based on our true age-gap. I ended up feeding her the "hot date" excuse just to escape without any more questions, but I was sure she didn't believe me. It wasn't like I ordinarily broadcasted my love-life. Consequently, it wasn't my most trustworthy moment either, but a necessary misdemeanor from my point of view.

Chapter 2

Voodoo Dust

Narrated by Trémeur DuChaine

"Eerie is the road often traveled by the loner," was something my mother used to say to me as a kid whenever she caught me kicking rocks by myself. I never knew where she got it from, but these days it was fitting as I drove up that Livingston backroad. I had a hunch, one that took me to a house Veleta and I had passed the night before on the way to Mary McCullup's home. Unlike Mary's house, this particular one was closer to "Cape Cod" style, and in decent shape for being nearly a hundred years above ground. It was the Watsons' residence, home of the assumed guilty party, now deceased.

"Ole dawg whatn't nothin' but a damn mutt! He ain't never hurt anybody! I don't care what them ole racist-ass fools up the road say!" This was what "Ole Man Watson" contended after I'd approached him about the incident. "It was still *my mutt*, though," he said. "Them fools shot my dawg for nothin'! And ain't shit we can do about it either." Rocking in a patched-up chair on his front porch, he didn't seem to care it was early evening. And by his foul mood, he had plenty more to get off his chest. "Now, we been here *way* longer than everybody else—all these fools. And they *still* been tryin' to run us out o' here. From plain ole hard looks to the damn county tryin' to trump up all kind o' crazy-ass property taxes." He looked towards the house at the end of the gravel road. "To them makin' all kind o' bullshit-ass noise complaints. *Shi-ee...* it's been as quiet around here as a tree fallin' with nobody around to hear it. And it been that way ever since we moved here." He rocked to a complete stop as his eyes inflated. "But you know what?"

I leaned in with nearly the same intensity. "What's that, Mr. Watson?"

"We ain't goin' nowhere. We here to stay." His mouth switched to a confident grin while his chair went back to rocking.

Meanwhile, standing behind the front-door screen was a handsome kid, an older teenager in fact, who rolled his eyes and himself back into the house once I noticed him. I had a strong feeling I was looking at Lolly Baker's distraught boyfriend, the reason she may have been tracing back home through those woods. Now, "intuition" did not come with any of my viral traits; I preferred to think it had been with me since birth.

Mr. Watson glanced back when he heard the screen-door slam, then rolled his head and eyes back around towards me. "And these here kids," he said, "we try and teach 'em how things ain't never really been changin.' But they don't never listen."

I couldn't disagree. "Hmm... by the way, if you don't think it was your dog, what do you think did it?" I leaned forward again, expecting nothing less than pure entertainment from his assessment.

"*Welp*—"

"Did you hear anything?"

"Uh, no... but you know, them ole black bears be rootin' around out there from time to time. That would be my guess. Shit, and my dawg probably whatn't doin' nothin' but runnin' that ole bear off—then tried to help that poor little girl out afterwards. That's what I figure. Poor thing. Both of 'em."

I knew from the bitemarks it wasn't a bear, but Mr. Watson's guess was more farsighted than any local law enforcement's efforts.

I ended up listening to more of his unique perspectives and intel, like how none of Lolly's relatives had taken too kindly to her "takin' up with my boy," was how he'd phrased it.   And his *boy* was actually his grandson, not his son. I also learned, according to Mr. Watson, how Council-President Slim Baker really felt.

"Ole *Slim Jimmy* didn't give a squat on a pointed rock about Lolly," Mr. Watson said, "and that there was because of her daddy." He paused to check behind himself before lowering his tone. "Her daddy was the downright drunk o' the family, and Lolly beared the brunt of his wrong-doins.' Plus, I'm sure they got wind o' her and my boy off seein' each other from time to time—black boy and a white girl and all. But ain't nothin' wrong with that, right?"

I shook my head with my chin shrugged, also smiling inside for guessing right about his grandson. But it was hard to believe Slim's feelings had *truly* been transferred onto Lolly. "Anyway, thinkin' all this mess might be somehow tied together, ole Slim called in the *big boys*," he said while pointing at me, "over his own Sheriff, another deadbeat-ass relative." Mr. Watson paused with a look more suspicious than curious. "Now, you gonna tell me whatever you find out, right?"

"Mr. Watson, it sure has been a pleasure talking with you." I stood up and pulled a card from inside my blazer. "Here. Please take one of my cards. And don't you hesitate to call me if you hear anything else."

But he stared at me with one brow lifted and a grunt. "Mm hm..." Suspicious until the end.

The moon was full by the time I'd left Mr. Watson's house, and just enough light was hovering for me to roll up the road with headlights off. Mr. Watson, a wise *old brother*, had painted a neighborhood picture I needed to see, while also re-introducing me to a "hatchet" not even a treaty could bury—racism. Although, very few Vs of any ethnicity had ever shown much concern on the matter. For instance, since becoming V, I was rarely approached with this sort of racism anymore—never directly. Except for the occasional "stop-and-frisk" over the years, our current ostracism happened to be of a less oppressive variety—for obvious reasons. But there were always moments, like tonight's, to remind me of those sometimes happy, but often dreary days of my African American humanity.

Stopping at the edge of the last lot, it was time to give Mary McCullup and her nephews another shot. As I exited the vehicle, my luck seemed to be changing. Tonight, a shiny black sedan was parked on the far side of the house, almost out of view, while a light was beckoning from one second floor window.

I was sure my approach was as silent as the night air, until my foot hit the first porch-step. It wasn't that I was too noisy; it had more to do with the porch-lamp switching on and the front-door creaking open, as if I'd been expected. Behind the screen-door was the weathered face of a short elderly woman, one whose eyes rang familiar, taking me back nearly forty years to the late seventies. As young as she was back then, her eyes were wary but unafraid. Now staring up at me were those very same eyes, just as fearless, demonstrated by how boldly she had opened the door. The report and deed may have had the owner's name as Mary McCullup, but I remembered her as Rose, and even her scent was just as familiar. *And Rose, a racist?* I couldn't figure out what the old man was talking about. Rose had never struck me as that.

On this evening, as I stood on her front porch, I wasn't sure how much she'd actually remembered from those years, or how much of a spell she'd been under, so I composed myself before making somewhat of a reintroduction: "Good evening, Ma'am. I'm Detective Agent Trémeur DuChaine with the

Louisiana Bureau of Investigation. May I ask you a few questions about the incident three nights ago?"

"The what?" She practically sneered at me.

"The incident with the Baker girl? Have you heard anything about it?"

"Hadn't heard anything about a Baker girl," she grumbled as the door began to close.

"Uhh, as in Lolly Bak—er." The door was now closed and the lamp switched to off. I was left standing on an empty porch now gone dark.

As if Rose's response wasn't perplexing enough, I was downright distraught by the time I was back in my car. I sat inside thumb-tapping my steering wheel for nearly ten minutes before deciding to phone-in for a "midnight" search warrant. My finger was hovering over the last digit just before I switched to stretching my chin. *Wait a minute...* I had a better idea. This night may have taken an awkward turn, but if I was anything of a detective, I wasn't going to let it ruin my fun.

With moonlight still guiding me, I was out and softstepping towards Rose's rear lot with only one other thought: *And why not? I've come this damn far without permission.*

Deep in the backyard were a few dilapidated barnsheds and makeshift chickencoops scattered about. I heard the chickens scrambling around, but it wasn't from my presence. From the largest shed straight ahead, a deep guttural inhuman moan floated over the yard. One more, and the chickens went from scrambling to clucking, while the night shifted from awkward to weird. Turning around to the sound of a faint heartbeat and a moving shadow, I was about to get an explanation. It started and ended with the lady of the house blowing a handful of green powder up my nose. "What the hell!" I shouted—staggered back and forth. *What kind of shit did she just hit me with?*

Whatever it was, it traveled up my nose, into my eyes—blinding me from everything. *I* was usually the one in touch with my surroundings, the one able to detect motion, no matter how small or slight, but Rose had me somehow beaten. She was short, but nowhere near the smallest individual, so how she had gotten so close so fast had violated the new age of physics.

I swiped and smacked my face like a dirt-filled rug, now staggering completely backwards. As my eyelids grew heavy, I cranked down to my knees wondering, *Was that Rose?* And raging, "Did you just hit me with—*Voodoo dust*?"

The answer was in my next move, me hitting the ground and my conscious going dark.

Chapter 3
Luck and a Pocketknife
Narrated by Trémeur DuChaine

One of two fluorescent bulbs twitched into a steady glow overhead, enough to awaken me from whatever was blown up my nose. It felt like only a few seconds had passed, but based on my current predicament, it had to be much more; I was face-up and shirtless on a steel lab-table. Woven straps around my wrists, ankles, chest and head had me anchored down; my strength was zapped. And by the split rafters above, I was inside some kind of barn-shack and not alone. Muffled sounds around me shaped into voices with bad intentions. Although Rose's voice wasn't among them, she was definitely the one responsible, but I couldn't figure out why she'd done it. Whatever the reason, she'd made one big mistake: it was going to take far more than a few woven straps to keep a Vampyrian down. I was going to be out of these things in a blink.

It was time to do something I hadn't done in many years: I *growled* like a beast, feeling my strength burgeoning and my canines stretching from my gums. I then heaved my chest with all my might—but not a *got-damn* thing happened. The straps were just as tight and I was just as weak, so I heaved again, and again and again, only to end up completely out of breath. Either these straps were steel-reinforced or I was no longer the Vamp I thought I was—long removed from practice. When my breath returned, I figured out the reason why: that Voodoo dust Rose had hit me with must have been a "miracle" drug to take down a V.

"What was in that shit?" I mumbled, dizzied by all my attempts to escape.

My energy may have been depleted, but my sense-of-smell was still heightened. Inhaling another mass of chemical fumes, I was able to cut my eyes just enough to see beakers, syringes, scalpels, centrifuges and heart-monitors. The barn-shack was a lab, and the crappiest one I'd ever seen. Most walls were naked down to the studs, while others were covered by assorted panels, some crooked. From behind the stringent odors seeped a different kind of scent, a sweet aroma I usually tried to ignore—the sweet aroma of human blood that used to drive most Vampyrians to starving depravity. Nowadays, it was the sensation that drove many to those therapy sessions I'd mentioned; and right now, it was making for one huge-ass psychotic break.

That sweetness reached its peak when a lean, hump-backed elderly man wearing a lab coat stepped between two boys, each maybe seventeen- or eighteen-years-old. The slimmest teen was holding a shotgun; the stout one, a chain-saw. Both must have been Rose's nephews, seeing her now standing in the background in a humbled posture, nothing like the woman who'd just attacked me. It was all still daunting, nonetheless, and now even worse as those prior inhuman moans resumed, this time much louder from deep in the barn's shadows.

I couldn't deny it; the entire scene had me pretty spooked, especially when the old man made his intentions fully known. "Perhaps you shouldn't have come here alone, Detective DuChaine," he said on his way to a side-table, where he stopped and lifted a few scalpels and bone-cutters one-by-one. "But I'm glad to see such a willing participant in the name of science. You will make a prime subject for deconstruction. And don't worry, Detective, your name will live on in the annals of medical history as the one who saved an entire race from extinction." The classic mad scientist whipped himself away in dramatic fashion. "Now, off with his head!" he said to the heaviest nephew, who stepped forward and yanked the chainsaw's chord.

I was nearly out of my wits when the saw rumbled towards me. *Off with my head? Deconstruction? Sounds like this motha' fucker has plans for some kind of reverse engineering shit!* As wooden stakes through the heart proved long ago to be nothing but V-acupuncture, decapitation was the only way to silence me forever. But this mad scientist apparently had no idea what would happen afterwards, and I had no desire to be his first demonstration. With time ticking, I glanced down, but saw nothing but an empty holster at my side. My piece was now laying atop a table beyond my feet. And as the nephew approached revving the motor, I saw and heard more than the chainsaw smoking and screaming.

The Rose from before had returned, her arms lifted towards the roof, her voice raging into a crescendo: "Praise to the true gods who will raise from the dead their chosen people! And as the chosen ones, the son of Satan's head we offer as atonement... atonement for our failure to enshroud the heretics who have opposed you! And for this, we ask that your chosen Aryans rule the Earth once again and forever more!"

I couldn't believe my ears. *Rose? With a bunch of got-damn Neo-Nazis? When did—how did this happ—*

With the steel table turning into a sacrificial alter, I no longer had time for the how's and why's. That's when it occurred to me: they may have disarmed my handgun, but they apparently didn't check everywhere. My hand was just close enough to work another weapon right out of my pants' pocket—my pocketknife. It may have seemed like an uncanny stroke of luck, but a sharp blade was something a brother from the seventies, especially one from the country, never left home without. Meanwhile, between Rose's incantations and the inhuman moans in the background, no one noticed me rapidly cutting away at the strap.

The humpbacked scientist stepped aside for Rose to issue the last command. "To Varuna, Indra and Agni," she cried out the names of gods they'd stolen, "we deliver to you the son of Satan!"

As the chainsaw fell, I'd cut through just enough strap to rip right out of it and block the spinning bar with my forearm. Seeing my own flesh splatter into the nephew's face, I slung the chainsaw into the back wall. A second later, I was totally unstrapped and off the table; Rose's dusty potion had worn off.

The nephew gasped, but before he could move, I grabbed his throat and bared my teeth. It would have been easy to tear into his throat, but some interesting things were going on around us. Mainly, from the corner of my eye, I noticed the other nephew with his mouth wide-open, obviously freaked-out by the whole scene. But I saw neither Rose's or the scientist's face—only their backsides as they raced out of the barn.

"Move it, Mary! We'll finish him off later!" I heard the scientist shout.

"But, but, but, what about Wilbur and Billy!" Rose yelled.

"They'll be fine! Let's go!"

It was just from a mere glance, but never had I seen two humans move that close to V-speed—much less two over seventy-years-old. My arm was already healing enough to employ my own special trait. Not exactly hypnosis, it was still effective in solving odd mysteries, and this was the oddest ever. With my hand wrapped around the nephew's neck, I grabbed his forehead with my other and dove into his mind. *Metaphysically, that is*. Once inside, I sifted through the waste to find only the memories I needed, and inside those was a dark secret—a man hunched over a body in the woods.

Chapter 4

Buried Thoughts

Narrated by Trémeur DuChaine

Right before my eyes, Lolly Baker was alive but
not well. Pinned beneath a man I assumed to be
human, she was gurgling for her life. Taking a
closer look, the man could have even been a V,
except he was oddly gnawing away at her throat
instead of siphoning from it. It was something I
had never seen before, and surprising since the
intake mechanism was usually automatic.
Whether first-timer or not, no training was ever
needed to know where to puncture and how to
drink—like genetic memory.

There was a reason I was there: my hand
was still attached to the stout nephew's forehead,
deep inside his memory like an invisible guest—
a silent guest. From the nephew's perspective, I
witnessed the attacker pause and turn his head,
displaying something else I'd never seen before:
a full row of skewed fangs, all nearly equal in
length and dripping blood. He snarled, while exposing a hideous skin-peeled face, dark veins
pulsating from temple to throat, and a hairless

rippled skull. Neither human, V, nor animal, this thing was something different.

"What we gonna do, Billy?" the stout nephew asked the other one.

"Shit, I don't know, Wilbur."

"Well, brother, you got the dang gun! Ain't you gonna shoot 'um?"

But Billy paused. "Now hold on just a second." And several seconds did pass as the beast turned back around and dove back into Lolly.

"What are you doin'? Ain't we gonna save that girl?"

"What? And kill him? Shit... that ugly mother fucker right there is our ticket outta' here, while she ain't nothin' but a tramp-ass whore out here messin' around with a bunch o' black-ass s'owns-o-bitches!" Billy paused even longer, waiting for Lolly to gasp her last breath. And by the end, he had never lifted his shotgun. Instead, he went to his pickup bed, returned dangling a heavy-duty chain and began whistling a hypnotic tune.

After a hard twitch, the man-beast dropped Lolly's limp body before turning and hobbling over to Billy, where he humbled himself enough to be chained and loaded into the bed of the truck.

Flashing through Wilbur's mind like the pages of a book, I ended at him and Billy later returning to the murder-scene, both of them now with shotguns in their hands. This time, the Watson's dog was sniffing and whimpering around Lolly's dead body. It was an opportunity Billy couldn't pass up; he raised his shotgun along with a hideous grin towards the dog. "Say cheese, boy," he said just before blasting the dog with a load of buck-shots.

With me deeper inside Wilbur's mind, both he and I had tensed up at the blast. We next watched Billy turn-on his cellphone's flashlight, the only piece of modern technology found in these parts. He began backing up, stirring the leaves on the ground with his foot.

"What'cha doin'?" Wilbur asked.

"Coverin' a few tracks, dummy," Billy said before hurrying over to the dead bodies, where he squatted to wipe the blood from Lolly's throat.

"Now what in the hell are you doin'?"

Billy went on to smear Lolly's blood onto the dog's muzzle. "I seen this here on that damn forensic show."

Wilbur shook his head. "You's a real genius, ain't—"

Before he could finish, Billy had leaped to his feet so fast, even I felt his fear as he jumped back and re-aimed his shotgun.

"You fuckin' s'own bitch!" Billy blurted at the bodies.

Blocked from view, Wilbur raised his own shotgun. "What happened?"

"Fuckin' dawg tried to bite me!"

It turned out the Watson's dog had been resurrected, having taken one last nip at Billy's finger.

"Do you much blame 'um?" said Wilbur. "What'cha gonna do, shoot 'um again?"

"Hell yeah!"

"Why? It ain't like he gonna tell no-body!"

"No, but this here'll teach 'um a fuckin' lesson for tryin' to maul me, *and* for takin' up with the wrong color folks!" Billy had mustered up just enough frustration to unleash the fatal shot, with me feeling more than both boys' emotions, but somehow the buck-shots too.

Back in the barn-lab, Wilbur and I were both lying on the other side of the room—Wilbur now as motionless as Lolly, and me wondering what in the hell had just happened. Feeling my own ribs, I realized, my side really *was* filled with buck-shots.

Billy had risked it all to blast me off of Wilbur, but at a severe cost.

"Wilbur!" Billy cried out. "Wilbur, you alright there, brother?"

There was no answer. Billy didn't know it, but I knew right away there was no heartbeat either. Wilbur was dead. A few pellets wouldn't have killed him, but as I looked closer, buck-shots weren't the reason. Wilbur lay crumpled in a corner with his neck twisted and broken from just my sudden twitch. None of this mattered to me at the moment, since I was already beyond rage. I rose to my feet and heaved my entire torso, popping buck-shots out of my skin as my fangs stretched longer than ever. Meanwhile, those hideous moans still grew louder, now agitating every one of my senses.

With eyes wide, Billy stepped back and shot me straight in the chest this time, but that only staggered me. I kept towards him, until stunned by what happened next: the man-beast, the same one from the woods, had lunged from the shadows and straight into Billy's throat. Not only was he the source of the hideous moans, but obviously the mutated result of their first reverse-engineered V attempt. While the beast clamped down, Billy squeezed off one more shot from just reflexes alone—not only accidentally shooting me in the leg, but also causing the beast to flinch deeper into his neck.

As one-sided and brief as their struggle was, it gave me plenty of time to limp away and grab my sidearm. I loaded it with a special cartridge no one here had recognized. In fact, no living human knew of Vyrotellum cartridges, tranquilizing agents to Vs only. Sure, I could have whistled Billy's taming tune; it was fresh in my memory. But I was certain *my way* was going to last a lot longer.

I approached the mutated beast, who dropped Billy like an empty sack, but protected him like it was his last meal. And when I raised my gun, something else became noticeable. Even under the twitching lights, the mutation's own twitches were now incessant compared to those in the woods, and obviously painful. Again, I noticed something I didn't catch before while in Wilbur's brain: the mutation was now wearing an electronic collar to keep him confined—the source of every twitch.

In truth, I felt sorry for the poor guy; I even paused to wonder: *Does anyone know where he came from, how he's lived, and who he's loved? Hopefully, our Human/V alliance will somehow have him restored to normal.* Then just as he was about to lunge in my direction, I made up mind. I pulled the trigger, figuring a regular dose of Vyrotellum would lay him to sleep instantly, and that it did. But seconds later, it was doing more than just tranquilizing him. After a series of convulsions, his body went totally stiff, while from across the room, I heard no heartbeat. The only thing left alive was that damn collar, which never stopped buzzing.

I stood in awe as his row of fangs slowly shrank to human size and shape, and his rippled scalp returned to a smooth bald finish. What was once a mutated beast was now a man again. *That was amazing! What I have is from a damned virus, but this is some kind of magical shit!* Except, this man on the floor in front of me was dead.

"Fuck," I mumbled. "Who's going to believe me now?"

In just those seconds after I'd pulled the trigger, I had had my entire story already prepped and ready: *mad Neo-Nazi scientist and his gang of "woodrats" concocted a formula to create a mutant Vampyrian strain; mutant monster got loose and killed the town's head honcho's niece; backwoods "Billy Bob" and "Bubba" framed the neighbor's dog, figuring dead dogs wouldn't talk; while they all eventually fell victim to a chain reaction of events like falling dominoes.* But now with only dead civilians lying around me, I was the only one left standing—the only one with an empty hunch. Come to think of it, who would have believed me even if the last domino hadn't have fallen?

I found the rest of my clothes tucked away in a corner, and to my surprise, neatly folded. I couldn't for the life of me figure out where Rose had found the generosity to even consider doing such a thing. After redressing I paused before dialing on my cellphone. *Wait a minute... there's no way this is a job for the typical L.B.I. contractor.* This mess required a more unique style of cleaner.

Both my chest and leg had healed up while waiting for Henri ReGett, a legendary "cleaner" in V-circles. Luckily, residents in this neighborhood were no strangers to late-night gunshots and other creatures only hunted by night. This gave me plenty of time to think with no interruptions. I even took time to search the main house, but found no signs of Rose or the mad scientist, and no signs of the shiny sedan that was parked on the other side. With even more time, a few other thoughts came to mind, one being: *What better place than a dump to conduct such a controversial experiment?* It may not have been a total success, but it was much more than expected from any human.

Once Henri arrived in his dinged-up van, I poured out my story as he started cleaning. Even he, a V with nearly one hundred years' experience, scratched his head in between laying out body bags. "That there is a story I ain't never heard before," he said with a stiff Cajun accent, "but I know you to be one who shoots straight from the hip, Agent DuChaine, so I figure I have to believe you. Plus, it make plenty o' sense. You and me both know how the Klan and them new *Swastikas* still racin' to be top dawgs. And since we went full plasma-bag on 'em, ain't no hope o' that happening, is there?"

I took a deep sigh. "I know, but nobody really expected them to get *this* far with a plan B either."

"Huh," he chuckled. "Did either one of us expect to be a V by now?"

Henri's question may have been lighthearted and rhetorical as he kept cleaning, but he definitely knew about the dark side of Louisiana culture. Like me, he was from Lafayette, but that's where our commonality ended. Henri was an early nineteen-hundreds Cajun. Not only that, he was one who'd been to quite a few Klan meetings. To elaborate on racism and more, being turned had a tendency to change one's point of view, especially with regard to prior allegiances. And in those days, with it came a certain amount of indifference to the entire human plight—sometimes total disdain. The adopted V-family was the only group who'd take new Vs under its wing and coach them along, while bestowing upon them its last name. An "un-legal" name was our word for it.

I'd only seen Henri twice before this night, so I didn't know his name prior to "ReGett." But I knew he had been cleaning human crime-scenes in and around Baton Rouge since the Armistice, with some as far down as New Orleans. He was so damned good at it, the next time I looked up he was finished. Each nephew was body-bagged and draped over each of Henri's shoulders, and the deceased mutant had already been loaded into the van.

"Well now," Henri said, "I can't advise you on what to do with this here lab, but I guess you'll have to figure that one out for yourself."

Henri ReGett had left me behind with a mystery too complex to relay to human ears. That's when my cellphone rang, displaying a number every V in South Louisiana knew by heart.

"Yes?" I answered without hesitation.

"The Council needs to see you, DuChaine. Immediately," a rare but familiar male voice said on the other end, and he wasn't talking about the L.B.I. or a city council.

"Yeah, but can't this wait until tomorrow night?" I wished he could have seen me trying to rub the hair right off my head.

"No. Tonight." His tone was as abrupt as his discon-nection.

Only one council operated this late at night, and I was sure they weren't happy about what had just transpired. It was no surprise that Henri had pre-reported the incident to them before arriving; this was his customary duty. Yet per my adoptive family's protocol, we had only sworn to *answer* the Council's call, not to always *comply*. But as emotionally and physically spent as I was, I felt no choice but to hear them out, regardless of the time—for the night was a Vampyrian's day.

Chapter 5

Two Kids from the Flats

(a.k.a.—Those Consequences)

Narrated by Delroy Jackson

It was late 1975 when I returned home to Louisiana from the war. Many soldiers had already returned a half-year before, but this particular war hadn't quite ended when history said so—not for us arriving home this day.

It had been a long ride from South Carolina, the place our return-flight had landed—the place we'd received America's true reaction: pure vitriol. Throughout the trip, I didn't know why, but some of us had still filtered to the back of the bus where I'd sat with my head pressed against the window. Perhaps it was where we could express our real feelings quietly in peace. Although most of the ride, I'd sat there with nothing to say, and only two memories running over and over through my mind. The first being Viet Cong SKS and AK-47 bullets shredding through the reeds of South Vietnam, capped off by the one that had found temporary lodging in my thigh. This might have sent most folks home, but a brother was simply patched back up and sent right back to the same mother fucking jungle. My second set of memories involved my beautiful Tasha, the girl I'd left behind—the real reason I'd never lodged a bullet into my own skull. I was fortunate to return with only one gunshot-wounded thigh, and just as fortunate to step off the Greyhound with only a slight limp.

The fanfare was light when we deboarded at Lafayette's downtown bus station, but not much more was expected. Very few people in the laidback deep South carried either joy or spite for our cause. For the most part, parades were replaced by indifference, especially for a bus carrying Negro veterans. But just as I'd prayed, Tasha was one of the very few people there waiting, her smile dissolving all my pain. Her beautiful face and perfect brown frame met me with a soothing hug, reminding me I was still alive, followed by a passionate kiss for the letters I'd sent.

Tasha and I were good, virtually picking up where we'd left off. Both of us from the Flats, we were surrounded by an abundance of French Creoles and Cajuns, but we were cool with mostly everybody; we got along as best we could. For me, Vietnam and all the books I'd read between gunfire had made me as close to worldly as a brother could be, while Tasha was slightly older and already smart beyond her years. We were good, but the rest of the story about the seventies you know: love was free. But that kind of love came with consequences. And *man, those consequences—man*, did they cost.

It all started several months later when Tasha and I had heard about a jazz festival more than a hundred miles away in New Orleans. Its reputation had been growing so fast, we decided to take a trip in my fresh and clean '72 silver Thunderbird. With the top down, we were the envy of the highway, both of us drawing the ire from those who believed they alone owned the road. There *were* the occasional pullovers by state troopers to help reinforce their claim. These had always been expected, but never comfortably. If it wasn't for my "Yes, Sir" act and my working "war-veteran" into the conversation, we'd probably still be on the side of that highway today.

There was more drama along the way when Tasha asked me, "What's up with that cough? Are you getting sick?"

"What cough? What are you talking about?" As much as I appreciated her concern, I'd never heard myself cough, not until that very moment after she'd just pointed it out. That's when it exploded out of control.

She threw up her palms. "*That* cough!"

I ended up coughing nearly a whole minute before I could muster-up an answer. "I don't know. Must be allergies."

Allergies were common in Louisiana, especially from one area to the next. I even coughed a few more times along the way, but the last time was when my beautiful passenger finally conceded. "Well, we're gonna have to go get that checked out when we get back."

I nodded towards her with a smile, and no doubt, I was looking at my future wife. From then on, I fought with everything I had to hold all future coughs to a minimum.

Once inside the New Orleans Fairgrounds, a popular horse-track except on this day, we grooved to the music of Professor Longhair, Allen Toussaint, Irma Thomas, Earl King and a few more. Their soulful sounds went on from early afternoon until evening fell. But the crowd was only modest by then, as it had been most of the day, which was surprising based on the lineup. That's how I knew those left behind were the true music fans. Either that or the fruity alcoholic beverages were wicked and sneaky.

As the sun reached its final moments and I gazed down upon Tasha, I knew it was time. I was going to look for a ring and pop the question the first thing tomorrow morning. My eyes may have even been saying it, but Tasha's eyes were somewhere else, staring in another direction. When I looked over my shoulder, in plain view were those consequences I was talking about. They emerged in the shape of a slim but curvaceous woman; her sinuous hips and hypnotic eyes seemed to catch everyone's attention, Tasha's and mine included. Beautiful in a psychedelic front-knotted blouse, the woman was fine from belt to bells in her jeans, her skin-tone as dark as ours while carrying Creole features. Without realizing, Tasha and I ended up *entangled* in her midst, both of us winding with her in between. It was like we both felt what was happening, but couldn't stop if we wanted—both of us under her spell.

By late evening, after the festival, the three of us ended up off the beaten path in the French Quarters, where we stumbled around with drinks in our hands. And with the trip this woman's weed was sending us on, we didn't give a shit. Still hugged up between us, her supply seemed endless as she kept pulling one joint after another from, *God only knows where!* She had even said a lot of things along the way, but all I remembered hearing was one: "I got the stuff dreams are built on, baby." That was just before sliding one beneath each of our noses. Those words hung in my memory more than her name, and if hanging with a nameless woman wasn't strange enough, an hour later was when things really got weird.

"Yo, I got to go sit down," I said before crashing down on a metal bench just outside Jackson Square, too damn "high" to feel a thing. Ladylike giggles then tickled my ears like blissful waves as Tasha and the woman took a seat on each side of me. They started talking to each other like old friends, but handsy ones, alternating from caressing each other's fingers to rubbing on *my* chest—my nipples, even—to tickling my ears for real. Everything they said after that was pretty fuzzy, until the moment I heard the woman ask my girl: "You mind if I take a little sip?"

"A what? A *sip*?" No longer with drinks in our hands, Tasha seemed confused, but did nothing to stop the woman from leaning over my face to steal a kiss. Her lips were so supple, even more so than Tasha's, but me saying it would have been as taboo as just going with the flow. So, I reciprocated, surprised to hear what Tasha really thought: "Negro, I know you diggin' on this."

Meanwhile, the chest-play continued from both until I flinched, but not from their little impromptu massage. "Ouch, shit." I may have mumbled it, but something hurt like hell.

This woman must have bit a damn hole in my lip! Yes, it hurt, but I was just too damn "chilled" to move.

"*Oooh...*" I heard Tasha say just before the woman moved from my lips to Tasha's—right over me as if I no longer existed. It was even more shocking to see Tasha offering absolutely no resistance, the most passion I'd ever seen in a kiss. I simply shook my head. *Damn. I didn't know my girl got down like that.*

The strange woman returned to me, this time slowly sliding from my lips down to my neck. And when she bit into it, the pain didn't last long enough to try to stop her. It just turned into a rush, better than both passion and the weed. Out the corner of my eye, I saw people passing by, not many, but enough to goggle at a dude seemingly having the time of his life. A few even cheered me on: "Go 'head, brotha'! Get yours!"

Soon after, Tasha leaned back and folded her arms as I gasped and jittered in ecstasy. "Girl, what you doin' to my man?" she asked the woman. "That's gonna leave one helluva' hickey. You alright, Del, honey?" Those were the last words I heard from Tasha before things got hazy, next blurry, then totally black.

I didn't know about the hickey, but I knew things were out of the ordinary when I woke up on that same bench, the morning sun scorching like a furnace. Louisiana heat, I was used to, but this was something different. And although things were blurry, I could tell Tasha and the Creole woman were nowhere around. To add to the confusion, my neck was throbbing; both my mouth and throat were crumb-dry. And because I'd been severely wounded before, I knew what it felt like to be down several pints of blood.

It took a few minutes for me just to begin to feel my bearings. It must have been Sunday morning, at least I hoped it was only Sunday morning, but I also began to worry about Tasha and Loretta. *Loretta! That's her name! Hopefully, they went to find breakfast because they couldn't wake my ass up.* That would have been perfect, since my stomach was churning like a gatling gun. But the passing minutes turned into half-an-hour with no signs of either woman, especially Tasha. I was sure she wouldn't have left me stretched out on a park-bench, if waiting patiently for me to come home from war was any indication. With the bench getting lonesome, I *had* to find my girl, but I couldn't do it on the most upsetting bellyache ever.

After wandering around the Quarters, a sausage biscuit from a convenience shop was all I could find to ease the suffering. I couldn't even wait to get out of the store to bite into it, but once outside, it became tasteless and foul—gross enough to barf it out on the street.

Several blocks later, I realized more than just my girl was missing. *Where's my car?* My silver convertible Thunderbird was also nowhere to be found. I walked around for at least another half-an-hour thinking I'd destroyed a few braincells, but a quick self-pat-down proved even my keys were missing. *What in the hell? Grrrr... There goes that stomach again.* But this time it felt like a wild animal inside. That's when I folded over and poured out every bit of my meal from yesterday. "Ohhh..." *I feel like dogshit! One minute I'm having the time of my life, and now this? Damn, those motha' fucking consequences!*

I ended up wandering around until nightfall, a few times back to the bench, other times from edge-to-edge of the Quarters. All the while, I refused to believe Tasha would have just left me like this. She *had* to have had a good reason. *Unless... Oh, no!* She could have been mugged, assaulted, abducted, or worse. I couldn't bear to think about it. I just knew I had to find her. *Grrrrr—* "Shit!   There goes my motha' fucking stomach!"

Chapter 6

Uptown Sunday Night

(a.k.a.—More of

Those Consequences)

Narrated by Delroy Jackson

Nearly an hour later, I was on St. Charles Avenue in an area called Uptown, up the river from both the Quarters and Downtown—a spot where Saturday and Sunday nights were the same. I remembered it from being there one Mardi Gras week when I was a young boy, back when things were more "tame." For a young black kid from the country, the Zulu parade—its Afro-centric theme, its glittery-gold coconuts tossed from massive floats—was an experience I never forgot. But tonight, only trolley cars railed back and forth along the median—a far less festive scene, and worse with my throat as dry as parched ground. *If only I could stomach some coconut water right now.* I'd tried real water a little earlier, but it just felt like it steamed right out of my pores without the sweat. Meanwhile, my stomach was crying, punishing me to the point of forgetting to find a payphone.

The hours had passed and night had fallen. By then, I was still on St. Charles, now leaning against a light-post outside a liquor store, still trying to figure out how to satisfy the thirst, the hunger, even after trying scraps off the street. I didn't need a mirror to tell how exhausted I must have looked, but no one seemed to care. The way their eyes bounced away from me, I was nothing but a funky ole *drunk* to them. That's when I heard it: a steady beat pounding my eardrums when one of them passed by too closely. I even perked up when I heard it, but it started fading the farther a strange man walked away. It took me more than a minute to realize I was following him, and I didn't know why. It's not like *I* got down like that. But the closer I got, the more he smelled like he'd just eaten dessert. *Finally, something that smells tastefully sinful—Whoa! Where did that thought come from?* The smell could have been coming from the bag in his hand, so I took a whiff. *No, that's meat.* Somehow I could tell, as if my nose were actually inside the bag. But whatever that other smell was, I was instantly hooked on it. In the meantime, the beat just kept growing and growing, drowning out the offkey tune whistling through his teeth.

By the time the poor guy noticed me moving in from behind, we were a few blocks off St. Charles, the very moment my instincts started kicking in—instincts world away from human. It was the smell of his blood drawing me in, and just like Loretta's pull at the fairgrounds, I knew what was happening, but I couldn't stop it. I pounced, knocking the man behind a holly-dwarf bush. It may have been in someone's front yard; that part was fuzzy, but when my mouth fell onto his neck, I also knew I wasn't trying to plant a kiss. What I didn't know, was how my teeth had gotten so deep into his throat, deep enough to feel my canines sinking through his jugular into his carotid artery. His blood started flowing through me, carrying a sweet aroma and a savory taste, while his every jerk made it so much more titillating. Even with him being my first catch, I still felt the entire process: one tooth sending a venomous blood-thinning agent through his entire body, as I later learned, while the other tooth siphoned nearly every drop.

The man begged for his life, but that only made me bite harder and deeper, until I felt him tremble like a dying fawn. Through the sweet rush, that's what his body felt like to me—nothing but ensnared prey. At the time, I had no idea that my last sip would leave nothing behind to host life or the virus.

To a few folks passing by, two men behind the bushes were no huge attention grabbers, especially in those days. But to two other guys who stopped along the sidewalk, it seemed like they knew something different was going on. One even commented in a slow melodic tone: "This one here is *pretty damned hungry.*"

I didn't remember his words until later; my mind was too crazed to register anything at that moment, but I did remember my reaction. I remembered hissing at them like a night-prowling beast guarding its meal from two more predators. How I knew they were predators was a mystery, because as attuned as I'd suddenly become to the scent of blood, theirs emitted no distinguishable odor. They *had* to have been after my take, but when the shorter one aimed a hand-weapon at me, the last thing I felt was a dart in my neck, followed by shadowy darkness fading to absolutely nothing.

"Relax, my friend. Won't keep you tied down too long." Those were the next words I heard from the same man's mouth, his cadence still melodic—as rhythmic as the spoken word. "Just have to let the urge run its course before detoxification of the mind, body and the spirit begins."

But neither of us was on the side of the street anymore. We were in a dark room with a coffered ceiling, where I was propped up in a chair, unable to tell if it was for a patient or a dead-man-walking. What I knew for sure, it wasn't the least bit hospitable. My wrists and ankles were shackled to it by steel clamps. He, on the other hand, was leaning against a bookshelf in the far corner of the room, while a young, sandy brown-haired woman, a maid perhaps, whose eyes were wary but unafraid, swept the floor around the chair.

And neither of them was frightening to me either, but I still hissed, more so at my predicament than anything, only to be taken aback by the man's appearance. In his high twenties with dark flowing hair, a rock star's face, and his shirt open to a thin beaded necklace above his bare chest, he looked vaguely familiar. At first I thought I was looking at white Jesus, except for the clean shave. But another celebrity quickly came to mind, and I had to ask him, "Hey, aren't you… Jim Morr—"

"Casio DuChaine's the name," he said with no delay, "but I get that a lot."

Okay. Back to the matter at hand—*my* hands were still clamped to his "executioner's chair." A few more yanks and more questions came to mind. "What in the hell is all this?

Why am I here? What do you want?" I didn't know what kind of fucking detox he was talking about, but my struggle continued, this time with an animalistic growl.

"Well, Monsieur, first let me pose something to you. Do you recall what transpired last night?"

"Wha'?" It all started coming back on his cue: the attack, the savagery, the stranger's blood flowing through me. *Did that really happen?*

"Oh, it happened," he said.

I couldn't believe it. *Oh, my God, what's happening to me? What on Earth have I become? And did this dude just* read *my mind?*

The guy named "Casio" tapped his chin. "You're probably asking yourself what have you become?"

"What the—hey, man, are you in my fucking head?"

My suspicion was met by a look just as doubtful. "No, not at all," he said with a faint chuckle. "It's just that I've seen this a few times now. The look... the same. The thoughts... the same. The reaction... the same. Don't need to be a genius or a mind reader to see it... to know it... especially since it's happened to me." From the lick of his teeth, exposing a hint of razor-sharp canines, I had a feeling what he was referring to, but no strong grasp of any of it yet. Still, he continued, "As for what *I* want... can't say I want anything but the best for you, my brother—considering *our* unique condition."

"Condition?"

"Yes," he said, rising up and pacing the floor. "You see, you have been bitten by... a creature of the night. And by your state... yesterday, perhaps?"

I still couldn't grasp what this dude was talking about, but my neck started to throb again just from the insinuation. So much so, I no longer felt any pain from my war wound, and my cough was completely gone, as it had been the entire day.

Casio peered at my neck all the way from where he stood. "But no bite-wounds," he said. "Possibly inflicted by someone extremely crafty. A 'venomous vixen,' no doubt." His eyes went wild just before flicking and lifting a Polaroid photograph for me to see.

The photo's clarity and definition were alarming from all the way across the room. More so were the people in it: me posing between Tasha and "the viper," herself. *But when was that taken? And how does this guy have it?* Until now, I'd completely forgotten when it was taken by a stranger—an older man at the Fairgrounds. I even remembered what the old guy had said when he had handed it to me: *Live it up, young fella'! Live it up while you can!*

I moaned her name, "Loretta..."

"Loretta?" Casio's eyes flared again as if I'd insulted him. "Oh, you mean, Lady Artreaux. 'Loretta' happens to be one of her aliases—one of her *many* aliases. She makes her way back to the bayou during peak seasons—when she's looking for a little bit of New Orleans flavor, if you feel what I'm saying." I didn't, but nothing was going to stop him from dragging on. "Although, I'm surprised to see her this careless when it comes to leaving a visual trail behind," he said while shaking the Polaroid. "But yes, Ms. Artreaux is her name. One of the most powerful of us all, she is, yet she prefers to be an independent force of nature." Now, I was even more confused, but on he went. "Well, anyway, some would call what she's given you a curse, an affliction, a virus even. Those of the 'old school' variety might go as far as to call it... a gift. But I choose to call it a special *gumbo* with a little bit of everything mixed up in it."

Finally, I was getting the idea. "A drug," I said, now starting to feel groggy, this time on my own cue. "She drugged me, didn't she? Then last night was a hallucination, wasn't it?"

"Never heard it called a drug before, but last night, a hallucination? It wasn't."

"What? Oh, shit! The man... is he alive?"

Casio leaned back against the bookshelf and stroked his chin. "*That...* we'll discuss later. In the meantime, why don't you go on and get some more shuteye."

Back on his cue, I felt my body growing limp, my eyelids falling. "If it wasn't a drug, why am I so sleepy?"

"Oh, that dart we hit you with last night—" He stopped and looked at the cleaning woman. "That'll be all, Rose."

The cleaning lady's eyes cut towards me on her way past a young Asian-looking man—the same cat I saw with Casio last night. Propped against the doorframe with his arms folded and the comfort level of a barroom patron, he must have been there the entire time, but I never saw him enter the room.

Moments after seeing Rose make her exit, Casio returned his eyes back on me. "As I was saying," he said, "the dart we hit you with last night was loaded with a heavy dose of Vyrotellum. Some call it an old-world potion; others call it a derivative of Voodoo or Hoodoo dust. We just call it... effective."

My eyes narrowed.

"Like a sedative," the other guy said.

"Yes," Casio said, "and it has a few strange side effects on new cases—a few residual lulls being among them."

"And when you wake up, we'll get you hooked-up with a nice nutritional substitute. You're gonna *love* it, dude!"

I couldn't tell if these dudes were psychics or puppet masters, because my growling stomach returned on the other guy's cue just before I dozed off.

When I woke up again, my hunger had subsided, but I wasn't sure why or how. Still shackled to the same chair, I glanced down at my arm for the answer; stuck in my vein was a tubed needle leading to a hanging bag of what looked to be blood. *Why are they drawing my blood? Are these sons of bitches experimenting on me?* Blood slowly draining from the bag instead of filling it had me rethinking: *Transfusion, maybe?* Except whatever it was, most of it was somehow going straight to my stomach. With my senses so heightened, I was certain of it.

I didn't know how much time had passed, but Casio and the Asian-looking guy were now in different clothes, each leaning over a countertop across the room.

Casio looked my way when I started to move. "Allow me to introduce my brother, Timothy," he said.

"Tim DuChaine at your service," the other guy said, but his attention was buried into some kind of electronic device.

I looked back and forth between the two. "Brothers? *Ri-ight...*"

But Casio gave no reaction, as I was sure he'd ignored many before me. "Feeling a little more leveled out now?" he asked while standing there with his thumbs in his pants' front pockets.

Despite the shackles, I felt extremely relaxed, but I wasn't ready to let either of these guys know it. I even sank deeper into the chair like a mud-stuffed pig. But somehow, I was craving a little more than a sanguine colored food substitute.

"And now, I suppose answers are what you seek," Casio said, on-time as already evident. "Then answers are what you'll receive, *but*... you may not like what you hear." He warned as if everything he had said before was a goddamn fairytale.

I opened my palms. "Like I have a choice." Yet two seconds later, the shackles snapped open.

"Got it!" Tim pumped his fist; his fidgeting with his remote control had obviously paid off.

"You do now," Casio told me. "But I hope you in-
dulge us by hearing what we have to say. A remedy for the
most insane moments."

The memory of what I'd done the night before returned, along with recalling Casio's words: ....*a hallucination?
It wasn't.* Consequently, I didn't budge; I was too damned
curious to hear his version of it all.

"Good." He nodded. "As I was saying earlier today,
you've been bitten by a creature of the night."

"A what?" I asked.

"A creature of the night, except this creature... hunts
by both day and night! She's a venomous snake in the form of
a seething pariah, one that's left you with something you will
never rid!" His version was now carrying *way* more drama
than before; he was the one now *seething* and festering. "You
can call it a permanent disease, a curse, a virus, or a—"

"You're a vampire, dude." Tim's face was as blank as
an unwritten story.

Although Tim's answer was more straight-from-the-
hip than Casio's, nothing had been made any clearer to me. In
fact, I was more clouded than ever.

Casio folded his lips and nodded. "To put it plainly,
but not like the mythical stuff you read or watch on television.
Well, maybe *some* of it is, but no coffins, aversions to crosses,
invisibility in mirrors, or shit like that." As crazy as he sounded, he'd switched his tone back to mellow and nonchalant, just
before lifting an ID card and reading it. "So, Delroy Michael
Jackson. Hmm... catchy name," he said with a smile.

I'd seen that look from many other people, but obviously, it was *my* name first. *And what's with this dude, Casio—always digging in my fucking pockets?*

"Although, you won't be able to use it anymore," he said, "considering last night's outcome."

I sat clueless. *"What?"*

"The stranger from last night…"

I remembered the night before, but I couldn't quite remember any other outcome—like all those images were blocked and sealed under a steel lid.

But again, Tim was there to pour it straight with no chaser. "Drained, siphoned, dripped, vacuumed," he rattled off.

And now, I was finally putting it all together, but still not wanting to believe any of it. "You mean I—"

"That's right, you left him as dry as a flattened tube of toothpaste."

"Hold on. Are you saying he's—"

This time, Tim dipped his head, interrupting with only a dead-faced nod.

"This typically happens with newbies and their first live kill," Casio explained further. "You don't know how to hold back the juices. No one's ever shown you how to slow-down on the draw. But that's why we've brought you here with us. First, to show you how to exist without one more milliliter of vibrant blood. Secondly, to show you how to restrain yourself if ever you do feel the lust… *for human vino.*"

Okay, it was all starting to sicken me now. *No, I couldn't have just killed a man! Not a civilian! That's not in me! I don't care what these fools are trying to pull!* But the images and the sweet taste returned with a vengeance, regardless of what these guys were pumping through my veins.

"I see something in you, Delroy Michael Jackson," Casio said, "something that can make you a precious member of the DuChaine family." He looked at his brother. "What do you think, Tim?"

But Tim was already two steps ahead; his fingers were reeling through the pages of a ledger book. "Hmm, the name, *Trémeur*, is available."

"Tray what?" I uttered.

"Yeah, sounds super cool too." Casio gave a few slow nods before looking back at me. "Oh, it's a records thing. We have ways for you to keep it for a *very* long time. You'll need it. I'll explain it to you one day."

That's when it hit me. *"Oh, ho, hooo... ha, haaaa!"* I rolled out of the chair while withdrawing the needle at the same time; its incidental blood splatter meant nothing to me. I pointed at each one of them. "Y'all motha' fuckers are crazy!" Lightheaded and wobbly, I somehow managed to recoup my manly strut by the time I found the front door. *"Man, I'm out-ta' here!"* What I thought was the front door.

"The front door is to the left, Delroy!" Casio called out.

I turned to the left. "Yeah."

As promised, neither guy made any attempt to stop me, but Casio did call out one more time. "And mark my words, Mr. Jackson! You'll be back! When the hunger turns to thirst, you'll be back! And when you *do* return, you will be welcomed! Like it or not—here—you have a *new* family!"

When I'd left Casio's 1800s Creole-style mansion, I felt more vibrant than ever—abated of all aches and pain. But by the next night, my mood had completely shifted. I ended up crouched in a shadowy alcove back in the Quarters, not far from the same park-bench. It wasn't pleasant, but it had become the perfect spot to hide the blisters. Yes, my outer skin was already crispy from earlier daylight. It was now beginning to heal, but *good God* so unsightly. For me, it was only an initial reaction, but if Tasha were to return, I couldn't have let her see me like this. Whatever disease was eating away at me, I couldn't expose her to it—not my Love.

I had to think about Casio and Tim just to get Tasha off my mind. *The crazy bastards still have my ID!* Judging from my flattened pocket, they still had my wallet too. But who could I have told? *The police*? Why would *they* have believed me, now a rank-smelling brother from the Flats. And where would it have eventually led—to a missing uptowner? I couldn't take that chance, so I remained squat in the dark.

While the plasma had kept me filled for nearly twenty-four hours, its impact was finally wearing off. I had to eat something, but like Casio had warned, it was feeling more like a cross between hunger and thirst. A flowing thick bloody liquor was all I could envision before rising from the shadows and into motion. *I have to prowl. I have to feed!*

The short time that passed afterwards seemed like hours, but my search ended in a deeper alley, one where I saw a derelict curled up against the end-wall. I smelled his grime and alcohol drenched cells all the way from the sidewalk, but still with a touch of sweet nectar in between. Sure, I could have tracked down a purer blend, maybe an unsuspecting tourist, but I was feeling guilty enough as my delirious state had hardened my heart as coarse as my skin, while my logic had turned cold and cruel.

There he lay, ready and waiting, his neck exposed, his pulse pounding like a drum, or was it mine? I couldn't tell. His snoring sounded like a lion's roar, but it didn't stop me. Before I knew it, I was leaning over him, my nose twitching and my canines lengthening. This time, I felt them tearing away from my gums. Yet as much as I was starving for the kill, the guilt returned. I had to find more of a reason than just a slab of drunken meat beneath me. *Any reason! The snoring! That's it, the snoring. It's killing my ears! He's got to go!* But just before gouging, my tears began to stream, tears I couldn't hold back. "This isn't me," I sobbed.

"What the fuck!" the gray-haired man beneath me yelled. "Get off me, you freak!"

Miraculously sobered, the old guy knocked me back as he rolled onto his feet, stumbling all the way out of the alley—leaving me behind fetal in a ball of anguish.

Soon after my epic failure, faded memories of my every step somehow led me all the way back uptown, where Casio's slender mansion was waiting. As I stood famished on his porch, the door opened before even having a chance to knock. In the doorway stood Tim with a bagful of plasma in his hand.

"Casio," he shouted, "our brother is home for supper!"

I stood before him humbled and trembling, finding it difficult to believe it was the start of my life as Trémeur DuChaine.

Chapter 7

Blood Does a Body Good

Landon Levy sat in his current-day prison cell without a hint of worry—surprising since he had been confined to solitude in a seven-by-seven-foot cell, smaller than the typical one. Its twelve-inch-thick wall was the only thing superior to most other cells, while an ankle shackle chained to the floor kept him even more grounded. In all, it seemed a bit hefty for a man of average height and a wiry frame. And he may have been bearded and unassuming, but he was a stone-cold killer-V with a voracious appetite, his veins having been filled with masses of human victims. Strangely, his hunger seemed to have increased after the Treaty, much to the chagrin of the V-Council prior to his incarceration:

> "We cannot let him carry on like this!" Louisiana V-Council member, Romney Higgins, urged of Chief Luriel Bahaj inside the Council's New Orleans Lakefront chambers.
>
> Middle-aged in features, Luriel and Romney both fit the mold of Council leaders, her wearing the V-C symbol as a scarf-broach—Romney's as a lapel pin. Luriel sat at the head of a large polished black-oak table, while Romney sat close to its middle. Facing Luriel at the op-

posite end was the more youthful looking Chief Security Officer, Efran Marques, who stood immobilized by Luriel's silence.

"Shall we bury this problem for good?" Efran asked her.

A long pause and stiff brow followed before Luriel finally responded, "No. Here is a prime opportunity to display our commitment to the Treaty. Find him, capture him, and have him delivered to the human's justice system."

"This will be dangerous for them, will it not?"

"Hmm... maybe. But we will give them a few pointers on how to keep him contained—none involving Vyrotellum, of course."

"Then *surely* they will die!" Romney said.

Luriel shrugged. "Then fuck 'em. Locking him up is what they've been 'dying' to do anyway. No pun intended."

"This, will be done," Efran assured on his way out.

"Oh, and Officer Marques?"

Efran stopped and turned in his tracks.

"We will revisit your original strategy if the humans fall short in their efforts." Luriel was now peering from under her brow, her lips tightened.

"As you wish, your Honor." Efran turned away like a man intent on maintaining his 100% success rate.

After being found, Landon didn't resist Efran's forces, eventually landing him in his supermax security cell inside the Louisiana State Penitentiary. Plasma now as his only nutrition, midnight marked the time for his post-meal walk into the currently empty prison yard. Dragging along in the traditional waist-chain, he was led by two rifled human guards in front of him and trailed by two large V-guards. The rifles were merely for the front guards' own sense of security, for there were many myths about Vs, but surviving bullets wasn't one of them; it was a *fact*. There was simply no true blood to lose. Although the bullets would have been great massage therapy for Landon, the two-hundred-volt prodding rods in the V-guards' hands would have at least stunted his urge toward old habits. This would've been the case if they'd reacted to Landon snapping his chains—if they'd reacted to him reaching up and snapping both human guards' necks—if they'd reacted to him falling to his knees and burying his teeth into the humans' throats one-by-one, draining both of them in less than five minutes. But the V-guards never reacted; not one flinched. Well paid to watch, they stood stiff-necked in place until the carnage was complete.

"Aaaah!" Landon exhaled in the end. "Now *that* does a body good."

Meanwhile, all the monitoring room guards had seen was Landon escorted into the prison yard by four prison guards. All four then stepped back and stared beyond Landon's standard ritual: him kicking dust for nearly thirty minutes, followed by them leading him back into the prison. The entire scene was the same as the night before—*exactly* the same as the night before. The monitoring room guards had had no idea they had been watching a looped relay uploaded by unknown sources.

Chapter 8

Some Things Never Change

Narrated by Trémeur DuChaine

After Henri ReGett had cleaned up the mess in Livingston Parish, I was pissed-off for every minute of my hour-long drive
down to the V-Council's New Orleans office. It was bad
enough they didn't believe in teleconferencing, but I just knew
they were going to throw one of those guilt-trips on me if I
didn't show up. I even imagined one of them saying: *We
made you who you are today, Agent DuChaine. You owe us
this much!* It was going to be the same old rabbit, just from a
different hat. But I always had a few memories to remind me
of something worse—like my mishaps in the seventies. There
was losing Tasha, never having seen her again—along with the
abducting *"demoness,"* who made the V-Council look like a
church choir. It was enough misery to get me to the Council's
lakefront mansion nearly in tears.

Once inside the mansion, I sat at the end of a long conference
room table with Chief Councilwoman Luriel Bahaj on the opposite end, and four other council members split on each
side—not even a quorum. The conference room lighting was
dim as always, its walls covered with portraits of council lead-
ers past and present. Behind me stood their Security Chief,

Efran Marques, the one who'd called me, whose stiff demeanor had rubbed everyone the wrong way—me included.

In crumpled clothes and buckshot-tattered slacks, I sat there and spilled the strangest ordeal of my young immortal life. And when I was done, there was nothing but five poker faces in front of me, Bahaj's being the stiffest. All four remaining members swung their eyes slowly towards Bahaj, who kept hers on me while tapping her pen on the table.

"That will be all, Mr. DuChaine," she said.

The other four sets of eyes were back on me now. But even after longing to get back home, I didn't budge; I could tell they were hiding something. "Excuse me," I said, "but I'm not quite finished."

"Oh. Is there more?" Bahaj asked.

"Well, not more to what happened, but there's definitely more I'd like to know—like does anyone here have any idea what's really going on? Any clues?"

"Clues?" she asked with a buckled brow.

"Yes. Clues!" My patience was already wearing thin. "As in clues to solving this mystery? As in how a despicable group of low-lives have been able to pull this whole thing off?" I wasn't used to name-calling, but the shoe fit quite well here. "You know, mutant genetics and them taking one of us down so easily!"

Bahaj's initial reaction entailed batting her eyes like she'd just been slapped in the face. She took a quiet breath. "Clues? No. But ideas? We may have a few," she said before going deathly silent.

Waiting for an answer—any answer—I put down my finger and did a little table-tapping of my own. "Well... is anyone gonna *share* them with me?"

"In due time, Agent DuChaine," she said. "That will be—"

"Hey, wait a minute! What do you mean 'in due time'?" I wasn't sure, but I believed my hand slapped the table because I felt it rumble.

The entire group was almost standing, until Bahaj's eyes went back to batting. "Mr. DuChaine!"

"Like I said, I get taken down by some kind of Voodoo dust!" I pinched the air. "Then I come this close to getting sawed into spare parts! Then I get attacked by some mutated... mutilated... *strigoi*-lookin' motha' fucker—"

"That's enough, Mr. DuChaine!" Bahaj's fists met the table, hers rumbling it and the floor. "I can understand your anxiety, but this level of disrespect will *not* be fucking tolerated!"

I exhaled, but with no apology.

"Now," she said, "let me remind you that although we have always been aware of the intentions of such overly-zealous groups, solving this particular mystery is in large-part *your* job... a job, need I remind you, that was facilitated by the esteemed in this room!"

"And here we go," I mumbled.

But a mumble wasn't inaudible in this room. Her brow simply buckled deeper. "Is this understood?"

As I sat there tapping again, ready to whip out my big *fat-ass* silver badge and sling it at her, Bahaj stood up and pressed her knuckles into the table—*literally*.

"Is this understood, Mr. DuChaine?" she asked. "Or shall we push to have you replaced?" She wagged her finger at me like a whipping switch. "Many other Vampyrian's have *far more* law enforcement credentials from their previous lives."

But her brow-beating had no effect on me. Perhaps it was my earlier ordeal; maybe it was thoughts of Tasha and "Demoness" Artreaux; or maybe it was the fact this could have been resolved by an email, that had brought out my rare side. Or there was always that Louisiana thing: *Woman, who you think you waggin' your finger at? You ain't my Momma!* Most importantly, there was also the fact that the DuChaine family was well-endowed enough to handle its own affairs—with or without the Council—so I saw my role in the new V-Unit as strictly voluntary. On the other hand, Bahaj may have had me by the balls just a little. I was emotionally invested now and she knew it. I rose to my feet without a word, re-membering something Casio had once advised: *It's not such a bad idea to keep the peace, Trémeur. You never know when you may really need them...*

Meanwhile, with arms folded and a staunch look on his face, only Marques was blocking my path out of the room.

"Is there a problem, Marques?" I asked with my fists clinched.

I noticed him clinching his too, but when his eyes flashed towards Councilwoman Bahaj, he stepped aside and let me by, no resistance. The entire scene reminded me of more of Casio's advice: *But beware… your best friend in the light… can be your worst enemy in the dark.*

The next day, a Friday, I was back in the Baton Rouge L.B.I. office where an emergency assignment was waiting on my desk. Escaped mass killer, Landon Levy, a V, had been spotted in Los Angeles. When I opened the file, I was stunned by the photograph. Although we Vs had many ways to remain anonymous, Levy's shades and afternoon shadow had almost done the trick, until he was seen on a fan-cam—second row, third quarter at a Lakers game.

A local detective was the one who'd made the initial ID, noticing Levy hanging out with a crowd already under watch. As for now, out of my folder fell a roundtrip ticket for me alone to Los Angeles, starting the next day with an open return date. This gave me only one night to squeeze in a special visit.

"Baby, the night's gonna be completely gone by the time you wake up," my girlfriend, Rayna, said in a groggy but sweet tone. Her soft lips against my neck awoke me from wasting an entire evening. And no, she wasn't using any special hypnosis, nor was she about to "fang" me, which wouldn't have been the worst thing. Rayna was all human, all five-feet-five-inches of her delicate frame. Although Casio and Tim had taught me long ago how to control my deadly impulses, I didn't need any of it when it came to Rayna. She had introduced me to many other ways to enjoy the warmth of human blood without one single puncture. It was enough to make me often forget about Tasha, who I'd searched for frequently throughout the seventies and the eighties, but not lately.

"Would staying in all night be such a bad idea?" I asked Rayna with a long stretch.

She nibbled on my neck a little more while cajoling at the same time. "*Staying* in? No. But if it turns into *sleeping* in... a *horrible* idea."

Catching her drift, I turned to kiss her lips, laced with extra sweetness from strawberries she'd eaten earlier. "Ooh, you're such a vamp," I whispered.

She chuckled as I flipped her over into my arms. Knowing exactly who and what I was, she always giggled whenever I said that. It was what made her so amazing. Since we'd first met in a quaint restaurant/bar, she could tell I was a V just from my off-tan. But it didn't bother her, as if fed up with desperate pleas from human guys—and she'd heard many. However, the same couldn't be said for her sister, Jacynthia, who'd taken up several meditation techniques just to get through every day her sister and I spent together.

I, on the other hand, had had my fill of women of my own kind as well. Not only had Demoness Artreaux dampened a brother's enthusiasm, but other V-women were only slightly better. It was their immortality that often led to empty passion for precious moments, but Rayna was *oh-so* the contrary.

That Friday night in her one-bedroom apartment, we remained in her queen-sized bed almost the entire time. Making love over every square-inch, her racing heartbeat kept me going. So much so, it wasn't until early a.m. the next time full words actually came out of our mouths.

"Tray, what's in California waiting for you?" she asked as our fingers touched, her eyes with the glare of a real hypnotist.

"The usual," I said. "You know, a few mountains, a little sun, a little breeze—"

"You ass!" She sneered with a light slap. "You know what I mean."

"…an endless coastline, a few waves, a few bikinis—"

"Tray!"

"*What?* Okay, okay. Just an escaped convict spotted out there chillin' harder than a bucket of ice." I couldn't always contain good ole country boy Delroy, the only side of me Rayna knew nothing about.

She sat up with a morbid look on her face. "And just how dangerous is this *convict*?"

"Mmm, not very."

"Is he a V?"

"Yes, it's a he, and yes, he's a V. You know my job."

She crashed into her pillow like a diving plane. "God! I hate thinking about this shit when you're out there!"

"You shouldn't have asked."

Later, I stepped out the shower around 3 a.m. Bathed of my V-Screen, it was the perfect time to beat the South Louisiana sunrise. I may have showered alone this time, but I wasn't going to leave without saying goodbye to Rayna, who was shuffling around in the bedroom. I was stunned when I walked in on her. This woman made any- and everything look sexy, including the plain terrycloth robe she donned on her way towards me. Yet it was what she pulled from her pocket that surprised me the most.

"What's this?" I asked.

"Promise me you'll come back here *first* as soon as you return. I mean, *immediately* after your flight lands." With a stern look, she handed me a freshly etched key. "I want you here and waiting even if I'm not."

"Wow... this is a *mighty big* step."

"Is it?"

"Yeah," I said, stroking my chin, and a little tempted to give it back. *I mean, God forbid she asks me to return the favor!* "Yeah, but baby, I'm probably going to have so much to do when I get back, and I'm not sure I'm gonna be able to wait around here for too long—"

"Then call me first." Her eyes flared as she grabbed my fingers and wrapped them around the key. "But just be here. *Okay*?"

I huffed. "Okay."

Still, she pressed. "Promise me."

"Aahh, alright."

"Say it!"

"Okay, I promise."

A deal sealed with her kiss, my resistance became futile.

It was only six in the morning when I made it to Baton Rouge's Metropolitan Airport. It was still a little dim and dusky outside, but the sun seemed to be making its presence known pretty early. I was fortunate to have refreshed my V-Screen before leaving the house, but I could always tell when I'd caked on too much. The stares from children's eyes usually said it all. This time, it came from a kid with only his mother's grip guiding him through the entrance. I didn't mind, though; expecting the west coast sunlight by journey's end, caking it on wasn't much of a stretch.

Onboard the plane, I sat in the typical aisle seat—no one between the window and me but empty seats. Meanwhile, most other rows seemed full, as if the airline had my name superscripted by the mark of "Satan" in their database. It couldn't have been the V-Screen, nowadays practically odorless. Even long after the Treaty, no matter what kind of badge I carried, many humans remained vigilant of whenever that fateful day might come—the day we Vs "renege" on our part of the deal. *I see some things never change.* Meanwhile, Vs like Landon Levy were of little help. In any event, from another aisle-seat two rows forward, that same little kid was still staring at me, his eyes now expanded beyond curiosity.

Chapter 9

Rogue Hunt

Narrated by Trémeur DuChaine

Hours of layover time in Phoenix had pushed my landing at Los Angeles' LAX to late that afternoon, but work was no longer on my mind. My first duty was to be a good boyfriend. "Made it safely... miss you already," I texted Rayna.

It only took a split-second for her to text me back: "Ditto, sweets. Can u talk?"

I was so excited and ready to talk, until a guy wearing a blazer approached me.

"Agent DuChaine?" He reached out and shook my hand without giving me a chance to respond. Either he had seen my face in a file-photo, or he too knew a good V-Screen job when he saw one. "I'm Detective Austin Flores, L.A.P.D."

"Nice to meet you, Detective." I wasted no time cutting to the chase. "Not many would have identified him so quickly." I was talking about Levy, and what I really meant was—not many *human* detectives would have identified him so quickly.

"Nice to meet you too, and a touch of biometrics does *wonders* these days." He opened his hand towards the bustling terminal. "Right this way."

Weaving behind Flores through the crowd, I tried to extract as many details as I could about my escort, like how his handshake was firm, indicating no apprehension around me. And like me, he was well-dressed enough to show how he missed very few details, especially by his next course of action.

"Hey, you feeling pretty spry right now?" he asked me.

"If you're asking if I'm jetlagged or not, I feel fine."

"Good. The Lakers happen to be playing tonight. How about we catch a quick game?"

"Sure, I don't have any other plans."

Honestly, as much as I'd loved basketball as a youth, I hadn't watched it much after that fateful trip to New Orleans, but this night had nothing to do with basketball.

Later, inside the Staples Center, Flores and I had been standing in the opposing team's tunnel the entire game. Only he couldn't resist the action on the court; his body jerked and quivered on every shot. But the rest of my attention was locked on Landon Levy, who was tossing down caramel corn like a kid, somehow upgraded to a *first-row* seat. When the game ended, he rose from his seat, hamming it up with potential victims on his way out. But I kept my eyes on him from the shadows, my thoughts on no one else but those within his reach. I'd never met Levy before, but I couldn't say for sure he didn't know me, or at least know *of* me.

Trailing Levy through the crowd, into the streets, and soon down a quiet boulevard, Flores and I saw no signs of the Levy we'd expected—a V on the prowl. That made me wonder: *Could it be? Could something about the L.A. weather have changed a tiger's stripes? Could Landon Levy now be...* domesticated? But I'd traveled too far not to bring him in, and domesticated or not, he was still a fugitive on the lam.

Flores and I stopped. Both of us pulled back when Levy turned and detoured into a bakery shop. *Bakery shop? Why in the hell would Levy, of all Vs, be into bread and shit?* It was no secret, some Vs ate almost anything as an appetizer, but I couldn't see someone as bloodthirsty as Levy being a caramel or muffin man. Human blood was sweet, but it was a different kind of sweet, a taste a muffin could never replace. Nonetheless, we waited nearly fifteen minutes for Levy to exit, continuing his original path as if we weren't on his tail at all. And when I took a stronger sniff, he was carrying a bagful of fresh-baked cookies, not muffins.

Finally, Levy turned into a parking garage, but before following him in, I halted Flores with a new game plan. "Listen, Detective, this may be as far as you need to go. I can take it from here."

Flores threw his hands up, a sure sign his prior confidence had taken a nosedive at this point. "Hey, no problem. This guy's *your* collar anyway. The other guys he associates with are *mine*. Plus, I got a pension coming up."

"Great, he'll smell you coming anyway," I muttered.

"What?"

"I'll explain it to you later. Just wait for me right here."

"Hey, if you're not back in ten, I'm calling for back-up."

"I will definitely be back *within* ten," I said on my way into Levy's darkened path.

Flores's reaction had come as no surprise. If Levy would've been the usual escapee, L.A.P.D. would have taken him at first sight. But most human forces were in no hurry to risk their own. Plus, with Flores smelling like oven hot pra-lines to any and all Vs, not even his bath of cologne would have masked his scent from Levy.

Several steps later, I thought my target had given me the slip, until my senses started to tingle. Like a gate, I swung behind a column just in time to avoid a series of crashing ob-jects. Dart after dart was flying my way and shattering against the concrete column. Along with every one of them came that acetic smell of Vyrotellum fuming the air after impact.

When the crashing tubes stopped, a voice echoed through the parking deck. "What are you doing here, DuChaine? Isn't this a little out of your 'human-loving' juris-diction?"

It was Levy, and apparently, he *did* know of me. *But where did he get the gun? From his ass? Oh! The fucking bag of cookies! The perfect masking agent.*

"Why would you think that?" I shouted. "From one L-A to the next L-A, it's not too far!"

"*Hmph*. Clever. A little quirky, but clever. Well, you think I didn't spot you inside the arena? Following me down the street with your sweet-smelling escort? I *figured* you'd be too afraid to face me alone!"

Enough banter. "Levy, I'm placing you under arrest," I said while drawing my own hidden vyro-filled sidearm, specially prepared for this kind of moment. "So, drop your weapon, come out peacefully, and I'll forget all about your little outburst here!" *That sounded pretty forceful. Very definitive. There's no reason he won't—*

Three more darts crashed against the column, but only holding me at bay for Levy to finish his point. "Didn't you hear?" he shouted. "I've been cleared of all wrongdoing!"

"Only in your dreams, Levy!" I didn't believe him, because why else would he be putting up such a fight?

"Ha! You must be pretty low on the totem! Or just fucking expendable, you piece of shit!" he yelled, followed by more darts crashing against the column. "Yeah, it looks like a few privileged humans are willing to pay a fortune to be turned—politicians, corporations, scum-ass supremacists— makes no difference to me! I'm more than happy to oblige!"

That comment was a shocker, but a little hazy. All I could envision was the Neo-Nazi "foul-up" just a couple of days ago. "That goes against the Treaty, Levy!"

"Treaty? *Treaty?* Were you thinking 'Treaty' when you drained a poor innocent guy to death? You know... Uptown? Off St. Charles? Does that ring a bell?"

What? How did he know about that?

"Oh, so you thought no one would find out!"

His agitation seemed as endless as his ammunition, and it was starting to work.

"That was an accident," I said, "and long before the Treaty!"

"Anyway, you think my benefactors give a shit about a freakin' Treaty? Oh, yeah, and I wouldn't be so cavalier if someone on your precious V-Council hadn't given me the thumbs up!"

"You mean the same V-Council that turned you in?"

"I don't know, but like you and all the rest, they don't have the *biggest* balls on the block!"

He sent a few more darts, but this time I answered with a few of my own, both of us still hitting nothing but concrete columns.

"But you know politics," he went on. "They tend to get a little *polyamorous*, don't you think?"

Hearing him chuckle, he was obviously more amused at himself than I was, but I didn't know what to think. It was becoming more than evident I was on this guy's shit-list too, and I'd never met him until now. What I did know was that I'd never received a cease-action order, so my objective remained unchanged. "I don't really care what you've been told, Levy, but like I said, drop your weapon, and come out—"

I was interrupted again, this time by a thunderous metal clank lighting up the entire parking deck. Seconds later, not one peep leaked from Levy's mouth, nor from mine. It took me nearly a full minute after that to creep around my column towards his. By the time I got there, my nerves were already rattled, but the foul smoky odor coupled with what I saw next left me clueless. *What the fuck!* His body, devoid his head, was on the pavement with fumes rising from his neck. Crumbled around him were concrete chunks, all below a huge open wedge at neck-level on the column. I looked all around, but saw nothing but a vacant deck. And when I looked back down, the fumes had gone from rising to overwhelming, leaving behind a huge mound of ashes where I'd just seen Levy's body. *Damn!* The odor was now tear-jerking. I'd already been told what *would* happen if a Vs head was ever removed, but I had never *seen* it happen before.

"What happened?" Flores was suddenly standing only a few feet behind me.

The smoke was so pungent, I'd never smelled him coming, nor did I know how much he'd seen. Also, it couldn't have been ten minutes. I looked back, disappointed for all sorts of reasons, but only one answer could sum things up: "He got away."

"Damn! What in the hell's that putrid odor? God! Is that coming from that pile of dust? Or is it a pile of *shit*?"

Flores cringed from the smell, but I was far too conflicted to come up with a crafty explanation. Traditionally, our mandate was to conceal the supernatural from all human eyes, but I had a simpler solution.

"Well," I said, "I really can't explain it to you, but rest assured, Landon Levy won't be a problem anymore."

With a blank look on his face, Flores offered nothing back but a shrug and a quick turnaround.

Soon after, Flores was driving me to my hotel with very few questions, giving me time to check all my messages along the way. "Damn," I mumbled. *I forgot I turned off my phone.*

"What's that?" Flores asked.

"Oh, nothing."

Turning it back on revealed some truth to what Levy had said. "Stand down," It was a message from my supervisor. "Assignment on hold."

Damn! Could Levy have been right? I sighed quietly, wondering if a different kind of dark force had reached law enforcement. More importantly, with Levy now deceased, how far would it continue to reach?

Later in my hotel room, me sitting on the edge of my bed, I used my personal cellphone to call for a local V-cleanup crew. The ashes and Vyrotellum residue left behind at the garage needed to be erased. Afterwards, I was ready to get some long-awaited rest, until noticing another message, this one from Tim, and it was marked urgent: "Tray, I found Tasha, Hit me back right away."

"What?" I held my breath. But the message was clear; it just took several minutes to sink in, and I still didn't know how to react. There were so many times I remembered her begrudgingly before eventually giving up; other times were just tearful. But Tim wasn't the quitting type. Finding her was a brotherly favor he was determined to fulfil; and that, it seemed he finally did.

I rocked back and forth on the edge of that bed for several emotionally-torn minutes before rising to my feet, lifting my head towards the ceiling and roaring, "Ahh sssshit! You got to be fucking kidding me!" It was a roar of both love and hate, and all the pain in between.

Chapter 10

Bonnie and Bonnie

Narrated by Tasha Whitlow

To some, the mid-seventies was a time two young black women cruising the countryside in a silver convertible was an abduction waiting to happen. But with the crispy cool chick sitting beside me in the passenger seat, it wasn't. When we'd met, she told me her name was Loretta, but later informed me it was just a façade. "A pen name destined to create one of my many true-life masterpieces," she had told me. I may have been hooked at first sight, but at that moment I was head-over-heels in love.

Phoebe Artreaux was the name she'd gone on to reveal, and with her, I never felt so alive, so infused with opportunities, those the boyfriend I left behind could have never offered. *God, bless his soul.* Yet what could a girl do but follow her emotions? I was now ensnared by Phoebe's energy. My boyfriend—my *ex-boyfriend,* that is, must have gotten over it. Afterall, he had never reported his silver convertible Thunderbird stolen.

What started as a brief drive for food along the French Quarters' fringes, turned into a long road-trip up the southeast coastline. With Phoebe pointing out landmarks from here to there, it was obvious she'd taken this route many times before.

Her tour-guide skills were just as captivating, until I started thinking about money. I'd left a damn management position behind in Lafayette just for her. I even asked her as politely as I could: "Umm, excuse me? Phoebe? What exactly are we gonna do about *money*?"

"*Money?*" She sneered as if she'd never heard of it. "Listen... don't worry. It's all under control," she said with one finger twirling through the air.

"Alright," I said softly, but it was going to take a lot more than a finger-twirl to make me believe it.

After an overnight stay in Jacksonville, Florida, our pitstop routine duplicated itself just like every stop before then: Phoebe sashaying into a gas station and batting her eyes at each cashier, male or female—ending with her walking out with change for a hundred when she had only presented a twenty. Along with it came me pumping a tankful of gasoline, never knowing if it was free or stolen. Either way, Phoebe seemed unbothered, evident by her victorious laughter as we drove off into the wind.

Oh, it was hilarious, but I had to shut her amusement down for a second. "Seriously, though," I said, "Girl, you gotta teach me your tricks."

She patted my inside hand gently and said, "It's no trick, but in due time, my dear. In due time."

Our stays at the hotel inns were no different. The next one was outside Charleston, South Carolina, where I noticed my previ-

ous error in judgement: Phoebe wasn't batting her eyes at all.
They were more like a rifle's scope, now locked into her next
target, an old white innkeeper.

"We'd like a room. No charge—" she started.

The old man raced from behind the counter before
Phoebe could say *please*. "Oh, yes, Ma'am! Yes, Ma'am!" he
said. "We aim to accommodate!" As if under a spell, he nearly cracked his back toting our bags up to our room.

I swear, Phoebe gave the phrase, "Power to the People," a new meaning. No man could have ever made me feel
as safe as she did. That evening, when she and I lay in each
other's arms, lips to lips in the bed, I felt even safer. And
when I fell asleep, her essence was so surreal, there was no
cause to dream. Until meeting her, I'd never been into the *girl*
thing, but there was something different about this one. I
wouldn't even call it a "lesbian" thing. Odd still, no warmth
came from her flesh, but there was a strange energy pulsating
from inside her that kept me attached. I had even felt it as far
back as the Jazz Festival in New Orleans, where we first met.
I never could explain it, not even to myself—not then and not
now.

But by early a.m., long before dawn, our connection
had been lost. I opened my eyes to a dented pillow and an
empty space beside me, but the bathroom shower was on.
Waiting with eyes wide for several minutes, the water kept
running, and I was getting lonely. Seconds later I was up and
knocking on the bathroom door. "Phoebe?" I asked like I was
apologizing.

More seconds passed until she finally answered. "Yeah?"

"You okay?"

"I'm fine!"

I couldn't help myself. I wanted to join her so badly, I grabbed the knob—not surprised it was locked, but more so by its slippery surface. A sliver of light from outside shined across the knob smeared with blood, now on my hand too. It was a bit frightening. "You sure?" I asked.

"Yeah. Why?"

"Because there's blood on the doorknob."

"Oh! I must've cut myself... uhh... shaving my legs!"

Strange... Phoebe's legs were already buttery smooth, and unless she'd slit an artery, a nick couldn't have drawn *this* much blood, so I began looking for a towel and an excuse. "Well, are you gonna let me in to wipe off my hands?"

"Yes, gimme a sec! I'll bring you a towel!"

Shit! Now I had to wait even longer, but this wasn't her first time. She had done the same thing at our last hotel stop—though, minus the blood on the doorknob.

The stakes were raised when we stopped in Richmond, Virginia. It was the first time we attempted to dine in a ritzy restaurant, the others having been Phoebe's favorite soul-food joints, just "holes-in-the-wall." Unlike in the others, stares from the many white faces here were harsh, but this wasn't the "sixties" anymore, and Richmond was no longer the capitol of the

South. These folks wouldn't have dared deny us service, but the front hostess did say something pretty interesting.

"I'm sorry, we're a bit crowded today," she said with a huge smile from ear-to-ear. "We do have one available in the back. Will that be okay?" It was the politest "cock-block" I'd ever heard or seen.

Phoebe panned the room with a side-eyed glare. "Hmm... I sure do see a *whole* bunch of empty tables all over the place."

"Oh, those are reserved," the hostess said.

As if triggered by the devil, Phoebe was back in hypnotic mode, her glare capturing the hostess's eyes. "You believe a table near the window has just become available," Phoebe told her.

After a quick glance over her list, that hostess's eyes lit up like a bulb. "Oops," she said, "I believe a table near the window has just become available. Right this way, please." Grabbing two menus, she led the way wearing her same smile.

Finally dining at our table, the leers and murmurs from the other patrons had lasted nearly our entire meal—all the way through dessert. Just the leers alone were as deafening to me as witch-hunt calls, but to Phoebe, she seemed to digest them as easy as the parfait sliding down her throat.

"Mmm... I do so love the taste," she said in the Queen's English, "but the nutritional value leaves much to be desired. Wouldn't you agree?"

I couldn't hold back my giggles, the other patrons' murmurs now reduced to silence. It gave me enough time to once again admire my captivating muse. No matter what she wore or the fit, she always managed to make it look sexy, and each time she was wearing something different. *Wait a minute.* I began to wonder. *How?* She'd been traveling with only *one* small bag filled with only *one* set of extra clothes the entire way, and I'd seen that set. We'd yet to enter any department store along the way, so I couldn't figure out where she'd been finding all the other ensembles—from her *magic bag*? But seeing her peaceful look across the table, I decided to save this mystery for another day.

It may have been amusing in the restaurant, but much later in our hotel room, both of us in bras and panties, I was serious as a vow when I sat next to her on the bed's edge. "Okay, Phoebe, I can't take this anymore," I said.

"You can't?" Her mouth dropped in terror.

"No, no… I mean, you've got to show me how you did that."

"Did what?"

"You know… that thing!"

"What thing?"

"That thing with your eyes! That hypnosis thing!"

She sighed in relief. "Oh, girl, I thought you were talking about—anyway, I really don't want you to get yourself wrapped up in that."

"That's what I'm talking about! What is it exactly I'd be wrapped up in? Tell me!"

She stroked my face with almost a mother's touch. "You're so nice... so sweet. You don't want to be like me."

"Did I *ask* to be like you? I just wanna know ... wanna know... you know..." I stammered until the Flats poured right out of me. "How to... make *motha' fuckas* do whatever the hell I *w'ont 'em* to do!"

Phoebe leaned back, laughing out of control. "Okay, okay! I'll give you just a taste of power, nothing more than a nibble. But you have to trust me, okay?"

"Girl, you already had my full trust since the park-bench." I clinched my entire body in anticipation. "Now show me!"

"First, give me your wrist."

"My wrist?"

"Yeah, your wrist. You just said you trust me, didn't you?"

"Okay." I held out my wrist, which she grabbed and slowly raised towards her lips and started to kiss it, followed by licking it in the very same spot. "Woman, I ain't got time for this now," I softly fussed.

But she was only marking her target point.

"Ouch!" I felt a prickling pinch. "What are you doing?"

"Quiet," she muffled with a mouthful of wrist, sucking it like the side of a dick.

Soon, it wasn't painful any longer; it was more soothing than the weed she also carried around in that "Magic Bag."

By the time my head bobbed in peaceful bliss, Phoebe disengaged, leaving two faint puncture wounds along my vein.

"Whoa... what was that?" I whispered.

She rose from the bed. "The taste I just told you about, so get up and get dressed.   That was just the ammunition. Now I'm gonna show you how to fire it."

I was still confused.   *"Shit,"* I mumbled, "this bitch done chewed a damn vampire hole in my arm."

Practically shoved through the door by Phoebe, *this* little fledgling led the way into a nearby convenience store. Phoebe had explained the process to me on the way to the door, having summed it up like this: "You have to pull them into you with your gaze until you both become one... until their hearts feel your compulsion, and there ain't shit they can do about."

Like wow, was my thought. "Yeah, I can dig it."

Just inside the door, she bulked her shoulders and quietly urged. "And remember—confidence."

"Right. Grrrr." I growled and bulked back.

"But don't growl."

"Oh."

Phoebe remained by the door like a giddy lookout while I scuffled to the front counter, my head swiveling back and forth. Standing behind the register was a man who looked like a boy, instantly making me feel this was going to be a breeze. But I felt nothing but my bottom lip trembling when I opened my mouth, and my hand shaking as I placed a twenty-dollar bill near the register. Gazing into the young man's eyes, I stuttered, "Ch-Ch-Change for a hundred... please?"

Our eyes locked, I knew I had him where I wanted him.

"Sure..." he said with an accommodating nod. "As soon as you place one on the countertop."

With Phoebe giggling in the background, I whimpered. "Sorry, change for a *twenty*?"

Once outside, I was livid while Phoebe squealed in tearful joy. "You should have seen the look on your face!" she yelled. "Like, *yikes*!"

"Damn it!" I gritted. "Why did you let me go in there and make a damn fool of myself?"

"I'm sorry! I couldn't stop you. There was nothing I could do!"

"Now I ain't got shit but change for a twenty and two goddamn teeth holes in my arm!"

Placing her arm around my shoulders, her mood switched to constructive. "Look, there's nothing wrong. Like I said, you just have to be more confident in your game. You have to believe it more than your victim." She pulled me clos-er. "Don't worry. We'll try again tomorrow."

For a second, it sounded like advice from the "Players" magazines my four older brothers used to have laying around all over the place back home. *Okay,* maybe I had been a little curious in the female physique back in the day. *Don't judge me!*

Chapter 11

Deserve's Got Nothing
To Do With It

Narrated by Tasha Whitlow

Phoebe had had the right idea after my first failed heist attempt, and surely my most embarrassing moment. It had been a long day, and I was far more fatigued than her, so we decided to end it with a stop at a late-night diner somewhere on the outskirts. With no host or hostess in sight, we found ourselves a booth near the front window. Luckily steak and eggs were on their all-day menu, and we were the only customers there. But it still took nearly fifteen minutes for the waitress to make her first appearance.

"I'm Ella," she said with slumped shoulders, not one "hello" and an already wry attitude. "What can I get you two girls?"

Phoebe and I looked at each other with eyes wide, both of us thinking the same thing, I was sure: *Girls*? Who was she calling, *girls*?

But even Phoebe was done retaliating for the day—simply rolling her eyes instead. "Steak. Extremely rare."

Normally, I liked my meat well done, sometimes medium well, but never rare. Although, the thought of Phoebe's order had me curious for some reason.

I looked up with a smile. "I'll have the same, and my eggs scrambled, please." My tone was far more polite than Ella deserved.

She "scribbled" a straight line in her pad and turned to Phoebe. "Eggs for you too?" There was not a Ma'am, a Miss, a hon, or the least bit of respect in her tone. I was shocked she didn't throw in *"little girl"* at the end.

Still, Phoebe had little to no adverse reaction, her eyes aimed outside the window. "Nope." There was only so much attitude battling a person could take on in one day.

It felt like Ella was taking forever after that, and Phoebe's attention was still adrift outside the window, but I was getting antsy. It had taken nearly thirty minutes for Ella to return with our orders, except each came with eggs over easy on the side. She planted two glasses of water in the middle after having never asked if we wanted any juice. *Lord knows* I wanted scrambled eggs and juice instead. I just didn't want to start any trouble. Afterall, we *were* still below the Mason-Dixon line, so I at least checked the rim of my glass for any extra saliva, thankfully finding none. But biting into the blood-drenched steak drove all my worries away. I never knew it would taste so good, so succulently raw, so perfectly natural—had me thinking how I should try new things more often. Taking a moment to exhale, I noticed Phoebe glaring at me with her arms folded and her plate untouched.

"What?" I blurted with my mouth full. "You ordered rare too, didn't you?"

"That's not what's eating away at me."

"Then what *is* eating away at you?"

She grimaced. "Girl, look! What's it gonna take for you to get *pissed-off?*"

"What are you talking about?"

"I mean, the eggs are runny. She didn't even offer us anything else to drink. Doesn't that spell *rudeness* to you?"

"Well yeah, but I didn't want our glasses to come back drippin' with nasty-ass spit! Plus, *you* didn't say anything either."

"That's the point. Why does it have to be me all the time?" Switching to a chastising finger in my face, she gritted. "Tonight, it's got to be *you.* I know I said tomorrow, but the tables have turned. The time is now! It's time for *you* to make *our* presence felt. It's time for *you* to compel her to do whatever the hell *we w'ont* her to do. So, as soon as that waitress shows her fat, blotchy hanging pale face again, you call her ass over here to exact *our* revenge."

I may have nodded like a maniac in agreement, but I was still scared shitless to start any trouble, no matter how right Phoebe was. In fact, what good was a new gift if I was never ever to use it? Fortunately for the waitress, two fine-ass *brothers*, as in *ethnic* brothers, fine from belt to bellbottoms, interrupted our plans by stepping into the diner. I knew I was into Phoebe, but I wasn't blind. With our table in their sights and no hesitation in their strides, they stopped at the edge, one with a respectful question: "You ladies mind if we join you?"

Still playing the fledgling, I didn't really expect them to stop at our table, so I didn't say anything. Instead, I aimed my disapproval in Phoebe's direction—a desperate attempt to compel her to say "no," but it bounced off her face like a spring.

"Sugar, I don't know what took you this long to ask," she said to the bold, young male aggressor, her deep southern accent renewed.

I couldn't believe it. *What is she trying to do?* I was so confused, and I knew she could tell, but it didn't stop her from scooting over and prompting me to do the same.

"I'm Renton," he said as he slid beside Phoebe.

Phoebe's brow crinkled. "Excuse me, did you say, you're *renting*?"

"*Renton,* with an 'o' and an 'n.'"

He could have been *Rin Tin Tin* for all I cared.

The other slid next to me—a bit too close for comfort. "And I'm Joseph," he said with his best Barry White voice. "And you are?"

"I'm Tasha," I said as flatly as I could.

"And I'm Loretta," Phoebe said, batting her eyes at Rin Tin.

Oh, I get it. The seducer had returned, and we were all about to become part of her *Masterpiece Theatre*, the Creole version.

For the most part, both men were gentlemen through-out the conversation. It just so happened this particular diner offered alcohol this time of night, but beer only. The guys paid for a round, a real classy move, until I soon felt a hand massaging me above my knee. Its grasp was far too big to be from Phoebe, and both of *my* hands were above the table. *Ole Boy Joe* was getting frisky, and it was definitely creeping me out. I'd given him no signs, no looks, no nothing. He removed it shortly after, but if he was to try it *one* more time…

Fortunately, the conversation remained tame, but minutes later, Joe was at it again, this time whispering in my ear, "Say, how about we finish this over at my place?" A whisper so light, I barely heard it, but Phoebe seemed to hear him clearly, her eyes already saying "yes." "I got something there to show you," Joe said, on the verge of chest-bumping me through the window. "Twelve inches of fun in my pants, baby. Waiting for you."

That's when the hand returned, higher up my thigh this time.

Past due to make a decision, I put both my foot and my fist down. "Look, I don't care what the hell you got in your pants! I ain't that kinda' woman! And to make it clear, I don't know you!"

Joe turned to Phoebe with a dazed look. "What's up with your girl?"

But she rolled her eyes back towards the window. "You got to ask her that yourself, my brother."

Joe returned to me. "What's up with you, girl? You know you been giving me the look all night long. Tryin' to get your hands on all *thisss*," he said, holding the "s" and his full *package* at the same time.

I was sure my blood pressure was rising. "Look, I don't care what you got in your pants or how big and long you *think* it is; I ain't touchin' *yo' thang* with *his* hands," I said while pointing at his boy, Rin Tin.

Joe had had enough, throwing his hands in the air and mumbling, "*Psss*, ole bitch-ass tease."

At this point, it wasn't his handsy-ness; it wasn't the word, "tease"; but when I heard the word, "bitch," my fists practically clinched on their own. "Hold up! What did you just call me?"

Meanwhile, Rin Tin was patting the air in front of Joe. "Yo,' cool down, man.'"

But it was too late; the sacred line had been crossed. With a piercing glare, I gritted in Joe's face. "*Negro*, if you ever call *me*... or *any* other woman... a bitch again, I bet you better take yo' ass outside, pull out yo' *stanky-ass* dick, and yank it until you rub the skin right off it! Now, call me a bitch one more time!" I dared him.

From the corner of my eye, I saw Phoebe's mouth hanging open. Rin Tin's hand was clamped over his own mouth, and Joe simply looked at me apologetically, but still softly cursed, "Bitch," blatantly disobeying my request—or was he?

I gritted again, every nerve in my body vibrating. "Why you motha—"

Joe, on the other hand, rolled from his seat before I could finish my sentiment. He strolled away as cool as he had walked in, stopped outside the door, and then *definitely* obeyed me. Joe pulled down his pants and started shucking himself like a cob of corn.

Both Phoebe and I had our hands over *our* mouths at this point, while Rin Tin squealed towards the front, "What the fuck are you doing, man?"

Even Ella joined in from the middle of the diner. "Oh, my Lord, what in the hell is he doing? Dan, you gotta see this!"

An old white man looked up from behind the counter. "Boy, get on away from here with your nasty self!" he said.

Once the word, "boy," finally registered in my brain, I couldn't dispute Dan on this one, but he wasn't finished.

"They oughtta have his dang ass roped to a tree!" Dan shouted with a death-seeking grimace.

Now that wasn't nice, I thought, but Phoebe seemed to think even worse of his remark, if the slice in her eyes was any indication.

Everyone cringed when Joe yelled towards the sky, "Ahh! Why can't I fucking stop!"

Rin Tin stood up, intent on running to his friend's rescue, but was halted by something more frightening. A police squad car had simultaneously rolled into a space right in front of Joe. By the time the sirens flashed, Rin Tin was out the diner's side door and completely out of sight. Meanwhile, Joe had to be wrestled to the ground and handcuffed just to stop yanking—a blessing in disguise.

When the squad car eventually pulled off with Joe in the backseat, Phoebe and I were still sitting stunned at our table. It took a few more seconds for her to turn my way with a quizzical look. "Well, that was interesting. How does it feel?"

I nodded. "My nerves are tingling a little, but it feels pretty good." I felt more alive than ever. "I can't help but feel a little sad for that slimy bastard, though, but overall... I feel pretty hyped! Hey, will he ever stop?"

Phoebe shrugged. "Sure. I mean, if he stays cuffed forever, or until he works the skin completely off—whichever comes first. Of course, there's the little matter of him eliminating the "B-word" from his vocabulary altogether. That's all."

"*Da-yam...*" Then I wondered. "Hey, can these... uhh... spells be removed, or uhh... reversed?"

Phoebe stroked her chin damn-near as if she had a beard. "I don't know..." She switched to a chuckle. "Huh, huh—who on Earth would ever want to do that?"

My eyes rolled, but to a dead stop. "Hey, wait a minute ... was this what you did to Del?"

"Who?"

"Del. Remember? My boyfr—my *old* boyfriend back in Louisiana? Did you compel him in some kind of way?"

"Oh, yeah, him... Something like that," she muttered. "So, what do you want to do next? Are you ready to get the hell out of this little shitty-ass racist outhouse?"

"Been ready. But I'll be damned if I leave here without my scrambled eggs and juice, and maybe another steak." I looked towards the kitchen and yelled, "*Ohh, Ella!*" Little did

I know I would be the one creating the masterpiece this night. I needed a pen name.

Later, back in the hotel room, I'd fallen asleep just as soon as my head had hit the pillow, but I was awoken again by the sound of running shower water. And like before, it was nearly two a.m. and the space beside me was empty. Feeling the cool sheets was when I noticed something else seemed amiss. A faint streetlamp revealed my bite marks were completely gone, but I was too tired to question anymore. Instead, I fell back to sleep in total acceptance of my dear's incessant urge for cleanliness.

A few hours later, we were both up and packing our few bags with the television on, but only I stopped when I heard a reporter announce: "A community is in terror after an iconic local diner was hit by a horrific double-death early this morning." I turned up the volume just as two older white faces engulfed the screen. The reporter continued: "Owner of Danny's Diner, Dan Thornton, and waitress, Ella Burbank, were both found mauled and dismembered by some sort of animal. Remaining details are too gory to repeat, but a few local customers were interviewed for their reactions."

"Da-yam!" I blurted and pointed at the screen. "Phoebe, look!"

She stopped and looked. "What?"

"Isn't that the diner-owner and the waitress from last night? Wasn't that the diner? Danny's Diner?"

She shrugged after only a glance. "I don't know. I never looked at the name of it. And that *might* be them. Why?"

"*Lord...* they were mauled and dismembered! By some kind of animal, they said."

Phoebe shrugged again before walking away. "Some people get what they deserve in life."

"Phoebe!" But I stepped back, appalled.

"Well, I'm just saying."

"I mean, Ella was a bit rude, but no human being deserves *that*!"

"I just believe certain forces in the universe have the final say, so in that case, maybe 'deserve' ain't got a goddamn thing to do with it," she said on her way to the bathroom.

"I know. But damn."

She came back from the bathroom flapping a few face-towels in her hand. "Plus," she said while stuffing them in her bag, "I'm sure that ole coot of an owner done lynched a few of *us* back in his heyday. And the waitress? Guilty by association."

As possible as it sounded, I was still a little shocked by Phoebe's harsh judgement, but I remained glued to the screen until she finally broke my trance.

"Anyway," she said, "let's just finish packing and get the *fuck* out of Richmond. This place nauseates me. And as you can see from that report—too much goddamn drama."

Chapter 12

A Big Bite Out Of

A Big Apple

Narrated by Tasha Whitlow

New York—where we "Soul Sista's" took our talents next. That was Phoebe and I, but since I was still in training, Phoebe utilized her skills to find us a low-rent apartment for the price of "none." Located in a place lovingly referred to as *Da Bronx*, the neighborhood seemed a bit borderline, but I still trusted her instincts. And whenever she was out on one of her mysterious night-runs, her free-flowing ways had rubbed off on me enough to make my own. I decided to go to the avenue's corner store a couple of blocks away. The "corner store" was what we called it in Louisiana; the corner "bodega" was what they called it here in New York. Whichever, this hot pretty thing from the Flats boldly strutted her stuff into the bodega. It was when I exited that reality struck, and my mood changed.

The first catcall came from a man passing by: *"Brown sugar! Come on and cum on me-ee! Brown Sugar!"* I knew the song, but *that* version definitely wasn't a hit.

The next man was hanging outside his car window while still driving. "Psst! Psst! Hey, how much? C'mon, how much?"

But things didn't really get scary until another stepped out from the shadows—straight into my face. "Hey, hey, hey," he said, while a long stream of cigarette smoke fumed from his mouth. "Looking for something good tonight, baby? I got what you need." Honestly, since he didn't pullout any weed, I couldn't tell if he thought I was a prostitute or was trying to be one, himself. Either way, he was awful at it. After that, he kept pressing towards me like he couldn't stop.

Thoroughly revolted, compelling him away was the last thing on my mind. I fled from his foul breath and turned on the first available cross street, a dark path that grew even darker the faster I walked. A few more steps and I discovered the reason why: what I thought was a street was nothing but an alley dead-ended by a brick wall. Looking back revealed even more trouble: three male figures approaching from the avenue. "Oh, shit," I uttered. It was doubtful if any of them were the guys I'd just encountered, because these kept approaching without any words, but I didn't need to hear them speak to know their intentions. Meanwhile, my newfound boldness was now trickling down my inner thigh.

With thoughts of Phoebe, my new love, flashing in my brain, I turned completely around with only one thing left to do: I stared into the first man's eyes and shouted, "I think y'all need to stop and leave me alone! I said, 'Stop'!"

Either I didn't really believe they would stop, or there wasn't enough light for them to see my hypnotic stare, because all three kept coming until the first grabbed my face.

"You think you just gonna drag that sweet little round ass through our turf and not pay the toll?" he said, lifting me by my cheeks until my heels left the ground.

Now nose-to-nose, it was the perfect opportunity for me to attempt another trance, except I was speechless. Just as his other hand slithered up my skirt, a loud swish breezed around the alley on an otherwise still night. A crunching snap later, one of the other thugs hit the pavement; my attackers were now down to two.

The first one turned his head with me still in his grip. "What the fuck?" he mumbled. But it didn't stop him from squeezing my cheeks tighter.

Another heavy breeze later, the second thug vanished, leaving the first one standing in awe. With his mouth hanging, he finally returned his attention to me, giving me a clear view to his frightened eyes, and one more chance to offer my opinion: "Mister, I don't know where you come from, but I'm gonna assume wherever it is, you ain't got no love from your mother. So, what you're gonna do... is take your goddamn hand off my face, then take your ass out of here, find an old-ass woman to serve, and lick her dusty crotch until you choke to death on her crusty-ass cum, you son of a bitch. Now!"

After my heels retouched the alley, he let go of my cheeks. "Aw, man," he said on his way towards the avenue, where he punched the air in disgust. I even heard his mumbling sobs from where I stood: "Fuck, how come I gotta go lick on some old ass bitch? Damn!"

Once he turned the corner, I exhaled down to my knees
and quietly praised, "By the grace of God, I've been spared."
But at what cost? Not only was I standing in a dark alley with
a piss-drenched leg, but one of the thugs was still on the pavement where he lay motionless near a garbage can. *What kind
of grace are we talking about here?* The next moment, from
behind me in the corner of the alley came the loudest slurping
and gurgling noises I'd ever heard. Just enough light emerged
to see a woman with her back to me, and the second thug,
twice her size, dangling and jittering in her arms. It was the
weirdest make-out scene in the oddest of places, but when his
body slumped all the way to the alley's floor, I realized, sex
was *not* on the agenda. Afterwards, the woman looked at me
with a furtive glance, the man's blood pouring down her chin,
her blouse soaking in it.

Oh, my God! I gasped when I saw who it was. "Oh,
my God!" I said it out loud.

"Oops," Phoebe said. "I'm *real* sorry you had to see
me like this."

"Oh, my God! What did you just do?" I was quivering by now.

"What do you mean? I believe I just saved your digni-
ty, if not your life. Now, give me a little graceful credit too,
will you?"

I gob-smacked my face. "Oh, my God! Did you
just—"

"Drink all his blood? Yeah, I kind of did."

"So... you *are* a—"

"A vampire? Yeah, I kind of am."

"Oh, my God! You mean he's—"

"Dead? Yeah, he kind of is."

"Oh, my God!"

"Hey, what are you all shaken up about? You think you didn't just dish out a little death penalty of your own on that first guy?"

"What am I shaken up about? I, I... well... take your pick!"

I stumbled back dizzily, not only from this night, but from the myriad of unexplained moments: Del's neck being sucked on, the twilight showers, the blood on the doorknob, the tiny bagful of new clothes—obviously stolen—the diner mauling, and now this. Luckily Phoebe was there to catch me from completely fainting, although I'd never seen her move. She was apparently also as swift as the wind. Now limp in her remarkably strong arms, her face was starting to blur as her eyes locked into mine.

"Honey," she cajoled, "I think you just need a little rest right now."

"Whuh..."

"Whuh...," was the last thing I remembered slurring before waking up with the sun beaming through our apartment window. My eyes aimed at the ceiling fan, I was lying above the covers with all my clothes still on, wondering if last night was all just a dream, a horrid nightmare. Meanwhile, Phoebe was sitting on the edge of the bed with an unflinching stare

into my eyes. It was hard to tell if I'd passed out last night, if she had compelled me to sleep, or if she was trying to compel me right now, but it was obvious she was waiting for me to say something.

"Well," she said as her eyes suddenly drooped, "what you saw last night was real. I'm still a—"

"A vampire?" I was groggy but aware.

"I kind of am."

"Am I in danger?"

"Honey, oh, no. You, in danger? Never! I could never harm you!" She laid her hand softly on my shoulder. "In fact, you're as safe as can be right here in my hands."

I couldn't help myself; I sat up and brushed her hand away. "But Phoebe, you're a *stone killer.*"

She flapped her hands. "Whoa, hold on, hold on. Only those who deserve it, mostly, get… you know…"

"Killed!" I shouted.

"*Shh!* Keep it down, will you?"

"But last night, couldn't you have just *compelled* them away?" I was now amazed, myself, at how comfortably I was debating my point as opposed to fleeing for my life.

"Yeah, I *could have*, but there's this *one* little thing," she said, pinching her fingers together. "I was pretty hungry. That kind of tension works up a *real* appetite, you know. And I *am*… a vampire. A Vampyrian, to be exact. I need my blood live and flowing. Some of the myths *are* true."

Phoebe was so deathly calm and convincing, I was almost a proponent just that quickly—at least a halfhearted one.

Yet a recent topic had resurfaced. "But I'm sure he didn't deserve *that*, did he?" I asked.

"Well, there are some who slip up, and some mistakes can get somebody killed out there in those streets."

"Yeah, but… Hey, wait a minute… does that make *me* one?"

"No, I told you I will never hurt you."

"No, I mean, am *I* a vampire?"

"Hell no! What would make you say such a thing?"

I held out my arm, which I'd forgotten no longer displayed any bitemarks, but still, I stretched it out in front of her. "My wrist, remember? You bit it."

"Oh, woman, please," Phoebe quipped. "It would take far more than a nibble to turn someone. I just gave you a little bit of an advantage, that's all."

"And what about Delroy?" I blasted.

"Who?"

"Del, my *boyfriend*?"

I remembered him going a tad bit pale after she'd "made-out" on his neck. *Relax, he'll be fine,* was what I remembered her telling me after he'd dozed off on that bench in the Quarters. And I had believed her, chalking it up to booze and weed.

"Oh, him? Relax," she reassured, "he's not dead, technically…"

"*Technically?*"

"Well, it's complicated."

"Try me."

"It's like… it's like… it's not quite death, but… maybe to *some* it's a curse. To others it's a gift—one your boy, Delroy, is gonna thank me for one day. However, if you want to go back home to *Del*," she practically *icked*, "who won't be quite the same man you once knew, I'd be more than happy to take you back. I can even make you forget everything from the *Jazz Fest* until now, if you'd like. *Or*… you can come with me to a special place I call… home."

Her eyes danced, finally displaying some degree of a soul. But me, I crashed back into the mattress with no clue how to respond.

Chapter 13

The Tragedy of Bahati Ambimbola

Narrated by Tasha Whitlow

Heading east on I-495, riding in the passenger's seat of Del's convertible was my response to Phoebe's offer. I'd only known her a few weeks, but our hearts were now connected. Plus, after her unplanned confession, I was now doubly intrigued—introduced to a whole new world I just *had* to know more about. And as crazy as it sounded, while Phoebe had finally gone to sleep the night before, I'd spent most of those hours in the mirror whispering homemade incantations to myself—desperate attempts to dispel Phoebe's slaughtering ways: "Please make me forget what I saw. I compel you to forget. Please make me forget. I compel you to forget."

Today along our highway journey, those images had already been buried deep in my mind, but were starting to resurface. It was now time to face my fears—time to know the real Phoebe Artreaux.

"Phoebe?" I asked.

"Yes, dear?"

"Tell me about yourself. I want to know everything. I mean, everything. Like, how it all began."

Phoebe took a deep breath and said, "Okay," before telling her dramatic story:

"*Sooo*... I was born Bahati Ambimbola in the late 1700s on a British-Caribbean Isle. My mom, Daliah, was an Afro-Caribbean princess, and she was the most beautiful—"

"Hold up a minute!" Her sensitive tone for her mother was no doubt a heartwarming beginning, but it was the rest that already had me lifted in my seat. "You mean to tell me that *you*... are what, close to *two-hundred-years old*? And the daughter of a *princess*?"

"Yes and yes. My grandmother was a Caribbean queen, and my natural grandfather, a slick-talking merchant from France."

This explained her smooth brown blend with Creole features.

"Now, listen up," she snapped, "'cause if you think things are hard for a sista' now, you ain't heard nothin' yet." She went on to explain how regardless of her royal ancestry, by battle or by treaty, dominion of the islands was in constant flux. "From British to Spanish to French rule, sometimes in reverse and back again, ultimately, it led to my family and me being captured in the melee and sold into slavery. I was only eleven when it happened, but I remember vividly how my father fought to his death to defend our honor, taking down as many enslavers as he could with his bare hands. He fought like a warrior was supposed to!"

Seeing Phoebe wipe her welling eyes was the answer to a question I would have eventually asked: *Does a vampire ever cry?*

"Umm… anyway," she said, finding the strength to struggle through, "my mother and I eventually ended up in southeast Louisiana, but by then, the sick-ass traders had already taken turns on the both of us, many times—many ways, before even reaching the mainland." Her trace of emotions was mild compared to my own fountain of tears. "Don't fret," she said with a few rubs on my shoulder. "It gets better."

"It does?" I sobbed and wiped my eyes.

"Yeah. Because I may've been too young to conceive, but thank God He forbade me to have a little bastard for one of *those* stank-ass bastards—traders and slave-masters alike. I should say, *Momma* forbade it. You see, she managed to brew up a nice little island potion to kill the possibility. Luckily she was able to find similar herbs from the Louisiana swamps, and they must have worked for the rest of my blood-flowing years, because never did I ever conceive." She jabbed her finger through the air like a sword, her tone more one of gratitude than defeat.

"Excuse me, but how exactly is this *better*?"

"How? Here's how: as many damned times as those white mother fuckers mounted me, then *and* the years after, all the way into my twenties, I would have rather die before bearing even half a seed of their sick, perverted souls," she professed, grimacing into the flowing air, only to contain herself a few seconds later. "Hey, don't feel bad for me. It was either

hate them or hate my mother. And it wasn't going to be her."
She paused for me to gather myself too, but quickly went on.
"Anyway, a few years into my twenties, I am sad to say I was
separated from Momma... traded to an upstate plantation on
higher ground. It belonged to a worldly Irishman named, Kelvin O'Mallory—"

"Wait a minute," I said, "did you ever see her again?"

"Momma?" Phoebe took a deep breath and a long exhale, followed by a few silent gulps. "No." Not even the
flowing wind could cut the tension in the air. "What was I
saying?"

"You were talking about... Kevin *O'Mallory*?"

"Yeah, yeah—*Kelvin* O'Mallory."

"Oh, sorry."

"No problem. Now, O'Mallory never touched me like
all the others, I'll give him that, but it didn't settle my suspicions any. I wasn't sure why he had even selected me that day
on the block. Later he told me. 'I saw something in you,' he
said, 'something strong in your spirit.' Funny he said that, because I'd never known him to be really spiritual—not that kind
of spiritual. In fact, rumors had started that he was dragging
slaves into one of his back-sheds and torturing them worse
than going to hell and back. So, I decided to follow him to that
shed one night, where I peeped through a crack and saw him
fang-deep into a strong young man's ribs. Marvin was the
man's name, I believe, and he was panting in ecstasy. It was
kind of hot at first." She chuckled lightly, a reaction with
which I failed to share with her. "Well, when O'Mallory

turned to my stumbling around outside," she said, "those elongated canines dripping in blood nearly made me water myself. But I ran away so fast, my bladder never had a chance.

"Now, all of us had heard tales of vampires and creatures of the night, but I never thought I'd be the first to see one, and this one ended up being one like no other. I'll get to that. But what I saw *that night* was actually an opportunity. Then, whatever he saw in me before, was personified when I, a shy but grown woman at the time, built up the courage to approach him in his study one night. 'M-M-Massa' O'Mall'ry,' I said, 'Can I asks you somethin'?'" Phoebe paused like an instructor with a point to make. "You do know we had to talk that way so the slave-masters wouldn't figure out how smart we really were, right?"

I didn't, but I nodded ridiculously. "Mm hm."

"Anyway, he just said, 'Yes, Mattie?' Mattie—that was my slave-name at the time. I raised my head high and let him know: 'I knows what you is, Massa' O'Mall'ry, and I w'onts to be just like you.' It was that calm demeanor of his that gave me even more courage to say what I had to say—that and the fact I had seen Marvin the day after the shed—walking around like nothing had happened.

"Anyway, O'Mallory looked at me with a flat stare, not the least bit fazed by my question. 'I know you do, Mattie,' he said, 'and I know it was you outside the shed. I have to say, it doesn't surprise me that you're approaching me on the matter, but I also have to say "no" at this time.'

"Shit, I thought he would have been flattered, but I was at least excited to hear the option was still on the table, but I still asked, 'How come, Massa' O'Mall'ry?' You wanna know what he said to me?"

My body tensed. "What?"

"He said, 'Because there's too much hatred in your spirit. I can sense it, and I'm not the kind that legend would have you believe.'"

I was amazed, not by O'Mallory's response, but by Phoebe's recall of almost two-hundred-year-old conversations like they had just happened yesterday, along with her masterful narrative skills—all while consoling me and never swerving over the roadway lines. And the story didn't end there.

"O'Mallory was right," she said, "and what he was saying was that he wasn't a killer, and I knew that. I sensed it. More importantly, he was only a gentlemanly feeder. He knew when to stop, how to control and withhold the virus, and even how to compel every victim to forget it had ever happened."

One word in particular had caught my attention. *"Virus?"* I blurted.

"Yes. What the legends don't tell you is that the word, Vampyrian, was originally an alteration to the stigmatic term, "virus-carrier." Anyway, based on O'Mallory's refusal, I had to devise another approach. So one night, in the cleanest, skimpiest slave-sack of a gown I could find, I tiptoed up to O'Mallory's bedroom, where I dropped it down to my ankles."

I froze in anticipation.

"*Child*," she said, "that man may have been a gentle-manly feeder, but he was still all *man* when it came to a wom-an. In his bed, I fucked, I scratched, I dug in, watching his gashed skin heal just as fast, but watching him moan after eve-ry raking dig. I must admit, for a second, I even felt a little something, because ole *Massa'* O'Mallory was different, even different from most Vampyrians I'd go on to meet. But it all changed once he finally sank his fangs into my neck, the mo-ment I was waiting for, and it was pure ecstasy, pure danger, pure inebriation... until I passed out."

I gasped. "Oh, no!"

"'*Oh, no*' is right, because when I woke up, I found myself standing butt-naked on the edge of a broken hill, nearly thirty-feet above an adjacent ravine. At first, I thought I was in a dream, until I turned around to the sight of guess who?"

I opened my mouth with only one obvious person in mind.

"O'Mallory!" she blurted, beating me to the punch. "And you wanna know what he did next?"

"What?" I felt my jaw hanging.

"Girl, do you know that mother fucker shoved me right off that cliff with no remorse."

"What!"

"I must have broken every goddamn bone in my body landing on that rugged ravine-bank, but I was somehow still alive. I even lay molded over the rocks thinking to myself: Aww... I thought he was different."

Even I agreed. "Aww…" I was also just as deep into one remarkable-ass story, and gladly, it still wasn't over.

Phoebe shrugged. "Yeah, and then I died."

"What! *You died*?"

"Mm hm."

At this point, I figured it was just a euphemism, so I gathered myself and humored her a bit. "Okay, what was that like?"

"Death? *Anh*. I saw weird little cloaked spirits scurrying around… waving their hands all over my body. None of them touched me, though. Looking back on it, it was like some reiki bullshit."

"Whoa…" I didn't understand her complacency here, but having been around her every day now, I knew she wasn't joking.

"Whatever they were doing must have worked, because I soon recovered and lifted myself to my feet. That's when I was *really* amazed, but still butt-naked.

"After that experience, I used every sense I had to find my way back to the plantation—back to O'Mallory to get answers. I could have just run away in the other direction, but I was *sooo* furious! I used my eyes, now able to see in the dark; I used my ears, now able to hear a butterfly's heartbeat; and I used my nose, now able to smell O'Mallory's housemaid's leftovers. Whenever a wagon passed by, I was able to slip into a ditch and hide without a sound, while having no idea how fast I was really moving.

"Finally, I was back on the plantation, where I snuck into my outside quarters, which was nothing but a shanty shared by eight of us. Fast asleep, nobody even heard me creep in to find another night gown. Shortly after that, I was back in the 'big house' facing O'Mallory again, this time back in his study. Frustrated as hell, I asked, 'How come you just did what you did to me?' And by the way, I was acutely aware I had dropped the 'Massa' prefix.

"He stood up and walked slowly from behind his desk—stepped in front of me, looked me in the eyes and put his hands on my shoulders. And this is what he said to me—he said, 'You had to know what it feels like to die—so you would know what it feels like to resurrect yourself. Now, you are a *true* O'Mallory.' I didn't quite understand what he meant, so he clarified: 'No, no, no. No longer an O'Mallory by chattel deed, but by clan.' He finished with a proud grin—like I was *real* family."

"And that turned you into an Irishwoman?" There was no sarcasm intended in my question; it just came out that way.

"Huh, funny. Well, at least an Irish-Vampyrian. That's what *he* thought. He went on to show me several things. You see, O'Mallory was what we call an 'Old-Worlder,' one who carries the most powers, and a few had rubbed off on little ole me, a shy little slave girl from across the sea."

"You talk about him in the past tense. Are you saying he died?" At the time, we had only scratched the surface on lifespans.

"Hmm... I'd say eventually he disappeared. I don't know to where, but I definitely knew other Old-Worlders didn't take too well to his benevolent philosophies." She gave a transparent shrug before resuming her story. "Anyway, I listened to him. He went on to show me how to feed instead of kill, how to control it, how to display compassion. But you know what? *I* had other plans."

I clutched my chest and gasped. "What did you do?"

Phoebe gritted again. "I left that shitty-ass plantation as Phoebe Artreaux, and tracked down every last one of them mother fucking scoundrel rapists, ripped off their fucking heads, and drank them dry from their mother fucking gullets," she said with an angry side-eye in my direction. "And I'm not just saying that to be metaphorical."

I knew that side-eye wasn't meant for me, and shockingly, I was suddenly no longer as squeamish about her actions. After hearing her trials and tribulations, I was beginning to understand, and I too was enraged.

She continued on, also telling me the name, Artreaux, was in honor of her grandfather, Bernard Artreaux—an "homage to his conniving ways," as she respectfully put it. And by the end of her story, the ride that started with me as her new lover, was now one with me as her "ride-or-die."

Chapter 14

Our Days and Our Nights

Narrated by Tasha Whitlow

Thirty minutes later, Phoebe steered into a winding driveway through a sprawling ten-acre lot, landscaped and manicured like a postcard. Speaking of plantation living, the house's style was close, but more Dutch Colonial than Antebellum. After swerving to the driveway's end, she rolled to an abrupt stop. "We're ho-*ome!*" she sang with her hand flipped in the air.

"What?" It made me wonder: She had to be up to something else, like maybe we were about to *steal* a home? I was *so* not in the mood for it. "Where are we?" I asked her.

"A little place called East Hampton. Surprised?"

Between her life-story and snoozing the rest of the way, how could I have noticed the road signs? "Uh, yeah... considering we were just in a shithole in *Da Bronx*."

"Well now, I do have to scour those neighborhoods time has forgotten—for obvious reasons. I mean it's not like I can go out for dinner here or in Manhattan, you know. I can, but it just wouldn't be... *prudent*. So come on."

After touring her house and property, I was even more stunned when I discovered it was backed by East Hampton's beach. Two-hundred-years of Bernard Artreaux's ways had apparently made for quite a living. The house at the end of Daliah Lane was to become home for the rest of at least my days.

Over the years, Phoebe and I did make a few trips back to Louisiana, each time by airline instead of road trip. Since Phoebe desired never to be tracked, even I had to travel anonymously, taking on the simple name, Terresa Jones, as my travel alias. Fake I.D.'s and passports were easy in Phoebe's world, so we ended up flying detection-free to Lafayette to visit my family, who was definitely suspicious of our union. Later, after my mother had passed away, I intended on returning, but found no need to rush. Those intentions soon turned into faint wishes as the years moved on.

My time with Phoebe in the Hamptons was heavenly, and I'd learned much more about all things V, but never had Phoebe given any thought to "turning" me completely. The power to compel she had gifted me in Richmond had lasted, but with it came no extended life. For the most part, I agreed with the decision, except in my weakest moments, those confronted by her ageless beauty as my back began to hunch.

There were still our excursions to Manhattan for either shopping or night-play, where I allowed her to be herself without compromise. "Allowed" may have been an overstatement, but knowing she'd gone through slavery and more, I often viewed her affliction as a gift—just like she'd once said. But somewhere in the middle, I did manage to change one of my concessions; I coerced her to stop the killing. Afterall, the Human/V Treaty had formed and had seen some success, suddenly making draining someone dry pretty difficult to hide. Plus, all of Phoebe's enemies were either dead by God's hands or hers, so what was the point? Then came a commercially bagged plasma called, "Alive," which wasn't really alive, but enzyme-enhanced with something called Ichorstim, something specifically for Vs. Yet Phoebe still thrived on live contact, the lively flow, as she frequently lured her prey to fancy hotel rooms, sipped them O'Mallory-style, and in the end, compelled them home without a mark or a clue.

Life had been a blast the whole while, but now my time was coming to an end. A genetic thing, most of the women in my family rarely made it far beyond seventy. It was a blessing just for me to have been on the incline towards eighty, but Phoebe's feelings were starting to wane. She was now reconsidering our personal pact.

One day while I lay in bed, groggy from heavy meds, she begged to turn me, to which I responded: "No, baby… this is far from my weakest moment, no matter how I look in it."

A tear ran down her cheek. "And, sugar," she said, "you look *fabulous*."

"You're much too kind, but I think I need some rest."

"No problem, sweetie."

She was ultra-comforting, leaning over to kiss my forehead like the mother I'd lost, which got me to thinking about home, my original home, and all those I had left behind. And it had been years since I'd thought about one person in particular. "Delroy…," I muttered.

"What's that, hon?" Phoebe answered from a seat in the opposite corner of the room, where I heard her shuffling through some old newspapers. It wouldn't have surprised me if she had heard me clearly, but her superb hearing had always become selective when it came to this subject.

"Delroy… Where's Delroy?"

There was a long pause. "New Orleans was the last I heard, actually."

"I need… to see him."

The shuffling continued before her voice dragged. "*Why?*"

"I have to… I have to… apologize to him. I've never apologized to him. I've always wanted to, but the years just kept passing—and I … and I… just couldn't… just couldn't face him." It wasn't like I could have told him the real reason back then, and it wasn't going to be any easier now, but I had to try to confront him about it; I had to apologize.

Phoebe's pause grew longer. "Are you sure that's what you want to do?"

"Yes. I'm certain."

"Okay, I'll have a message delivered for you. Maybe find his email address?"

"No, I have to say it in person. I owe him that much."

I heard her huff. "I'll see what I can do."

"Now, please?"

"Oh, alright."

When the papers finally stopped ruffling, I heard her on her cellphone as if she already knew the number.

"Phoebe, is that Del?"

"No, babe."

She returned to the call for what seemed like forever, until I could take no more. "Phoebe?"

"Hold on," she told whoever was on the line before asking me, "Yeah, hon?"

"Is that Del?"

"No, Babe. Yeah, I'm back—Timothy? Sorry about that. She's getting a little—"

Okay, I'd heard enough, and I didn't know who Timothy was, or why she was talking to him instead of Del, but those were the last words I heard before falling into a deep sleep.

Chapter 15

The Choice

Narrated by Trémeur DuChaine

The next morning I was on a plane from Los Angeles, but not heading back to Baton Rouge. After calling Tim the night before, I found out it wasn't his research that had located Tasha. He had actually received a call from Artreaux, the demon princess herself, who'd told him Tasha was very ill and wanted to see me. *The nerve of that bitch!* Not Tasha, *but that bitch of a monster!* I could never have cursed Tasha, the one I once thought was going to be my wife. I could never have blamed her for anything. *It's obvious she must have been compelled all these years, and now the demoness is allowing her one last wish from her dungeon!* So, I was on my way to New York State instead—on my way to rescue Tasha if only for her last breath, and on my way to destroy the one who killed Delroy Jackson.

This time looking out from a window seat, I no longer cared about the ticket back to Baton Rouge. My plan now was to get back by my own means, and with my return date open, I didn't care to call in either. I'd never responded to my supervisor's text, so as far as he was concerned, I was still on the hunt for Landon Levy. But his incessant string of text messages that followed made me wonder: *Is he more concerned about me, or the ones in search of more power?* Perhaps he was just determined to follow orders, but it didn't matter now; I didn't return those messages either.

Then there was Rayna, who'd only left one more text since the one after I'd landed in Los Angeles. We had an agreement that if ever I were to go dark while on assignment, she wouldn't press, but she *would* have carte blanche permission to contact Veleta to check on me, if done after a week's time. Obviously, this trip didn't qualify, but I had to admit to myself, I didn't know what to say to Rayna. No matter how I would have worded it, I was sure she would have read right through the guilt—these feelings for Tasha having resurfaced after being buried for so long.

My eyes still above the clouds, I refocused on Tasha, who had yet to be turned, a fact Tim had made sure to confirm with the demoness. I'd seen quite a few loved ones transcend to old-age and beyond, and surprisingly, those optics had never bothered me. But now, I had no idea what the next few hours would bring. It made me think about a few trips back to Lafayette after I'd been turned—remembering a different set of optics. Back then, I saw my relatives again, but they never saw me, and for good reasons. Prior to the Treaty, the virus was a never-ending "sentence," a disease of mythical horror. And prior to V-Screen, the sensitive pale but ageless skin would have been a dead giveaway. The only plus was that post-virus effects were slimming all over, if not muscle-tightening—what modern folks called "shredded," and what made some of us no longer recognizable. Nonetheless, I wasn't going to risk letting them see me in either of these forms, especially with the sinful taste of my one and only victim still in my mouth. In turn, I'd either watched everyone by cover of night, or from the shade of trees on a bright day, as was the case when they buried my mother. *Whoa*, how that moment hit me. I'd never gotten the chance to tell her how much I missed her, how much I loved her. Fast forwarded to Tasha, the sight of her alive was probably going to carry some consolation, but the years and the possibilities were gone, which left me once again enraged to the core.

It was late evening by the time the cab driver pulled into Artreaux's neighborhood. This was my second cab, and I'd kept my presence in the backseat silent the entire way, cloaking my ultimate intentions. I even stopped the cabby a few streets over, from where I barely made a sound to the demoness's front door with a special delivery hidden inside my jacket. Her door slightly open, I looked for signs of hidden cameras, but saw none. Besides, I had heard a lot more about her over the years, so I didn't expect someone of her extrasensory depth to be caught off-guard. *Why would the most powerful V on this side of the Atlantic need security anyway? A thief would be nothing but a fast-food delivery.* Suffice it to say, I didn't bother knocking.

Once inside it was me who was taken off-guard. The house may have been occupied by a voguish young woman, but its eclectic motif was that of a grandmother's cottage, except with an unusual twist. As I approached the stairs, antique lamps highlighted walls full of ancient weaponry of all kinds:

old-west rifles, muskets, crossbows, swords, assault rifles and anything else needed to kill someone in every era.

Landing on the top stair was when my hand went inside my jacket. I was prepared to share my gift with the lady of the house at first sight. My rage was now obstructing my original mission to see Tasha. But from here, all I heard were sobs and sniffles—softening my stance as I entered an open bedroom, the only one with a light on. Beside the bed with her head in her palms sat the demoness, wearing her same beautiful body from Jazz Fest days, but sobbing like someone with an actual soul. Under the sheets was an old woman, still and stiff with a coldness I felt all the way from the doorway. She had a face I wish I could have remembered, but I knew it was Tasha, and I knew I was too late. My heart sank.

For several moments, the demoness Artreaux and I had passed no words between us, until I could hold back no longer. I ended up saying something I thought I would never say to any woman, "You heartless bitch! How could you do this to her?"

Artreaux raised her face with an incredulous look. "How could I do what? Love her?"

"*I* loved her! You were just a motha' fuckin' trick-ass… life-wrecker!"

"No, no, that wasn't my intent."

She was trying to convince me, but all I could envision was the look on Tasha's face back at the Jazz Festival—not one from curiosity when we first saw Artreaux, but more like raw infatuation. Unnatural forces *had* to be at the root.

"Compelling her to leave her home, her family! And me!" I raged.

"No, you're wrong! I did *not* compel her!" The pitch in her voice dropped me to silence.

"I didn't compel her," she said, her tone now softer. "She was always free to leave, but she *chose* to remain with me." "What?"

She gritted. "I said, she was not compelled to stay."

I was speechless until looking at Tasha's cold but peaceful corpse. "Well, the least you could have done was *turn* her!" I didn't know what I was saying at this point.

"I couldn't. I mean, she refused. And I respected those wishes, as well as her wish for me to summon you. What, do you think I *wanted* to call for you?"

"Hmm… then if none of this was your intention," I grumbled, "why did you leave me *fucked up* on a bench, you fuckin' demon-ass whore!"

She cleared her eyes and pointed at me with a stern look. "You should be thanking me for that!"

"*Thanking you*? Why in the hell should I be thanking *you* for something like *that*?" I aimed my thumb at myself. "Something like this!"

She gritted with all her might. "Because of the cancer!"

Once she said that, I felt my nerves jerk to a stop.

"Because of the cancer," she repeated. "I could smell it fuming from your pores, flowing from your breath. Even over the alcohol and all the herb! It was on the verge of metastasizing out of control!"

And now my nerves quivered.

"Yeah, and afterwards," she went on, "I even felt your essence, your most painful memories. And brother, Agent Orange wasn't very kind to Delroy Jackson. Plus, he *did* go on to do more important things, didn't he?"

I didn't know what to think, utterly speechless, but I wasn't going to give any credit to *her* for any of *my* life and thereafter. I didn't even need to say it.

"Anyway," she said, dropping her forehead back into her hands, "I can understand how you feel, so if it's my head you want, that retractable sword inside your jacket is not gonna do any good." She paused to point. "Use that one right there. I'm ready to go peacefully."

Up until now, I'd never noticed the fully sheathed Samurai sword laying above the covers at Tasha's feet. Before that, I, myself, had wondered if the trinket in my pocket would have worked at all. I'd purchased it from a Craigslist collector just before my second cab to East Hampton. I knew it wasn't the Old World-forged steel I needed, but I didn't care; my plan was to keep whacking away like a yard-hack until reaching my goal. Yet with the demoness offering me an easier option, I slowly grabbed her sword and unsheathed it, while she bowed her head and lifted her ponytail, exposing her cervical vertebrae. As much as I hated what I'd done to my helpless victim years ago, the one on St. Charles Avenue, I'd killed before in

'Nam. Ending the demoness's second life wasn't going to be difficult.

Prepared to see ashes-to-ashes and dust-to-dust, something else came to mind, something that stopped me from cocking the blade. "Nah," I said before slinging the sword back onto the bed. "Why give you the satisfaction? Why allow you the glory of joining Tasha before me?" I gazed back at Tasha's body and mourned to myself. *Tasha, you're the woman I once thought would be my wife? Goodbye, my love.*

Leaving the house with other matters to attend to, I heard Artreaux yell all the way from Tasha's bedroom: "Ahhhh! Damn you, Trémeur DuChaine, you son of a bitching prick!"

With the evening's outcome far to the left of what was planned, I couldn't wait to get back home. And what was Artreaux trying to do, reverse *all* her wrongs into one right? *Cure me of cancer, my ass.* That's when I remembered the coughing: *Damn... it did stop after that.* But still, I couldn't wait to get back to Rayna and fess-up to my covert behavior. From the backseat of yet another cab, this required more than a light text. I speed-dialed her instead, only to catch her voicemail. "You know what to do," it said, her voice pleasantly curt before the beep.

I took a deep breath. "Hey, baby. I wrapped up my business in L.A. earlier than expected, but I had to take a little detour before coming back. I'll tell you all about it when I get there. Love you."

There was a twitch from the front seat, just before the cabby's eyes cut furtively in the rearview mirror. She too could tell it was the first time I'd said it. You know, the "L-word."

Along the ride, my mind shifted back to Tasha, but surprisingly, now for only a few seconds at a time. It seemed the years had given me plenty of opportunities to pre-mourn. Closure was all I was lacking, and it happened to come faster than I thought it would in the end. Now I just wondered how Rayna would take it—all of it. Then it dawned on me: *Will the big L-word soften the blow? Not that I planned it that way, of course.*

Chapter 16

For a Gift Given . . . .

Narrated by Trémeur DuChaine

I was in a window seat again on the flight back to Louisiana, but Atlanta, Georgia was to be the first stop on the itinerary, and a surprise storm had turned the trip into a turbulent one. Meanwhile, my feelings for Artreaux had gone from disdain to indifference, a monumental improvement, while my mind was back on the office, back on those who may have been on-the-take. Every coworker's face crossed my thoughts, from higher-ups to forensic scientists, all of them over and over. Even Veleta's face appeared once, but I shook hers away instantly. She was the most unflappable human I'd ever met. The rest had spines closer to that of an earthworm, and *that* was being generous.

"Can I get you something to drink, sweetie?" a woman standing in the aisle asked.

My little quandary was so engrossing, I'd never noticed how much time had passed, or that the turbulence had long leveled off. It wasn't until I looked up at the flight attendant's perky smile that I noticed the vacant seats beside me. *Okay, this is getting fuckin' ridiculous.* Even with a window seat, risk-management was still on the airline's mind.

"Sure," I said. "Vodka. Neat, please."

Accepting her offer was far out of the ordinary for me. Afterall, to a V, most alcoholic beverages carried the potency of a single grape, but I saw no other way to bring an end to a week full of deathly dilemmas.

"Not a problem, hon," she said.

Fortyish and confident, her accent was so deeply southern, it felt like I was back in Louisiana already, and further away from those dilemmas. After she poured my drink and rolled her whiskey-wagon to the next row, I opened an on-flight magazine, another way to idle my time away. That's when both my drink and the cart made a jump; the attendant nearly toppled into someone else's lap. As for me, the magazine was the only thing that saved my slacks from a good soaking. The turbulence had returned without warning, followed by a choking engine and a boom, and down the aisle went that cart and that attendant. Another engine choked, then down dove the entire plane. The fasten-your-seatbelt lights were far too late, and most fallen oxygen masks went untouched as screams and prayers filled the fuselage. With my stomach pressing up my ribs, I knew no one was going to survive this one, not even a V. A fall so gripping, I couldn't focus enough to make my peace, and I couldn't believe *I* was going to be the one reconnecting with Tasha long before Artreaux.

Fortunately, I had passed out before we made impact, sparing me a memorably gruesome death. But when I opened my eyes, it was dark, yet I still felt so alive. There weren't even any burning flames around me—no wreckage in sight. All I saw was a hazy drift, more like a heavy fog rather than smoky fumes. Even stranger, small creatures were moving around me like scavengers, but these creatures spoke, whispering foreign incantations. I didn't know what to make of them, but when I looked closer, they were fully cloaked with bony hands protruding from their sleeves—now looking more like little reapers. Not once did they touch me, though. They simply kept circling me until hovering and finally vanishing into the night.

Afterwards was when the fog cleared to a smoky scene, the charred field of flaming parts I'd originally expected to see. And in the dark, I was still able to make out a few human skeletal remains here and there. Raising my arm, I saw another skeletal remain—my own. Most of my flesh had been burned off my bones, but I didn't feel a thing, only numbness as I stood up, trembling on my rickety femurs. Although not in great pain, I was still confused, delusional even, but in the distance shined a light of hope—one I felt compelled to follow.

The few cooked muscles left on my bones carried me all the way to a light-post outside an old-fashioned gas station; the "ESSO" sign was still standing. I could have sworn I was looking at a mirage. *Shit… I thought those things had gone extinct.* But by the grace of God, it was there, and so was an old-fashioned payphone by the door. The crash in the distance may not have scared the two station attendants away, but a steaming skeleton walking in their direction did the trick— the chance I needed to get to the phone. And if there was one thing a guy from my era knew how to do, it was how to make a collect call.

"Tim?" I said when the call went through. "It's me." The pause that followed lasted so long, I thought I'd been disconnected. "Tim!"

"*Tray?*" he finally answered. "Where are you calling from, and what's wrong with your voice? You sound like... *death.*"

"Yeah, the jury's still out on that one, but I need a huge favor, bro."

With dawn looming, more strange things and sensations started to happen: my flesh was regenerating as quickly as the little flesh I had left was falling off. A few missing bones were even starting to fill, but I was now more vulnerable than ever. It was long after firetrucks and E.M.U.'s had made it to the crash-site, one where I was never found—a good thing since I would have been one huge-ass dilemma for human rescuers.

After scraping along into a wooded area far from the crash, and after Tim had made a few calls, I waited patiently. *When is my rescue coming?* It arrived a little later as a limousine rolled to a stop across the road. Out emerged the local Atlanta V-Council's service workers, most wearing U/V suits, as if prepared for this exact situation.

By late morning, I was heading back to Louisiana on a private V-jet, where I was treated well and made comfortable. So much so, it had me reconsidering Casio's previous advice. *If this is how they treat me in the light, I may have to bear whatever happens in the dark.*

With a Vampyrian doctor providing me ointments and medicine onboard the jet, my flesh was continuing to regenerate at a remarkable rate. Even without true blood, things like flesh, skin, hair and limbs all tended to regrow like a five-o'clock shadow. Meanwhile, lying on my backside with only a towel covering my "junk," I was hoping there was another matter the doctor could shed some light on—hoping psychiatry was also her specialty.

"Doc?" I asked.

She straightened up with a pensive look behind her glasses. "Yes, Mr. DuChaine?" Her features were Ethiopian with an accent to match, and the youthful look of someone who'd been turned back in med-school.

With only strands of vocal cords left, I may have struggled, but I was determined to find an answer. "While I was out, I had a weird dream. I... I saw and heard little people all around me—but more like... little goblins."

The doctor didn't pause. Multitasking, she finished the last few lines from a piece of paper in her hand before asking, "Goblins?" Her voice even carried only mild surprise.

I, however, used all my remaining strength in a desperate attempt to massage the vision from my brain through my temples. "Or maybe... little reapers or something."

She heard me clearly, but when she saw what I was doing, she rolled up that piece of paper and pressed it under my wrist. "Careful," she said, gently prying my hand away from my forehead. "The flesh and muscles may return rapidly, but the skin will take quite a while. As for goblins—weird?

Yes. Although, not unheard of. Realm Walkers are who you're referencing, and very few of us have claimed to have seen them. It has been said they appear in your weakest moments—to determine your fate."

"My fate? Are you saying this is fate's way of being *kind*?"

"Perhaps, but the Realm Walkers do not determine whether you live or die. They determine *how* you return."

"*How* I return?"

"Yes. Weaker, the same, stronger. Or perhaps more gifted even. And judging by the rapidity of your healing, you must be one of the lucky ones."

"*Huh*, fat chance," I said, "considering my unlucky path to luck."

"Relax, you'll be fine," she assured, standing to her feet. "Now, get some rest. Doctor's orders."

No matter how long I'd been a V, there were even more optics that never ceased to amaze me—like how this doctor's college-girl-looks had come with a sage's wisdom.

Throughout most of the trip back to Louisiana, I thought of nothing but more of the doctor's orders. Remaining inside by day was one of them, which now seemed cruel under the circumstances. I had no idea exactly how long it would take just for all my muscles to return. And as much as I wanted to be with Rayna, I couldn't let her see me this way. Afterall, judging by my body, I was expecting nothing short of a horror picture for a face. Seeing it would have surely sent Rayna to an asylum, and maybe me too. I was even planning on staying away from all mirrors.

The V-jet had landed me directly on a private airstrip outside New Orleans instead of Baton Rouge, where Casio and Tim were waiting to pick me up in Casio's S.U.V., just one of his many vehicles. Calling in family at a time like this seemed to be the best move, but as Tim soon reminded me, not always the most pleasant. When I got into the backseat wearing a U/V suit, I eased the hood back behind my neck for relief. From the passenger's seat, Tim began snapping his fingers, already toying with an analogy.

"Hey!" he said. "What was the name that guy was called in that movie?"

"What movie?" Casio asked.

"Oh! *'Crispy'*!"

Casio snapped and pointed too. "Yeah, yeah, yeah... *Spawn*! That was it!"

Tim cupped his mouth. "That's that shit! That's that joint!" With no mercy, he lifted his eyes towards the rearview mirror and rasped. "'Hello, my little *'Crispy.'*"

Not at all surprised, I leaned back to rest. "Man, fuck both you motha' fuckas."

"Aw, man, we're just trying to cheer you up," Tim said. "You'll heal."

But Casio couldn't hold back one more snipe. "Eventually." *True, but still a snipe.*

Moments after their smiles had straightened, Casio eyed me through the rearview. "How did things go with Tasha?" he asked. "How is she?"

It was clear Casio wasn't going to look at the road again until I gave him an answer, a lengthy one I assumed. But just a glimpse of my own bulging eyeballs in the mirror sent me back under the hood. "Dead."

"Oh… I'm sorry to hear—"

Casio had cut himself off, obviously sensing I had nothing else left to say. In fact, none of us spoke another word about it ever again.

Chapter 17

. . . . One is Taken

Narrated by Trémeur DuChaine

Nearly a week had passed at Casio's house, and most of it I spent drooping around in my old bedroom upstairs. But the whole time, I'd been following the doctor's orders to the letter. Like she'd predicted, my muscles had returned. I had official-ly graduated from skeleton to full anatomical model. Small patches of skin were starting to return to my face faster than usual, and the time had finally come. With a brand-new cell-phone and the courage to match, I began calling Rayna at least every ten minutes, starting with leaving a few messages until that dreadful moment—the moment when I heard: "You have reached a mailbox that is full or is no longer accepting calls from this number." *Maybe she's not answering this new num-ber. But I've been leaving beaucoup messages.* I tried texting her instead, but those also went unanswered, probably sent to nowhere. I couldn't help but wonder: *Could she have figured out I was in New York to see another woman? Can she be thinking, me saying 'I love you' was just a ploy? Or did she get scared off by the L-word altogether?* These questions only skimmed the surface of the deeper, irrational war going on in my head.

A few more days passed and I still looked "fried." From the rear-hall bay window in Casio's house, I watched the sun fall while exploring my only options: how to face Rayna—how to even reach her. *What am I gonna—*

"Hey, uh, Tray?" Casio asked just as his reflection in the window caught my attention. "Tim and I are gonna hit the Quarters. Why don't you join us?"

I was startled at first, having never heard him enter the hallway, but my eyes remained locked on the horizon just long enough to notice my own reflection. "What? Looking like *this?*"

"Oh, come on… you get dressed up real tight, no-body'll notice."

"Mmm…"

I was expecting him to snicker a little, but it never came; hands-out was his only gesture. "H'unh? What do you say?"

But I only shook my head.

"I understand," he said. "I tell you what, if you change your mind, here's a set of keys to borrow." He jingled them and hung them on a coat-hook on the wall. "Give us a call. Come out and join us. Or shit, go anywhere you need to! Just get the hell out of the house, will you! Your sour attitude is stinking up the joint."

I sat there with no answer.

In the reflection, his eyes widened. "Okay?"

"Yeah," I said. *Anything to get you off my ass.*

"Uh h'unh… I suppose anything to get me off your back, right?"

He huffed before making his way down the stairs, leaving me behind wondering: *Got-damnit! He's got to be holding out on everyone! Fucking with our heads. I know that son of a bitch can read minds.*

From surprise to exacerbation, my exchange with my eldest brother was silently more turbulent than he could have ever known, but five minutes after I heard the front door close, I already felt my options starting to change. Fortunately, I still believed in a God, which had me thinking about the gift I'd just been granted. Glancing at the coat-hook, I saw the keys to Casio's Aston Martin—a *definite* sign from above.

Minutes after my encounter with "divine intervention," I was in the Aston Martin racing all the way back to Baton Rouge. To us DuChaine brothers, the term, "borrow," could have turned out to be a very long time. Driving over ninety-miles-per-hour, I was really risking it because there was no telling how the state troopers, whose attitudes had changed very little since the seventies, would have reacted to a skinless V racing up the highway. *Well, at least I don't have my **other** skin to deal with at the moment.* Regardless, I wasn't ready to reveal myself as L.B.I., considering I still hadn't announced my return. In the end, Casio's car got me all the way to Rayna's complex in less than forty-five-minutes, and with no consequences.

Before I'd left New Orleans, I'd changed into loose-fitting clothes, nothing too clingy, per more of the doctor's orders. I'd even grabbed a soft ski-mask just in case, but in my haste to see Rayna, I darted out of the car leaving it behind on the passenger's seat. Honestly, I was probably going to frighten her one way or the other anyway, which did nothing to ease my nerves.

Most apartments in Baton Rouge had no secure entries, and Rayna's was no different—the reason I'd made it all the way to her breezeway before being slowed by a tangy venomous odor, an odor a human wouldn't pick up even if his nose was inches away. With Rayna's unit on the top level, it could have been coming from anywhere, but it only intensified the closer I got to her door. Nervousness soon turned into fright by the time I approached, especially when just like my phone calls, my knocks went unanswered. The key she had given me came to mind, but—*Oh, shit*—it had been lost in the plane crash. Luckily her doorknob was unlocked and jiggly—*if I can call that luck. And I know that smell.*

Easing the door open revealed light coming from her bedroom. "Rayna?" I called out as I entered. "Rayna? Are you in here?"

All I heard were my own shoe-soles clumping through her living room, crunching over her bedroom threshold, then my own gasp at what I saw next. A woman's body was face-down in Rayna's bed with bloody sheets twisted all around her, and by the residual odor, a Vampyrian's natural blood-thinning agent was relatively fresh in her lifeless body. I wanted to sink into the floor when I started to put it all togeth-er, refusing to believe it was Rayna's body. But I had to make sure.

I was barely breathing when I crawled onto the bed and rolled the woman's body over—no time for crime-scene eti-quette. It was definitely Rayna, cold and pale, her neck stran-gled, twisted and bitten. Just the shock of it all was enough to repulse me completely off the bed. Screaming to the ceiling was my next reaction, followed by my legs buckling and drop-ping me all the way back against the wall. *How much more can I take?*

Seconds after hitting the wall, I was jarred by another scream, one shrieking through the entire apartment, a scream that wasn't my own. Hunched in the bedroom's doorway was a woman with her hands over her mouth. I had been too dis-traught to even hear her enter the apartment, and now more so when I realized it was Rayna's sister, Jacynthia. And judging by the scene in front of her, her worst fears had finally come to pass.

"Aaaaaahhh!" she screamed again. "What have you done to her?"

I held out my palm, desperate to halt where her thoughts were going with this. "Jacynthia, wait! It wasn't me—"

But she wasn't listening; her mind was already made up. While her screams turned into airless gasps, a man and a woman, most likely Rayna's neighbors, had already heard the noise. Both now stood behind Jacynthia with their mouths wide open.

There were many options I could have taken at this point, but crashing through the window was the first of the moment, and I took it. From four stories up I jumped, hitting the ground in full stride towards the car.

Back inside Casio's vehicle, it wasn't until I reached I-10 West did I turn on my headlights, hoping no one else had seen me rush out of Rayna's complex. By the time I crossed over the Mississippi River Bridge, I began to absorb everything I had just witnessed. "Damn it!" I banged on my steering wheel. *I could have searched for her essence! That's if whoever did it wasn't "Old-Worldish" enough to suck all of it away.* But there had been no time anyway.

I remembered the fang-bites and signs of strangulation. With bruises underneath her chin and wounds in her lower jugular, only two things were evident: one, a V's desire to accumulate blood in the neck; the other, the scabbed fang marks, a trait not left behind by *my* unique maker, but one left behind by most others, especially by the most barbaric feeders. But therein lay the issue: Levy was dead, and there was never any word of any new serial feeder. *Who could it be?* After several blank moments, only the white supremacists came to mind. Afterall, Livingston Parish gossip had it that Mary McCullup had never returned home since the night I was last there. I'd even heard that Ole Man Watson had claimed to have seen "absolutely nothin' and nobody." And apparently for his own reasons, didn't even care to mention my name. As for Mary's crew, troubling questions raced through my mind: *Have those low-life motha' fuckers somehow perfected the strand and sent out another mutant-V to settle the score? Sent out a monster to murder the woman I love? Can someone so devolved be that crafty?* These few questions brought me back to the scientist's last words: "We'll finish him off later!" My logic may have been warped, but if there did happen to be a connection between his pledge and Rayna's murder, then they had practically succeeded in finishing me off. I was no longer able to hold back the tears.

As I continued to mourn, Rayna's final images became too difficult to fathom; so horrific, I had to get away from both Baton Rouge and New Orleans. I would have driven across southwest Louisiana, across Texas, and all the way to the west coast if it wasn't for Rayna's voice in my head—her passionate plea for me to stop and gather myself.

Taking an exit into Lafayette, I drove all the way to a spot on a bayou where Tasha and I used to sit. We used to sit there and stare at the constellations, each of us competing to see who could identify the most. On this night, an hour must have passed while sitting in the damp clearing, me staring up and naming those constellations again, none of them changing any time soon. As sappy and quaint as it was, it had briefly taken my mind off current circumstances—signifying the best of times. It was also a place I was longing to one day share with Rayna. Now it was the last peaceful plot for a man on the mend, but by tomorrow, a man marked with a murder rap.

It wasn't how the world was going to view me that had me concerned. I could have given the truth a try, could have gone into work tomorrow and tried to solve this case by legal means. But why? Since I knew I'd have to step outside the lines to find this killer. So, I stood up with renewed strength and a silent pledge: *Rayna, baby, I'm gonna find out who did this—if it's the last got-damn thing I do!* I knew exactly how to start my search and where to go, and it wasn't going to involve leaving Louisiana at all.

Chapter 18

It Happened One Night

Max was a truck-driver on his regular route, a two-lane highway outside Opelousas, Louisiana. Like clockwork, he pulled over at his favorite truck-stop for his favorite almond-covered cinnamon roll, large enough to hold him until morning. It was a little chilly outside, yet he didn't feel a thing but the cream dripping down his chin.

On the way back to his cab, Max was approached by a lean man from across the parking lot. The man's long leather overcoat, his pale weathered face, slickened black-dyed hair, and long-stranded goatee made him the strangest fellow Max had ever seen. While his long, hardened, claw-like fingernails made him downright frightening.

"Excuse me, Sir?" the stranger asked with a whisk of a smile. "I thought you might be the best person to ask."

Max paused with even more to consider, like the shiny dark limousine parked in the distance. "Yeah?" He heaved his chest to front his defense.

"Would you happen to know the quickest route to U.S. One-Ninety?"

The stranger's accent was slightly foreign, but his pleasantries were clear enough to work on Max, who calmed down as if those claws no longer existed.

"Sure, you almost there." Max's accent was blatantly Cajun. "Just keep on goin' that-a-way on this road right here." He pointed northward. "You oughtta be there in no time."

"Oh, am I that close?"

"Ee-yes Sir, you sure are."

"I guess you drive this road all the time?"

Max heaved his chest again, this time grabbing and lifting his beltline. "Yep, 'bout once or twice a week."

"Whoa! And it sure is dark. I don't know how you stay awake."

"Uh, I have a few tricks up my sleeve."

"*Whew...* I tell you, if I were in your shoes, I wouldn't be able to keep from veering over the lines. Those opposing lights would just draw me over—*nonstop!*"

"Well, that's why I'm the professional. Hey, I tell you what... you have a good and safe trip out there, you hear?"

"Hey, you stay alive out there!" the stranger said with a friendly wave on his way back to the limo.

Max watched the stranger step into the backseat as if he were the governor. It could have been just a sedan for all Max knew, but there was definitely a lone-driver in the front. But when Max turned around and faced his tractor-trailer, his eyes turned glassy—hypnotically glassy—as his memory of the limo, along with the strangers inside, faded to nothing. Dropping his cinnamon roll flat, as if he'd never bought it, Max witlessly trampled it on his way into his truck's cab. Meanwhile, that glassy stare remained as he revved up the engine and steered southbound off the lot.

Once inside the limo, the stranger's smile fell to the nastiest frown a person's face could carry.

"Where to, Mr. Ragori?" the driver asked with an extra deep voice, his eyes straight ahead.

From the backseat, Johannes Ragori, the stranger, and a master-of-suggestion, didn't have to stick around to see what would happen next. He'd never had to, not even after his many years of conversations with other strangers. Watching Max pull southbound off the lot, Ragori stroked his goatee along with a confident nod before turning forward. He now stared ahead also, while his accent shifted to heavy Mediterranean. "Hmm... as much as I'm intrigued by Louisiana and its politics, I think it's time to make our way to the airport. My work here is done."

Without hesitation, the limo's tires screeched off the lot, turning northbound towards U.S. 190.

Chapter 19

Deeds a Mask Cannot Hide

Narrated by Veleta Robbins

"Shit! Shit! Shit! I can't find my goddamn nuts!" I was livid.

"Veleta, baby, they're behind the cereal." Rob, my loving fiancée, pointed out with a mouthful and a layer of said nuts atop his bowl of cereal. And why *wouldn't* he know? He never could keep his hands out my jar. They were my favorite mixed nuts and fruit snack, my only pleasurable treat to get me going before work. And he, of all people, knew I would notice how much was missing. He would even hide the entire jar whenever I was in a hurry just to get me offtrack. A crafty one, that Rob.

"Babe, why are you extra jittery this morning?" he asked from our apartment's kitchen table.

Without sitting down, I answered with a mouthful, myself. "Ooh, I'm so pissed off!"

"Not a surprise."

"Shut up. Anyway, I told you how this new group treats me, right?"

"Yeah, but has the *dude zoot suit* not worked yet?"

"*Zoot suit*? It's *not* a zoot suit! It's well fitted, thank you very much. Anyway, they have me on this dead-end Lolly

Baker case, which looks like they barely give a shit about her. Another little white girl messing with the '*wrong*' crowd." I emphasized my point with air quotes before pointing to my brown backhand.

"They said that?"

"No, not in so many words, but I could read it on their faces."

"Oh."

"Yeah, and then they send my new partner off to L.A. on an escape 'Rogue V-hunt,' then told me I needed to stay behind for something else. Something else like pansy-ass, keep-busy work!"

From all that, Rob giggled away like Butt-Head. "V-hunt… huh, huh, huh, huh, huh, huh."

I just shook my head and sighed, expecting nothing any more mature.

"What escapee?" he asked.

"You know… that Landon Levy guy."

"Oh. Isn't he pretty *dangerous* anyway?"

"Yeah, but what are you trying to say? Because it's a little dangerous I shouldn't have been invited?"

I could see the fear in Rob's eyes, which I was sure came more from my burning ire than news of Levy. "Well…," he said.

"Well, my ass! Chasing down Vs is supposed to be *my job too*! I don't get it. Oh, and my partner, if I can still call him that, didn't utter a fucking word or lift a finger on my behalf. And I swear, getting anything out of him is like pulling teeth these days!" Just thinking about DuChaine was frustrating enough to drop my butt into a kitchen chair.

On the other hand, to make his point, Rob bared his own teeth. "Don't you mean... pulling *fangs*?" Okay, it was much quirkier than—*V-hunt. Huh, huh, huh, huh, huh, huh*—but it was a little cute.

"I know, right?" I said. "Anyway, my next assignment is another 'shit-show.'"

"What's that?"

"*Babysitting* a few political events—that's what I call it. Going to be working a few Danvers Stroy rallies. You know, that first V running for a human public office."

"A *human* public office? You're starting to sound like one of *them*."

"Sorry. That's also a consequence of the job."

"And just *what* are you supposed to be doing once you're there?"

"I don't know. Keeping an *eye* on things is what my supervisor said." I emphasized with a grandiose wink.

"Is that the way he said it?"

"Uh h'unh, just like this:" I deepened my voice. "'We need you to go over there and keep an *eye* on things, Robbins,'" I said with another huge wink. "Some real nebulous shit."

"Nebulous *and* safe."

We both paused, each of us crunching away like a woodchuck.

"Speaking of safe," Rob said, "will your new partner be attending?"

"I'on't know. I don't think he's made it back yet." I rose from the table and straightened my tie. "But why? What's he got to do with safety?"

Rob hemmed and hawed. "*Annnh…* maybe having a V with you at a V-rally might be... *safer*, don't you think?"

"Don't know, don't care. Plus, *babe… safe* won't get me promoted. It's tough out there for a sista,' you know? You wouldn't know nothin' 'bout that, though." Sometimes I just couldn't contain my Rougeon patois.

Rob stood up and slid around me with a muffled reply. "Hmph, you'll be the first to get a promotion *these days.*"

"What? Bite your tongue, white *b'oi!*"

"I'm your cute little white boy though, aren't I?"

"We shall see when I return." I stood up and slapped his cute little white-ass on my way out, at least to give him something else to think about.

I was almost out the door when he joked again. "Have a good day, my little *woman in black.*"

I was actually wearing a dark navy-blue two-piece suit and tie, but *I suppose* I was still a fan of the series. Plus, my coworkers viewing me as a "stud" instead of a "fem" didn't hurt my chances either—no matter how much the bastards talked behind my back. Meanwhile, even my fiancée remained a secret from them all.

The way Rob worried about me, I couldn't tell him *everything*. Keeping him worry-free was the only way I was able to drive to work with a clear conscience. I couldn't tell him things like what had happened to Danvers Stroy's opponent, incumbent Senator McAfee, whose car was flattened by an eighteen-wheeler in the middle of the night—McAfee and his driver included. But the trucker, a guy named Max Broucheau, whose driving record was impeccable before then, happened to have survived unscathed. The Sheriff's report had described the trucker as seat-belted, but found unconscious with eyes wide, and later with no memory of having even gotten into the truck. All he remembered was waking up behind the wheel just as he was drawn over the lines by oncoming headlights.

Accidents *did* happen, but I didn't want Rob overthinking this strange one—not now. It would have had my boo pacing a hole in our apartment's floor. Nonetheless, Stroy's "playing field" had been leveled considerably after the accident.

Speaking of fields, I was standing outside one several weeks later—an infield of Stroy's supporters in Lafayette's University of Louisiana Baseball Stadium. It was the last of Stroy's rallies I was scheduled to "babysit," and except for the location, it was pretty much the same—as bloviated as *fuck*. Night rallies were for obvious reasons for those of his type; there was only so much V-Screen to go around, as my *ex-partner* had made me keenly aware.

After DuChaine's girlfriend was found "tooth-picked" and drained to death—God rest her soul—Trémeur was now on the new V-Unit's most-wanted list. But I knew his nature better than anyone. He was no killer, no matter how equipped for it he was. And although I'd been ready to drag him across the rails before, now I would have staked my reputation on his innocence. *So why won't he at least try to find some way to reach out to me?*

Tonight, flanked by an entourage of stout men of varying heights, Stroy stood behind a platformed podium with fists pumping, fueled by the crowd's energy. His entourage seemed to be more security than staff, each wearing dark gray suits with even darker turtlenecks. Yet there was one in particular who gained my attention—this one, not so stout. In fact, he was lean, regal, and slightly taller than the rest. If his stature wasn't imposing enough, a black balaclava and shades were screaming, fear him or die. I couldn't understand it; the spotlights were bright, but definitely not U/V-potent enough to warrant such P.P.E. Still, there was something about him; I just couldn't put my finger on what.

V or not, Danvers Stroy was cut from a different cloth. A twentyish-looking Creole mulatto, he drew unusual crowds for District Three. White Knights, Neo-Nazis and anyone else who would have never supported a mixed human, had all stood in line to support the mixed V, his superiority their only desire. Now inside the diamond, they all stood in rows shouting randomly:

"V-Power! V-Power! We want it!"

"Make it happen!"

"V-Power! V-Power!"

"Change them got-dang laws!"

"Now, now!" Stroy waved them down near the end, his voice almost deafening through his mic. "Look, I can't promise you *that* per se, but I *can* guarantee: every last one of you will be endowed a power very few have known! The power to control your own destiny, your own resources, your own jobs, and your own communities!" But raising his fists to only mild applause, a low hum of a murmur, and only a few whistles, his sentiments swung in a different direction. "The power to live longer and stronger!"

On that note, the low hum escalated to a ridiculous roar, the crowd taking this as a promise to change the laws—laws prohibiting the perpetuation of immortality in any way. The morality disputes had become as numerous as life-in-prison versus the death penalty. Although "live feedings" had been greatly reduced, past deaths from these feedings had traditionally outnumbered actual conversions by double figures. Meanwhile, neither outcome was ever considered ethical, with the "turning" of a human still being totally outlawed.

While the roars continued, a swarm of activity was rising from behind the crowd. A separate group, all wearing advent-colored overalls, was advancing over the outfield. We knew them as the "Sons and Daughters of the Lost." The Treaty may have reduced human deaths, but not completely eliminated them. Eventually, descendants of the victims began to take a stand, with their numbers reinforced by growing sympathizers. These victims went on to become the Sons and Daughters. Tonight, however, *they* were the threat.

"Those from hell we must repel! Those from hell we must repel! Those from hell we must repel!" they chanted in unison.

"Hell is exactly where you all belong!" a Stroy-supporter shouted back, followed by others turning around to confront their opposition.

Agent Dunst, my new partner, leaned into my ear. "Exactly *which side* are we protecting tonight?" Dunst was no V—*shit*, he wasn't even a clever human—but his question happened to be on point.

"Would you believe it? The pale ones tonight," I said.

Dunst panned our surroundings. "Come again?"

"The *unnaturally* pale ones."

Paused by the agitated infield, Stroy fanned the panic and leaned into his mic. "Everyone, just calm down! No need to fear! Every man and woman—and everyone in between are all entitled to an opinion of their own!"

It didn't matter; the agitation quickly expanded into angst and resentment. A few combatants bumped chests and tussled, until gunshots from the Sons and Daughters sprang into the air. A few shots were aimed and fired barely over the supporters' heads, causing them to flea left and right in the infield. With nowhere to duck for cover, Dunst and I had no choice but to crouch and draw our weapons.

"Everyone, to the exits!" I yelled.

Supporters and protestors steadily crossing our sights, Dunst and I held from firing, giving me a chance to eye the platform. Even Stroy and his entourage were making an early exit—although much more under control. In retrospect, I didn't understand why he even needed much extra protection, especially from bullets. Regardless, shielding him was that lean *balaclava fellow*, who stole my attention again. His steps, his mannerisms, both I'd seen before. I had to find out who he was, so I vowed to myself I would do just that when the rally was all over. Then I figured, why put off until tomorrow what I could do that night?

I was set to chase the guy down, but a few challenges still stood between us. Some of the supporters had remained behind to battle the Sons and Daughters, but with too few local officers present to arrest anyone, I lifted my sidearm into the air.

"Everybody, L.B.I.! Drop your weapons!" I shouted, but the battle only intensified. *Right...* "Police! Drop your weapons! I said, 'Drop your weapons!'" But with all my attempts falling on deaf ears, I pulled the trigger. "Police! Drop your weapons!"

Now coupled with warning shots, the word, "police," had taken on a new meaning, sending everyone panicking in all directions. With the demonstration meeting an early end, my mind returned to Stroy's entourage as I weaved through the scattering crowd, while my only remaining delay came from Dunst.

"Hey!" he shouted. "What was that all about? And where the hell are you going?"

I glanced back but my feet remained in motion. "Keep things under control here! I'll be right back! And don't shoot anyone!"

Dunst shuffled back and forth with his eyes bucked. But as commanded, he held back as I chased Stroy and his crew, all of them now rounding the edge of the patio boxes. And leading the way was *Mr. Balaclava*, my new mission assignment.

By the time I caught up, I was still too late; Stroy's limousine was riding away with the lean, mysterious bodyguard in the front passenger's seat. I stopped and peered as if *I* were the one able to see in the dark. His window down, his shades now off, his eyes now exposed and aimed in my direction, it was just enough for me to figure it all out. The man staring back at me from inside the mask, I knew was none other than Trémeur "Tray" DuChaine.

Chapter 20
The Things I Hear;
The Things I See
Narrated by Trémeur DuChalne

My face all healed up, I stood in my old bedroom at Casio's house staring out the window. The room had remained vacant ever since my stint in Baton Rouge, and had seen little use since his and Tim's overnight guests rarely needed a separate room. From mine, my thoughts carried me back to the night of Danvers Stroy's truncated rally about a month ago, the night I'd last seen Veleta. I was masked that night, but even under the ski-mask, *she* knew who I was; I could tell from the mixed emotions in her eyes. In this case the mask had served its purpose, one some might have thought duplicitous, but I was only sparing everyone from a skinless face with a permanent grin. Hiding the face of a cold killer, *accused* killer, that is, was just a collateral perk. Veleta had to have been on my side either way, because the L.B.I. had never approached Stroy or me afterwards.

I also remembered little things, like putting my shades back on, trying to hide my eyes as I stared into the rearview mirror. It was one of those stretched blind-spot reducing mirrors, wide enough to see everything from the backseat to the trunk. That and the lowered partition window allowed me a clear view of Stroy, who was buried so deep into his browser, he never noticed Veleta or the small crowd that had accumulated around the limo. Then there was his conversation with his campaign manager from California—Koncadia Wessler—who'd been nestled away in the backseat the entire rally, now one seat over from Stroy:

"Danvers, this is going to create quite a stir," she warned. Koncadia was a slender woman, a jet-dyed brunette with extremely large eyes, virtually animated, but a V not to be taken lightly.

Stroy sat impassively, offering a light shrug to the remark. "What, that little episode? Nonsense." He triple-tapped his browser screen. "It says right here, we're already miles ahead of the next candidate, whoever that is. What happened tonight is only going to tickle the public's fancy—their sympathies... We'll have double the supporters once the story unfurls."

"Yahoos, all of them," Koncadia mumbled.

"Ah, yes, the working class. Someone once said, 'He who controls the workers, controls the world.'"

Koncadia tapped her chin. "Hmm, I can believe it, but who said that?"

"Oh, a cretin he was. But it was a great saying, nonetheless. Well, they're all yammering for a taste of immortality anyway—putrid humans."

"Which reminds me—I've never asked, but do you have any plans on conceding to their wishes?"

"*Hmph,* I don't know. I don't really give a squat. Um, maybe. Afterall, the longer they live, the longer they vote, right?"

She raised one brow. "Perhaps."

"Any who, it didn't hurt that the seat was graciously vacated."

Graciously! More like *murderously vacated* was my hunch. From just a few rides in his limousine, I already knew Stroy's handprints pretty well.

"Yes… quite a stroke of luck," Koncadia oozed, proceeding as if she had no clue. "You must still have friends in very high places."

Stroy's response was a dive back into his browser before addressing me, someone he had previously only greeted with head-bobs. "So, how are things going with you, Mr. DuChaine?"

It was a classic "redirect" if I'd ever seen one, and had come without him even lifting his eyes. Mine, on the other hand, shifted back onto the road. "Fine, Sir," I said flatly.

"Mmm hmm. You know, I was once in the very same position where you sit right now, believe it or not—what seems like a lifetime ago." He paused, waiting for a question which never came. "So, what exactly do you plan on doing after we win this election?"

Rarely was I at a loss for words, but the seconds passed until reaching my verdict. "I don't exactly know, Sir."

"Well surely you can't return to the L.B.I. Although, once I'm seated, I'm certain I can facilitate your impunity from the crime which you've been accused. However, if I go through the bother, I think your skills would be much more suitable for a... how shall I say? A higher plain of government—on occasion, of course."

Stroy was a member-at-large for the V-Council, but his campaign was neither sanctioned nor supported by it. Yet he was sure of his chances for a reason. After a few weeks on the new job, I'd been hearing quite a bit as a fly on the wall. Stroy's campaign contributions had been led by Ivander Oxley, a man not nearly as wealthy as his profile had indicated, but a man associated with New Orleans-based Zandamoor & Company, a "new kid" on Big Pharma's block. This new kid wasn't the only company waiting to commercialize immortality, but it was the only one to notice dark-horse candidate, Danvers Stroy.   In fact, I was probably sitting among the deep pockets responsible for Landon Levy's escape. Truthfully though, I didn't know if I'd given a shit at that point, and Stroy had probably sensed it. As far as I was concerned, both Tasha and Rayna definitely could have ben-efitted from it all, so I had no choice but to nod to his little hints.

No matter how noncontentious things were between Stroy and me, our connection had been severed once I was spotted by Veleta. In truth, I had only volunteered for security to get closer to the supremacists—to get a beat on Rose and the mad scientist's location, and to ascertain their level of involvement in Rayna's death. If luck would have prevailed, I may have even caught a glimpse of one of them in the crowd. But no such luck had ever occurred; neither their faces nor names had ever surfaced, and the time to move on had come. I was left with me no choice but to continue the search for Rayna's killer by other means.

Still staring outside my bedroom window, a tremendous scream, more like a roar, broke my thoughts. I raced down-stairs to the sight of Tim kneeling on the grand-room floor, Casio trembling in his arms. My face must have been spelling complete fright as Tim looked up.

"He gets like this sometimes," Tim said. "Anxiety attack."

Strange, after all these years, I'd never seen Casio like
this, so I rushed in to help by holding his other shoulder and
wrist. Inside us Vs, the pulse had been replaced by a pure energy so radiant, one U/V-ray could have sent someone into
instant shock. But with others, it fluctuated with mood, and
based on Casio's rage and feverish warmth, I feared he was
about to burst into flames.

"Hang on, my brother!" I cried out.

But he roared again, a look in his eyes enraged by the
air in front of him.

Grasping his wrist tighter, I never expected what happened next—a memory invaded my mind:

It was 1971 and I was shirtless in a bathtub full
of water, my body too limp to move. But this
wasn't from fatigue or relaxation, for impinged
in my neck were the fangs of a redheaded woman. Still, it was her perfume that actually stood
out the most. Its aroma took me back further in
time, to the moment I'd met her in a bistro bar in
central France earlier that evening. After an hour
of drinks and conversation, I never even had to
contrive a clever trick to lure her away. Just her
creamy skin tone, tight blue dress, and stream-
lined calves had drawn me all the way back to
my own apartment. She'd actually led the way

as if she'd been there before, but she hadn't; she just knew. And lucky for me, my real girlfriend was off somewhere else God only knew.

As if no time had passed, I was back in her mouth and wriggling in bloody bathwater, me being turned for the very first time. It was all becoming so clear. Before that moment, I'd stood on stages the world over versing music-backed poetry to tens of thousands, mostly women, all randomly screaming out: "We love you, Jimmy!"; "I'll die for you, Jim!"; "I'll kill for you, Jimmy!" The last one was a little morbid, but it was all totally mind-blowing, only to now end up lifeless in this thirsty chick's mouth. The world would go on to believe I'd overdosed in that tub of water, never reported as blood-filled, but—*wait a minute, what am I talking about— 'first time'?* It was 1971, but Delroy Jackson wasn't turned until a few years after that, and definitely not by a redhead. I had never been to France either, not back then, nor was I ever a rock star named Jimmy—or even a poet.

Miraculously, I was suddenly standing at the bathroom's doorway, now horrified to see Casio lying limp in that bloody tub, his arms hanging over the rim. *Whoa! He* was the one who'd met that treacherous redhead—*not me!*

Back in Casio's grand-room, releasing his wrist, I would have fallen on my ass from dizziness if it wasn't for Tim shouting me back to reality: "Damn it, dude, we don't need you zoning out too!"

Judging from their same respective positions, I must have blacked out for only a second, but it felt like I had lived half a life in Casio's shoes. Looking back down, Tim and I both sighed in relief as Casio drooped peacefully until his breathing returned to normal.

At the sight of it, Tim's tone instantly reversed. "What did you do?" he asked me.

I thought about it deeply but had very little to offer. "I don't know."

Even Casio sat up slowly with bewildered eyes. "Brother, whatever Voodoo you just pulled, you'd better consider using it wisely," he said, apparently having also felt me probing around in his head. Strangely, on top of that head was a light stream of gray that wasn't there before.

Having sat with Casio for a while, I went back to my room and reflected on what had just happened. I had just read my brother's essence, the deep recesses of his most feared memories. *But how did I do that?* This had never happened with a Vampyrian of any kind—only with humans. Just like the doctor had told me, it had to have been because of the plane crash, not to mention the little reapers. As I stared at my hands, I still felt the energy tingling, but had no idea the magnitude of its reach.

A week later, the ballots were in, and Danvers Stroy's camp wasn't surprised by the results. He was now the nation's first V-Senator; his sights, most of us knew, were already set on the next step up. We DuChaine brothers were sitting comfortably in front of our widescreen when it was announced, followed by a glass of "Jack Daniel's" knocking it cockeyed across the wall.

"Shit!" Casio had hurled it from where he sat. "That imperialistic—Neo-Nazi-loving—egotistical bastard—is gonna make things tough for all of us when it's all said and done! Both Vs and humans!"

Tim and I only laughed in agreement. Afterall, both the television and liquor had come from distribution centers practically owned by Casio. Yes, he was a man well-vested in items suited for his own pleasure only.

Feeling facetious, I threw my hands behind my head. "Hell, you think Nam was bad!"

"Right," Tim said. "If living for God-knows-how-long isn't bad enough, soon we're gonna have to share every fucking minute of it with every goddamn body else!"

Tim's remark had slammed the nail into the proverbial coffin, but I had to silently give it a second thought. As uneasy as we and most other Vs felt about Stroy, he had actually made good on his promise towards my impunity. Even Veleta had had no more reason to search for me. But no matter what favor Stroy may have been expecting from me, it was still going to be considered with only a "grain of salt." Yet he never came back to me. But like Tim had implied, we had a long life ahead of us. I knew I hadn't seen the last of Danvers Stroy.

Meanwhile, I also knew I had to find my own work-grove, but like Stroy had once made clear, the L.B.I. was out of the question. Part of their terms was that the public's reaction to Rayna's death was so heated, I was never to return to service, not even to the entire city of Baton Rouge if at all possible. All former colleagues, Veleta included, were encouraged to avoid contact with me—*forever*. An "off-the-books" outlaw was their description of it, leading me to lay low in New Orleans to sort things out. I wasn't very worried about my house in Baton Rouge. Not much was left behind, just my car, and I figured some other DuChaine would hold it down until my return. Nevertheless, once again, giving up on finding Rayna's murderer was not under consideration.

Chapter 21

Freaks Come Out at Night

Narrated by Trémeur DuChaine

Convincing Tim to co-invest on a small building for a new private investigation agency was easy; getting Casio to chip in, however, was a chore. There was no fun in it for Casio, but it was perfect for me. Every kind of case was now in play, and who better to do it?

Located on Carrolton Avenue with the title, "The V Agency," resting above our entrance, my first case was not the epitome of an old private-eye movie. There was no devil in a blue skirt—no buxom widow under a black veil. Seated in front of me in my cramped office was a group of distraught parents and grandparents with a collective unanswered grievance. About a year-and-a-half ago, each of their young teenage boys had been gunned down by the cops. I even vaguely remembered details from the original news report: three African American teenagers accused of killing a young Caucasian man were caught and shot by three police officers.

The pain on my potential clients' faces was "crushing," but I had to do my job. "I'm sorry," I said, "but wasn't it reported that your sons shot first? I just have to ask."

"That was a flat-out lie!" Mr. Franklin showed no shame in pounding my desk. "Our boys were good boys, good students! None of 'em owned any weapons! Them guns were planted in their hands! And our boys ain't killed that white boy neither!" He turned to his fellow grievers. "Shit, I told y'all this V-ass motha' fucka' don't give a damn about our boys!" With Mrs. Jones rubbing his shoulder, he retreated with a long exhale. "I'm sorry. I'm sorry," he said.

I raised my hand halfway. "It's alright. And believe me, I *do* care. I wasn't always a V, and I remember." But I didn't know what to believe at this point. After hearing more of their trials and tribulations, the time had come for me to consider other essentials. "Well, I'm more than happy to take this one on. My rate is eighty-five dollars per hour plus expenses." I figured it was fair for a former soldier, former agent, and an all-around insightful guy. "So, I'm thinking at least forty hours for starters, and—"

Mrs. Etienne interrupted by sliding a slightly puffed envelope onto my desk. "Here's three hundred dollars—upfront and total."

"We ain't doing this for the money," Mr. Franklin added. "We just want justice!"

I nodded my approval, as well as hearing my assistant, Tim, clearing his throat in his cramped office adjacent to mine. The agency's name was actually *his* stupid idea, another reason I'd accepted their offer. It had already taken about two weeks just for these good folks to show up, following a perpetual stream of aspiring models who'd failed to read our agency's subtitle, along with a few veterans looking for extra benefits. Plus, I guess you could say I was adopted into money; none of us DuChaines needed much more of it. Consequently, my sentiments about the money were no different than what Mr. Franklin had expressed.

After a few days of diving deeper into the case, there was more to it than just accusations of killing a typical white boy. That white boy was Waldo Egan, son of Zandamoor's C.O.O., Harold Egan. Harold had taken his grief to various New Orleans City Council members, while promising to support every one of their challengers if the murderers weren't found immediately. In response, three young boys were corralled and shot on the edge of Audubon Park, while the rest became case-closed for the N.O.P.D.

Tim was the most capable cyberspace-investigator I could have ever hoped for. Having utilized his connections to V-sympathizers inside the police force, he gained access to a backdoor link into closed files. Now walking down Carrolton Avenue at dusk, I was gazing at a copy of those files in my cell-browser. A few things jumped out instantly: filed off, unregistered pistols were in two of the kids' hands; Waldo's personal but trivial belongings were found in all three teenagers' pockets; body positions were consistent with point blank, firing squad executions—positions I remembered from the war; and only vital organs were struck in all three—too precise for an actual gunfight. Scrolling through recorded documents yielded more suspicions: evidence log-recordings varied from black ink to blue ink and back to black on different pages—hints of documents altered or replaced at some point in time.

All of it was too perfectly deceptive to me, but unquestionable to others in the face of Harold Egan's threats.

I could have easily cornered one of the arresting officers and extracted the truth, but who would have believed me, and what judge would have allowed it as credible evidence? It was an interesting dilemma, one now placed on hold as my cellphone buzzed in my hand.

"Yes?" I answered.

"Detective DuChaine?" a man asked.

I knew the voice, one I wasn't very pleased to hear. It belonged to the V-Council's Chief Security Officer Marques, and just familiar enough to make my temperature rise.

"What is it?" I said as flat as I could.

"The Council is in need of your services."

"For?"

"Matters of this nature cannot be discussed over the phone, I'm sure you are aware. Will you be able to meet me at my office in thirty?"

Typical of the bastards. I no longer knew who to trust in the Council, but at least Marques did ask politely; our prior episode had obviously been chalked up to business-as-usual. And while I knew money wasn't going to be an issue with them, I was so damned tired of their shenanigans, my head was shaking like a tongueless bell, yet my mouth still said, "Sure."

Only twenty minutes after arriving, I was leaving the Council's lakefront mansion with another new case-file, explained by Marques as: "A simple surveillance case, wouldn't you say?"

But I'd offered nothing but an eye-roll and no answer on my way out. The task: keeping tabs on someone for any unusual activity. It sounded simple, but surveilling this subject without detection was by no means the same. There was no telling how many ways this guy could have seen me coming— perhaps by sight, by smell, or even by brainwaves—I wasn't sure. His name was Johannes Ragori, an "Old-Worlder" who'd flown in from Greece without notice or apparent reason, a definite red flag to the local power structure. According to Marques, Ragori's actual date of arrival in New Orleans was unknown, which I couldn't understand why; his appearance was much like his name—as "gory" as hell. In the file photo, he was lean with a weathered face, a long-stranded goatee and slickened hairstyle, both dyed jet-black. His fingernails were long, black and claw-like; and wearing a long black leather overcoat, he was the epitome of his stereotype.

The next night, with the name of Ragori's booked hotel in hand, I parked my car as far down and across the street as I could, but close enough for my eyes only to see. I stared at the front entrance of Royal Street's Hotel Monteleone for nearly an hour, until seeing Ragori step outside looking as lanky, ghoulish and as "vamped-out" as in his photo. Yet there was a twist this time: he was full of laughter with two young women hanging onto each arm, each woman carrying her own gothic style, and both seemingly entertained.

"Checkout Old Man Ragori," I mumbled. "But those chicks *got to* be hypnotized."

The night progressed with no one on the street passing one glance at the odd trio, and for good reason: a costume party was never out of season in New Orleans. From there to Bourbon Street, from Bourbon Street all the way to the casino, and from the casino to the river, I followed them on foot from far behind. The entire time, the women never vacated Ragori's side, making me pretty damn curious: *He can't have that much game.* And when they arrived back at the hotel, all three reentered even happier than when they'd left—a headshaking experience for me if there ever was one.

As for Ragori, based on his side-eyed wink in my direction, it seemed he relished in my disbelief. *What the—aw, man… I've been made!* It was a terrible way to end a tail, not that I was planning on divulging this part. Regardless, I wasn't paid to follow Ragori to his room. If he were to exit alone the next morning, the V-Council would have had to tune into the news to hear about any dead bodies left behind. And as for "unusual activity," after tonight, I no longer knew what in the hell that meant.

With no word of any dead or missing women the next day, I figured I'd check back on Ragori later that evening. In the meantime, I was up earlier than usual working from my home office, feeling more than refreshed. There was even an unusual warmth inside-out as the sunrays poured on me through my window.

"Well, look at you!" A male voice blurted from behind.

"H'unh? What?" I jumped in my seat to look around.

It was Casio announcing from the shadows as he'd crept into my doorway, a habit he must have shared with Rose. With all the surprises of late, I actually wondered if he'd floated there.

"Sitting there with no V-Screen on," he said. "Something has changed in you, my brother. You're becoming more... powerful." His brow wiggled in raw fascination.

Leaning back, I contemplated his assessment. "Hmm... I don't know about that." I hadn't given it much thought until that moment, but my U/V resistance *had* been making the sun extra friendly since the crash.

"Like your maker," he pointed out.

That was Casio, never biting his tongue about sensitive topics. But watching me dive back into my computer screen, I was sure he sensed my true feelings about it.

"Sorry. My bad. Well, anyway," he said, "I thought you might be interested in meeting someone who may be able to help you with one of your cases."

I swiveled all the way around in my chair. "I'm all ears."

"The case with the three young boys. There's a V in Gert Town—someone who would defang himself a hundred times if anything were to sneak past *his* knowledge."

"Oh, yeah? Who is he?"

"He goes by the name of Wesley Morrow. *Usually,* he does. Specifically, among us, I know he does, but there's no telling what name he fancies today. A bit mercurial, this one, and he's a lifelong New Orleanian—many lifetimes, in fact. An *old timer*."

"He's an Old-Worlder?"

"No, not an Old-Worlder. Just an old *timer*. There's no official title for it yet; it might pose kind of a conflict. You know, copyright infringements and all."

Chapter 22

A Pint of Wisdom

Narrated by Trémeur DuChaine

The evening came with an air as suspicious as that morning's. With my plans to follow Ragori on pause, I made a detour to Gert Town, a neighborhood just a short drive east to the other end of Carrolton Avenue, not far from where the young Egan had been shot dead. The incident had happened between there and Holly Grove, both neighborhoods any other Egan would have never ventured. In fact, Gert Town was somewhere I'd never expected to find another V, much less an *Old-Timer.* I had quickly discovered that many Old-Timers were as old as some Old-Worlders, the former only distinguishable by the Americas being their point of conversion. Yet significant wealth was expected one way or the other, but not all had managed their funds so wisely.

As I walked into the dilapidated address Casio had given me, I figured Wesley Morrow was one of the unwise. The structure was Building Two of a set of deteriorating quad-raplexes. Walking up the beaten concrete stairs, there was a dark-haired little white boy sitting on the top step. *Jesus,* I thought; he couldn't have been any more than nine-years-old—someone I expected to see here even less than a V.

As I shifted by him, his eye contact was relentless, making even a seasoned veteran like me uncomfortable. Honestly, the entire scene had me feeling pretty weird already. Reaching Unit D, just before knocking, I heard a high-pitched voice with a strong New Orleans accent. "He ain't there, black," it said.

Looking back without a clue, I saw no one else but that little boy. "Excuse me?" I asked him. "Did you say something, young man?"

"I said, 'he ain't there.'"

I figured he was just a kid imitating his environment, so I gave him a break, but not enough to keep me from knocking. Several times I knocked until hearing the voice again.

"What are you, deaf too, motha' fucka'?" The boy was still looking at me, and he had a little more to say. "How many goddamn times I gotta tell you, 'He ain't there!'"

"Alright, kid. I've had just about enough of you."

That's when he stood up and headed my way, all three-feet-eleven-inches of him, his arms braced as if ready to start something he couldn't finish. "You lookin' for Wesley Morrow?" he asked.

"Yeah…"

And when he plunged his hand into his sagging jeans' pocket, I flinched and braced for impact. After my encounter with Rose, I wasn't about be caught off-guard by another pint-sized human being. But there I stood, shocked when the kid walked past me, pulled out a set of keys, stuck one in the lock and opened the door.

"You just found him," he said. "Come on in, Detective DuChaine."

Damn! My thoughts had been so distracted, it wasn't until that very moment I realized he wasn't human at all; there was no sweet aroma rising from his body. And hidden in such a diminutive package, he also gave new meaning to the term, *Old-Timer*. On top of that, he'd addressed me as if he'd known I was coming. *He couldn't have known. Casio would have never told him without me asking him to.*

"You seem surprised. Have a seat," Wesley Morrow said—a little more graciously once inside.

I followed him into the most immaculate slum unit I had ever seen. "I am … *very* surprised." Taking a seat in the most comfortable antique side-chair I'd ever been in, I was actually jealous.

"Can I getcha' you somethin' to drink?" he asked. "Water? Beer? A bag o' the 'soupy red'?"

"No, thank you. And does everybody I've never met know my name?"

Like a kid, Morrow sprawled himself across the floor before tossing a tennis ball in the air. Over and over he tossed it, even while answering. "This 'body' do. Now, what can I do for you, detective?"

I finally settled in. "A little more than a year ago, three young boys were gunned down by the cops off St. Charles, not far from Audubon Park. You familiar?"

The tennis ball stopped while he shrugged his chin. "Yeah, I remember. Good lil' boys. They whatn't botherin' nobody. But it was a lil' late for good lil' H-Blood boys to be out, though."

"Then you know about the murder of Waldo Egan too?"

"Yep, I sure do. Saw it all happen, a matter o' fact." And the ball tossing resumed.

"What, the *murder*?"

"That's what you just asked me, whatn't it?"

"You *saw* the murder? How? I mean, where were you?"

"I was a couple o' blocks away. Bored. Just hangin' out."

"Sooo… who killed him?"

"Rafael Etienne—one o' them lil' boys."

His logic had me baffled. "Hold on, wait a minute. I thought you said they were all good little boys?"

"They was. You think killin' a privileged *piss-ant* white boy ain't a good thing?"

"Well, it's not legal, so let's pretend it's not good."

"*Shiii…* I'd suck the lil' rich-blooded motha' fucka' dry, myself, if the Council wouldn't be all ova' my ass about it." Meanwhile, the ball tossing never stopped. "Anyway, he was a good boy, though. Shootin' that rich dude ain't had nothin' to do with his mood. Had more to do with his command."

"His *command*?"

"Yeah, that's right. His command. You see, lil' ole Rafael was compelled to kill Egan."

"Compelled?"

"Mm hm.   Compelled by an Old-Worlder named, Ragori. A real creepy lookin' dude."

"Ragori," I whispered.

"By the look in yo' eyes, it look like you might know him, h'unh?"

"You can say I know *of* him, but you saw him on the night of the murder?"

"Yawp."

"And what were *you* doing there?"

"Like I said, I was fuckin' bored, so I was makin' my rounds."

"Okay, what did you see?"

"Well, ole boy was standin' a couple o' blocks away castin' one o' his old-world spells on the kid, like he knew the Egan boy was about to come around, and he did, just like clockwork. And with Ragori backed up in the darkness, Rafael stepped out without hesitation and popped Waldo in the skull with a straight bullet. Fired on 'um a few more times to make sho.' From there, Rafael wiped down the piece like a well-trained pro, and walked off like a pimp. Like nothin' had just happened. As cold-blooded as a Copperhead."

"Any reason why Ragori did it?"

"Hmm… I ain't too sho' about the why. All I know is that once it happened, ole "Poppa Egan" pledged all his support full throttle towards Danvers Stroy's campaign and his undercover promise to immortalize a few select H-Bloods. I'd say Egan had a lil' more motivation at that point. You know—

one o' them motha' fuckers with the thirst to live forever, but
without the real hunger." He stopped and curled his upper lip,
briefly exposing a tiny fang. "Now, all this is my speculation,
o' course. But I'm pretty good at speculatin' and shit."

I scratched my head, searching for more. "So, tell me
this, why didn't you come forward with any of this before—
right after it happened?"

"*H'unh?* Well, first of all, you know this here kind o'
information don't usually come for free, but lucky for you, I
don't give much a shit about Old-Worlders. Ole fools wanna
take over the whole world and shit, and change things over
here. I like things the way they are, though. You know, the
status quo. Even when I was turned, I found out one thing."
The tennis ball finally stopped. "You can take all the blood
out o' my body, but you cain't steal the blood o' New Orleans
from nobody."

Wesley's look was as serious as could be, but I could
barely hold the snot in my nose at the sight of this pouty faced
kid, now with eyes bulging.

"All that bein' said," he continued, "I still don't owe
nothin' to that H-Blood culture no mo.' I wouldn't even be
tellin' *you* if you was still workin' for the L.B.I. Oh yeah, I
know about yo' deal."

"Hmm... well, tell me this—why is Ragori back in
New Orleans?"

"Back in New Orleans? You mean right now?"

"Yeah."

"I'm surprised I ain't know about that one, but just to let you know, Ragori *was* an old-school assassin and shit back in his day. Used to take pride in doin' the jobs all himself, but when times changed, he changed with 'em. He started usin' other folks to do his dirty deeds. Now, after his first New Orleans job, I heard he developed a likin' for Creole honeys. Been back a couple o' times before now."

"Yeah, he was out with a couple of those last night."

"Hah! I bet he was lookin' like the most interesting old motha' fucka' in the world, whatn't he?"

I chuckled as I stood up, thinking, *No, that would be you, Wesley Morrow*, before tipping my head. "Thank you, Mr. Morrow."

"Glad I could help you, but I'll be holdin' on to that favor you owe me."

That comment, I shook off. "Hey, but tell me something else: why did you have your door locked when you were sitting outside only a few feet away?" As soon as the words left my mouth, I had a feeling it was a question I was going to regret asking.

"'Cause I ain't want nobody breakin' into my shit in case I was lucky enough to get snatched up."

"*Snatched up?*"

"Yeah. As jailbait."

"*Jailbait*? You say that like that's a good thing!"

"Can be. Dudes ain't the only H-Bloods who like to cuddle with cute lil' white boy bodies. They got *beaucoup* crazy-ass ladies out there too." His smirk was aided by a wig-

gly brow. "You know what I'm sayin'?" I believe his fangs
even started to stretch.

"No. I don't."

"You know what I'm sayin'! Man, I'm over two-
hundred-years old in a kid's body! A kid with a *baby-ass dick*!
So, you mean to tell me that bein' raised in the backwoods o'
central Louisiana, you whatn't never approached *loose-
scivously* by an older woman when you was a kid? A neighbor, perhaps?"

"No, not while I was a kid."

"An older girl cousin?"

"No."

Squinching, he dangled his pinky finger in the air.
"You mean none of 'em ain't never play with your lil' *thang*?"

"No!"

"An aunt?"

"Hell no!"

"Ahh! A big sister!"

"Okay, I'm out o' here. I have all I need." The rest I
heard from outside his door, the door I'd just slammed behind
me.

"That's it! A sister! I knew it! You *do* know what
I'm sayin'! You know what I'm sayin,' DuChaine!"

Those twisted taunts followed me all the way to the
stairs and beyond.

Chapter 23

This Date Was Over
Before It Started

Narrated by Trémeur DuChaine

After leaving Wesley Morrow's apartment, I headed to my car trying to shake-off his last few inclinations—more like a desperate plea—one heard and answered by "someone above" as my cellphone vibrated with a familiar code.

"Veleta?" I answered.

She wasted no time. "Tray, I think I gotta lead on your girl's killer!"

I was so happy she had interrupted my thoughts, and ecstatic to hear her news, but too distracted to hear someone behind me, and too late to react to the trigger releasing a dart into my lower back. The Vyrotellum traveled through my body like dry ice, dropping me face-first into a grassy side-strip, where I lay as stiff as rigor mortis. To my surprise, I was still conscious, but everything, even my face, was numb—barely able to feel someone's breath against my neck seconds later. And with my mind intact, I was also still able to smell something strange. As faint as it was, the odor carried only small traces of human blood, more like residue, but from blood I'd actually smelled before. Then came a gritted voice straight into my ear.

"Nice night for a drive, isn't it, Agent DuChaine?" It was definitely from a man. "And in the midst, perhaps you got a little hungry... had a craving for something sweeter than sweet, hmm? So, you journeyed your way through Gert Town thinking no one would care where you dispose of your scraps." Even under grinding disdain, his voice was vaguely familiar, but one with content as irrelevant as Morrow's parting words. I sensed him standing up before asking, "Don't know what I mean? Perhaps you'll have a clearer understanding when you awake in the morning. That's if your flesh doesn't ignite from the sun's fuse."

Sun's fuse? This guy may have known who I was, but he had as little idea about what I'd become as I had about what he was saying to me.

No matter how much I struggled for clarity, I had no chance when I heard the trigger snap again, my numbness intensifying. In the background, I heard Veleta's voice from my cellphone, which was now in someone's front yard: "Tray! Tray! DuChaine! What's happening?"

With my head turned flat, I watched a pale hand pick up my phone, but even my eyes were too immobilized to rotate or see any higher. The next thing I heard was my attacker's voice: "Detective DuChaine's phone," he answered like a seasoned receptionist. "May I take a message?"

His pleasant greeting may have silenced Veleta, but *this* woman wasn't the type to be silenced for long. "Who is this?"

"Ahh, Agent Robbins, I presume?"

"Who is this?"

"You can say I'm a fan of your... well, maybe not so much your work, but your courage in the face of such a blood-thirsty partner is most commendable. If that doesn't garner that coveted promotion you've been suiting up for, I don't know what will."

After another pause, this one even longer, she returned sterner than ever. "I repeat, who is this and where is Trémeur?"

"Oh! Well, Mr. DuChaine is a little indisposed at the moment, but like I said, I'll be more than happy to take a mes-sage."

"Veleta...," I slurred, not sure if it had actually left my mouth.

"Buddy," I heard Veleta say to him, "if you don't get my ex-partner on the goddamn phone right now, you will have hell to pay!"

"*Hmph*... that debt seems to be climbing to a point of inconsequence, if you can believe that, but you and I will defi-nitely be seeing each other sooner than you think."

After he disconnected, I saw my phone hit the grass before his voice returned in my direction. "I'm not finished with you, DuChaine," he said, "or the ones you love. And I believe I've identified my next victim."

Those were the last words I heard before I faded into complete darkness, as the Vyrotellum finally hit its spot.

I awoke blinded by a beaming light, but it wasn't from the sun, because it was still nighttime. Regardless, my reactivated senses were telling me I was on another one of those unlucky paths.

"Out the fucking car, DuChaine!" a man demanded from behind the light.

Several more lights were aimed at my face with cops behind each one of them. To me, the flashlights were a touch more annoying than the firearms in their opposite hands. All officers held their distances—standard procedure whenever a V was at bay. Although I didn't know why *I* was that V. But when a cold limp hand tapped me from the passenger's side, I slowly turned my head towards the reason: a bloodily clothed woman drained dry from the neck. *Oh, shit! Not again!*

The lead cop tensed up. "Get—the fuck—out of the car, DuChaine!"

I didn't know what was going on, but my recent antagonist's voice instantly came to mind: *And in the midst, perhaps you got a little hungry... had a craving for something sweeter than sweet, hmm?* Then my own thoughts emerged: *I gotta get the fuck out o' here!* I had to get away to find all the answers, every last one of them. *If I don't, these clowns won't.*

I was just about to exit with my hands up when the lead cop yelled, "Freeze, DuChaine!"

Confusing... "I thought you said to 'get out of the car'!"

"That was before I could tell what you're thinking!"

"Well, you know what? I *think* I'm gonna take you up on your first order! But before I get out, I want you to know, none of this was done by me!"

When I got out, our conversation no longer seemed to matter. The cops opened fire with all intentions on taking me out, but I was gone before their second round—missed and unseen by all of them. Down the street in a flash, I glanced back to see a "V-less" vehicle and a woman's corpse, both being riddled by bullets.

As the rest of the city was seeing its share of revitalization, Gert Town was still seeing more than its share of abandoned buildings, apartments and houses. Later that evening, I was sitting in one of those houses, my eyes peeping around the edge of a second-floor window. It only took one person emerging on a far corner to send me back behind the wall, where I noticed my cracked-faced cellphone in my hand. *Whoa... how did that get here?* A vague memory of me veering and snatching it off the ground in a cloud of smoke was the answer. *Wow... good deal, good deal.*

With my browser open, I scrolled down and witnessed the story unfolding: a string of murders had been reported all over the city that night, culminating at the woman in my car. "What the fuck," I whispered. *Not a good deal. Not a good deal.* "This has got to be a setup." By whom, I didn't know, but the scent of my attacker was still in my system, stronger than if he were still on my back. *I have to go find this son of a bitch!*

Just as my knees flexed, I was pulled back down by Veleta's code lighting up my screen again. "Veleta?" I answered.

"Tray, what happened? Who was that weird guy on the phone?"

"I don't know. I'm trying to figure that out."

"Well, where are you?"

"Somewhere safe—relatively speaking. Why?"

"What do you mean, *'Why?'* I don't know—the cryptic sounding guy on the phone, maybe. And have you been watching the news? You've been implicated in another murder—several as a matter of fact! What the hell is going on down there?"

"Shit, I'm trying to figure that out too, but you know it wasn't me. That's not what I stand for."

"I know, I know." She'd switched to calmness. "Just tell me where you are, and I can come help you."

I knew Veleta was one of my few allies, but now wasn't the time to involve her. This new perp was serious, and I couldn't risk seeing a friend go down. Plus, something seemed suspicious; she was calm, too calm. I heard a strange hum in the line, followed by two, maybe three other people breathing in the background. "I'll clue you in later," I said before hanging up, figuring I'd beaten the trace with three seconds to spare.

Chapter 24
What a Splendid Place for Death

Louis "Birdy" Morgan was quite a saxophone player in his younger days. He once backed up the greats like Eaglin, Prima and Longhair, but none of them were left to attend Birdy's funeral. Heavy alcohol and drugs had spanned a small gap between those years and now, but just like a bluesman at the crossroads, Birdy had found a way to outplay those demons. Yet all in all, life afterwards had soon yielded to a more plodded pace, making tonight's attendance fairly sparce. A few family members were spread apart in the pews of Lamotte's Funeral Home, but only for a respectful display of Birdy's legacy. With the organ playing from the rear balcony, they moaned in harmony the usual, "Aa-maa-zing grace... how sweeeet—the sound....," while Reverend Dukes hummed it from the pulpit.

The reverend rocked slowly from side-to-side, his chin high and eyes closed until the window above the balcony shattered and the organ came to an abrupt stop. When his eyes popped open, Trudy, the organist, was plummeting to the first-floor center aisle. After smacking the floor flat, she was followed by a clean shaven, middle-aged white man. But there was no flat smack for him, who stuck his landing like a gymnast, then rose up with welcoming arms towards the stunned gathering.

"My condolences," he said, "but what a splendid place for death!" Having leaped through the upper window, Landon Levy had returned from the ashes.

The mourners' collective astonishment changed to terror once Levy's fangs ejected. As he proceeded to feed, one-by-one, men, women and children all dropped under his attack, their bodies drained completely dry in a matter of seconds. Those who were able to make it around him to the front door found it just as impossible to escape; for on the outside, its knobs were locked by a crowbar bent by Levy's own hands.

No one walking the streets had heard the perilous screams inside, which all fell silent after Levy reached the emotionally paralyzed Reverend Dukes, the last human to fall.

Chapter 25

When John Met Rayna

Months ago Rayna Gutierrez was taking care of matters in Baton Rouge's Charity Services Office, located in a simple block building on the city's east side. Sitting behind a dull-faced desk, she thumbed through file page after file page in front of Gomez Guzman.

"Mr. Guzman," she said, "trajo su Formulario I-551 completo?"

"No está ahí? Estoy seguro de que lo traje conmigo." Gomez scratched his head, having assured her he'd put Form I-551 in the folder before he'd left home.

She kept thumbing away until taking a deep breath, barely able to look Gomez in the eyes. She had seen him for three Fridays straight with at least one form missing every time. She knew he didn't have Alzheimer's and that he wasn't the typical age for dementia.

"Mr. Guzman, Mr. Guzman," she said with a huge sigh, finding the strength to finally look him straight-on. "We go through this every week. It's only going to delay the process, or worse."

His eyes wandered through most of the words, but he nodded vehemently. "Si, si, I know."

"Now, you have only two weeks to get everything submitted." She fluttered two fingers in the air. "Understood?"

"Dos semanas?"

"Si, dos semanas. So, I'll see you next week with *everything* filled out and signed, right?"

"Si, si, *okaaay…*" He rose to his feet, his sigh even heavier than hers.

Rayna's Spanish was as scanty as Gomez's English, but she'd given her all. Born in Baton Rouge, Rayna had seen only a sparse Mexican-American population in her younger years, but recent times had seen seeds of movement from southeast Texas, along with a few of their Mexican relatives joining them. Rayna was doing her part by helping them at least one day a week—no matter how detached she had often felt.

Gomez being her last appointment, she wasted no time rushing out to her Maxima, where her cellphone vibrated just after slamming herself in. "Hello."

"*Eh-umm…* Attorney Gutierrez?" Clearing her throat on the other end was her friend, Mavis, prodding as usual.

"Hey, chica!"

"Oh! You're in your *chica* mood today, h'unh?"

"Yeah, girl. It's my pro bono day. *Gotta help my people out*," she said in rhythm. "You know what's up."

"I most certainly do. So, what'chu doin'? You finished?"

"I most certainly am. Why, where we goin'?"

"The *Lady Crew* is meeting up at our usual spot—for starters. You coming?"

"Yeah, I'll be there, but I have just *one* stop to make, and—"

"Where?"

"Girl, that's *my* business."

"Mm hmm... I know where *you're* going."

"Oh, please! I will see you all in an hour or so, okay?"

"Yeah, whatever. See you there."

"Bye!"

Twenty minutes later Rayna was executing the slowest "drive-by" ever, past a small house on Magnolia Drive, east of Park Blvd.—night and day compared to its west side. Small but expensive bungalows bounded all streets in the vicinity, all properties slightly high-priced for one particular agent's salary. That agent was Trémeur "Tray" DuChaine, who Rayna hadn't seen in days. Gazing at his house, she had fond memories of her few times inside, but she also remembered how sparsely furnished and barely touched it was. But on this late after-noon, there was cause for another concern: not only had she not heard from Tray, but the house was vacant for just as many days. She didn't want to admit it to her friends, but she had been passing by every one of those days, and every time, his one and only sportscar was in the driveway—dust-covered and parked at the same angle. This time was no different, except for another layer of dust.

The first couple of days, she stopped and knocked a few times, but to no answer. The evenings when she passed by were just as bad; none of the inside lights had ever been switched on. She'd even called his office a few times, but there was no way they were releasing any details. Next, per her and Tray's safety protocols, she'd called Veleta, who had had this to say: "Look... I wish I knew, but I'm in as much of the dark as you are. I can tell you this much, though—I haven't known him half as long as you, but from the little I've seen, I think he'll be alright. Just be patient, honey."

Veleta's advice was now rolling through Rayna's mind at the very moment her Maxima rolled to a stop, allowing her one last view of the house. Hanging onto Tray's last phone message, the one which he had expressed his love, she found it difficult to drive off. And when her cellphone buzzed, it was just the excuse she needed to stay. "Tray," she murmured, almost dropping the phone on her way to answering, until she saw it wasn't Tray's number at all. "Damn."

A good attorney knew not to answer calls from unknown parties, not even under duress, and Rayna was a *great* young attorney. But knowing the call was on its last buzz, the stakes had her one thumb-press away from answering, until *really* dropping her phone to a loud noise. Behind her was a blocked stream of irate drivers, blaring their horns and damning the fact Rayna had stopped in the middle of the street.

Her phone now sliding underneath her butt, Rayna sped away waving her hand outside her window. As rattled as she was, it only took her half-a-block to refocus on Tray—no longer focused on the phone or its mysterious caller.

Alexander's Restaurant and Bar was where Rayna met up with her three best friends, all now sitting an aisle away from the bar with drinks on their table. It wasn't the typical Friday evening "meet-market," but a place for them to relax without the "volleys and returns." However, far from relaxed, the ladies confronted Rayna's hand-pressed face and her dawdling straw.

"Rayna!" Charlene pounded the table. "What in the hell's wrong with you? All distant and shit!"

Mavis rolled her eyes. "You know she thinking about that man again."

Subsequent was Kim trembling from head to toe. "That *scary man*?"

Rayna sat up straight and took a deep breath. "No, no, I'm done with him," she said before leering at Kim. "And what do you mean, '*scary man*'?"

Tucking her head low, Kim trembled even more. "Scary…"

"You sound like my sister," Rayna said, "but let me tell you this, that man is more man than you can imagine."

Kim rebounded with a lifted head and a tainted smirk. "Oh, I can imagine a whole lot o' man. A *whole lot*." She even slammed the "t" with authority.

Rayna also rolled her eyes among the table-full of giggles. "Girl, you so silly," she told Kim before turning to the others. "Anyway... he always keeps it 'one-hundred' with me—never a lie. I mean, there are times when he's vague or just can't say, but at least he always makes sure I know why. Which is *way* more than I can say about these other jackasses out here."

"Hmm, strange that you say you're done with him, and yet you still speak of him in the present tense," Charlene said. "But why would he lie? That motha' fucka's gonna live forever! What does he have to lie about? What does he have to fear?"

Rayna waved a finger in the air. "Wait a minute. Are you trying to say that death provides mortal men the unlimited license to bend the truth as they see fit?"

"Ooh, alright, *Ms. Esquire*! But... yeah."

"Speaking of living forever," Mavis said, "what's gonna happen when you reach seventy? Eighty? Hell, ninety!" She dropped to a deep southern hush, her Rougeon accent surfacing when she said, "Teeth go'n be all fallin' out."

Rayna squinched. "What!"

"Titties go'n be all saggin'."

Charlene followed by staring deep into Rayna's eyes. "And that man gonna be as fine as he is today. Not that I've been 'checking' your man like that." But all her sincerity ceased when she double-winked across the table.

Kim dipped her head again, this time in shame. "You all are *too* much."

"*Lord....*," Rayna said. "Anyway, I have to go to the lady's room."

Watching Rayna roll out of her chair in disgust, Mavis leaped from hers with a woeful look. "Hold on, I'll go with you!"

"No, no, I got it."

All three ladies' jaws dropped. "Aww, come on, Rayna!" Their collective guilt had poured out all at once, but they held each other back, giving Rayna her space.

On her way to the restroom, Rayna was ashamed as well, but for reasons other than her friends' deplorable behavior. Her decision to date a V hadn't always felt fateful; she was a perfectionist day and night, nearly every one of her actions geared to achieve self-actualization. And who better than one of the most powerful beings on the planet to allow inside, thus giving her due validation. This was what her subconscious had always relayed to her, except for moments like this bringing it into the light.

Once inside the restroom, in front of the mirror, a single tear rolled down her cheek—again, having little to do with her friends' chastisement, but more so to do with memories of Tray, who she was now certain had met a tragic end. Those memories came to a halt when her phone vibrated. Swiping her face, her nose nearly pressed the screen before recognizing the number: the same wrong number from Magnolia Drive. "Shit." And by the looks of it, it was one of countless attempts. "Shit." Slamming her phone to the floor and stomping it from existence came to mind, but she had another idea. Scrolling through her menu screen down to the "Block" button, she tapped it, not even bothering to suffer through all the other attached messages.

After making herself up and heading back towards the table, Rayna was convinced *her* Happy Hour was over, but not quite for someone at the bar.

"Excuse me, Miss? Excuse me… Miss!" A man at the end of the bar was about to try again until Rayna turned her eyes in his direction.

A beautiful young woman, Rayna was accustomed to passes from any- and almost everyone. If she had to, she would have guessed this guy was in his late forties—his wrinkled clothes, simple wire-rimmed glasses, and full head of graying but rustled hair—all disqualifying him from being a Happy Hour regular. But she didn't have to guess, because as a staunch professional, her protocol was to return at least two lines of communication before moving on. "Yes?"

"I was wondering if a drink might cheer you up?"

"Oh, no thank you. I already have one, but thanks again." Her response was practically trigger-released, and her two lines were done; yet she was mildly surprised by his eloquence.

As if sensing it, he paused her with a light touch. "Oh, but *their* advice can only go so far." His words came with a head-nudge in her friends' direction. "What you need is a *man's* point of view."

Rayna stepped back and slapped her hand across her own chest. "Excuse me?" She was appalled, unable to believe a complete stranger had just put his hands on her. But his proposition did seem timely, as if he'd been sitting at the Lady Crew's table the whole time. "And how would *you* know what *I need*?"

"I know the look. You've lost someone. Someone very important to you. I, myself, am intimate with the feeling. I'm John, by the way," he said, extending his hand. "And you are?"

"On my way back to my table. It was nice to meet you—John." By no accident did she fail to return his gesture. When Rayna returned to the table, her friends' faces and eyes were still drooping. Mavis was the first to ask, "Are you okay, hon?"

"Oh, I'm fine," Rayna said while taking her seat. "Just had to sidestep some creepy old guy at the bar. Sorry, I'm wrong for that. He's not too, too creepy—just a little—and he's not *that* old."

Kim swung her head around. "Who?"

"Damn... don't look *too* hard, but he's right there at the end of the bar." When the other two women's heads popped up, Rayna shielded her face. "Oh, geese," she said. "Ya'll up in here lookin' like Springboks and shit! I may as well have just said, 'Look now. Look as hard as you can.'"

Charlene screwed her lips. "Okay, while you're getting all '*National Geographic*' on us and shit, there's nobody at the end of the bar."

Dropping her hand, Rayna slowly turned her head, seeing nothing at the end of the bar but a full glass of wine and an empty seat below it. She couldn't hide how a bit miffed she was, but whether the stranger was gone or in the men's room, as long as their paths had crossed, her decision to leave right away was certain.

By the time the Lady Crew had moved on to their favorite dance club, they were minus one with Rayna back in her apartment. She had never bumped into John-from-the-bar again, and nearly two hours had passed, but his words still resounded, making her think even more about Tray. Her cellphone chiming beside her bed was just what she needed to hear, and this time, it came from a number which made her gleam. "Hey, baby sis,'" she answered. "What's up?"

"Nothing much," her sister, Jacynthia, said. "What are *you* up to? You're in early for a Friday."

"Nada. Oh, but I just got back from Happy Hour with the girls. Decided not to do the party thing, though. I'm beat."

"Too beat for a little sisterly *company*?"

"*Tsss*, never. Why, you comin' over?"

"Might as well."

"Cool! Plus, I'm not ashamed to fall asleep on your tired-ass anyway."

"*Bitch! I...* am *the* most exciting part of your day— you best believe."

"Alright, if you say so. See you soon."

"Hey, I gotta drop something off at Mom's first, but don't give up on me."

"I won't."

After hanging up, it only took Rayna a few seconds to resume her misery. *I can't let go of him—not* this *soon.* Tray's final message, although it was brief, was again repeating itself: *Love you.*

Stripping down to her slip, Rayna stopped in front of the mirror, where she hoped to find the "fairest of them all." But this mirror revealed absolutely nothing. Instead, it told her the *real* story behind Tray's departure, as Rayna saw it. Pressing and tracing down her own tight contours, she paused at her waistline and pinched a mere eighth-of-an-inch. "That's got to be the reason," she mumbled before shouting, "I'm too fucking fat!"

"I don't think you're fat," a deep voice commented from just outside her opened bedroom door. "I don't think you're fat at all." John-from-the-bar was inside her apartment, his posture relaxed as if he had never left the restaurant. "I actually think you're quite an exquisite specimen. A *sweet*-smelling specimen." His unwelcomed compliment preceded a set of growing fangs, followed by a hiss and his lean body flexing in her direction, while his fingernails began to stretch like his teeth.

Rayna gasped at the horrifying sight of him; her entire body quivered. She could have sworn she'd locked her door. In fact, she'd surely done so, but now knew she was facing a creature strong enough to pop a latch without a sound. And while she'd thought she could pick up on any V's vibe, this one was a bit more deceptive. His V-Screen was even applied to human perfection.

No time for regrets, Rayna leaped atop her bed towards her cellphone on the other side—the only way out she could think of. However, John was on her in a split second, wrapping her up with one arm and grabbing her throat with his other hand, stretching her neck like poultry. Totally voiceless, Rayna felt the grip of pending death, along with John's fangs jabbed into her lower neck.

With Rayna in his grasp, John sucked her blood until she dizzied, but withdrew to deliver a message: "By the way... please do say hello to my dear friend, Trémeur DuChaine. Perhaps you'll be able to haunt him from the other side, or... maybe not."

Back into her neck like a viper's strike, John continued to suck until Rayna fell limp, drained of all flowing fluids. And when her body hit the floor, the Vampyrian heaved his chest. "*Ahh*... now that was better than an orgasm."

After straightening his now doubly crumpled clothes, John adjusted his nonprescription eyeglasses, which had somehow never left his face. Casually on his way out and into the night, they remained intact, serving his ongoing quest for nondescription.

Chapter 26

Issues

John left Rayna's apartment complex, now a virgin crime scene, in no big hurry, licking traces of blood from his lips the whole way towards his car. Another with an apparent score to settle with Trémeur, whatever issue he had seemed satisfied by the time he reached his gray mid-sized Honda. However, tugging his chin, memories from almost fifty years ago resurfaced soon after his rear hit the seat:

> Mid 1970s South Louisiana harbored a vast number of creatures, and Vampyrians weren't the only ones. In Metairie, just outside New Orleans, John Wilson Parker, a human, approached a large Victorian-style house for a special service call. It was early evening when he arrived at its front door, his last appointment of the day. A senior level HVAC technician, John also sold a variety of home warranties on the side, and a courtesy check was always his first step. It was a bit outside company policy, but he had always found a way to avoid discovery.
>
> Octavia Winstead, close to sixty and a couple of decades older than John, cracked open the front door. Not only was she home alone, but

she was also recently widowed, the kind John had always made sure to accommodate.

"Hello, Mrs. Winstead!" John tipped his head with a warm smile. "I'm here for a systems' service check."

Octavia opened the door wider, wearing a plain pullover, long tiered skirt and a smile as pleasant as his. "Well, hello to you too!" she said, filled with delight. "I thought you weren't showing up. Come on in."

"Yeah, sorry about that. I got held up for a minute on my last appointment, but I'll make this *real* quick for you."

Leading him in, Octavia opened her hand. "Well, where would you like to start." Throughout was an assortment of furnishings dating as far back as the 40s, a sure sign of the glory years she and her husband once shared.

John remembered her room-layout from his first visit as if he'd been there the day before. Loaded with a massive toolkit, he pointed his way towards the kitchen. "Let's start with your kitchen appliances." There, he removed and unfolded a large visqueen sheet, placing it neatly on the floor near the dishwasher and sink.

Octavia tapped her chin. "What's that for?"

He dropped onto his back. "Oh, I'm just gonna check your dishwasher's drain hose. Could get a little messy."

"I could have mopped it up, but—" Her eyes wandered. "Okay..."

Stretched across the floor, John took an occasional narrow-eyed glance, catching Octavia staring at his slight mid-drift, making him think, *Probably the first piece of skin the ole "crotcher" has seen since her old man died.* But he couldn't tell her that—not well-mannered John W. Parker. Minutes later, he was up and looking at the stovetop. "Here, take a look at this." He urged Octavia forward. "You see all that grimy buildup?" he asked.

"Uh... I think so."

"It can cause quite a fire hazard. Take a closer look." Stepping back, he gently pressed her closer until she leaned over it. "You see that?" He pointed to the rear burner. "It's pretty deep and packed in."

"Oh, my... that *is* pretty nasty. I don't know how I missed that. I mean, I clean it every day! Would you happen to be able to clean— *Oh!*"

"Yeah, looks like you're going to need a whole new... *burnerrr.*" Ending with a grunt, he wrapped his arm around her waist, while his stiffened organ was poked against her rear.

It probably wasn't the answer Octavia was expecting, but she couldn't hide how welcomed it was. "Oh, my..." Stroking his forearm, her breaths grew heavier, and when her panties fell, those breaths turned into moans.

Putting her desires to the test, John placed himself deep into a spot not designed for entry, the only spot he'd ever envisioned. It was the spot he had seen his drunken father enter his mother many times when he was a kid. For most of them, it was in their kitchen too, and extremely abusive. Whenever he had watched from a doorway's edge, he saw his mother's neck being choked, her head slapped. Honestly, hearing her wailing moans, he could never tell if she was enjoying it or not. And now he repeated it with Octavia, at least the choking and penetration, while watching her squirm.

"You like it, don't you? You like it, don't you?" John's attempt at sultry whispers was accompanied by more grunts, but not once had he waited for an answer.

Octavia's breathlessness was her only response.

John just kept thrusting and grunting. "You like it, don't you? You tight little whore!"

Finally, Octavia groaned. "No... no... John... I don't think I do. You're hurting me... Please... stop."

But John kept going, kept thrusting, and choked her tighter.

"John..., you're hurting me... Please stop," she begged.

"You want me to stop?" he mumbled.

"Yes... yes... Please stop."

"Alright."

Two more thrusts later, when John reached his climax and Octavia reached her threshold of pain, he obliged her wishes with a boxcutter from his bag on her counter, slitting her throat with it. Cranking her down to the floor, he watched her gurgle and twitch in a puddle of spreading blood.

Like the V, Landon Levy, John was just as bloodthirsty, but not for its taste. The sight of it had him so fascinated, he pulled up his pants and a chair just to watch Octavia bleed-out on the visqueen sheet. There he sat, intrigued for fifteen minutes until collecting other thoughts, like how this was his fifth time—his third widow. Sometimes he strangled them with a steel wire; others, like tonight, he used a blade whenever the call for blood beckoned. Either way, this part was something his father had never done.

Yet John's job wasn't over. Deep from inside his bag, he first pulled out a set of Tyvek coveralls, followed by a Gigli saw, the quietest means to carve a body into several pieces. With coveralls on, like a surgeon, he chained through her cooling limbs, sawing her up into enough parts to fill both her washer and dryer.

Over an hour later, after cleaning Octavia's kitchen like a professional, John dollied the washer and dryer outside one-by-one. Wearing a work-suit, bibbed cap, thick glasses and a beard, he was the most nondescript man in America. He even raised a friendly wave to a neighbor, who waved back as if John were the President. Along with John's look, he loaded up and drove off in a white van with absolutely no label across either side.

John's normal regimen was to bag the body parts and drive to a spot he'd felt no one would attempt to dig—an overgrown, seldom used cemetery. There was where he'd buried the other bodies—burying every part deep as if it were his mother's, a mother who'd left him behind with an abusive father—a mother he never saw again. John's younger self wasn't able to grasp the stress and disarray his mother was in, nor the pain from her decision to abandon him. And every resulting blow he'd absorbed from his fail-ure-of-a-father, was subconsciously redirected towards his mother. Afterall, it was just easier to do since she wasn't there to make her case. Now as an adult, John had often stood over each woman's grave—not in prayer, but fantasizing the day his own mother would feel the pounds of dirt from his shovel.

But on this night, after leaving Octavia's house, John was hungry, and totally comfortable enough to leave his unloaded van outside his Up-town apartment house. The cemetery had to wait.

After dressing down for the evening, John, a solitary soul, walked a few blocks until crossing St. Charles Avenue. He was even whis-tling a tune without a care until reaching his fa-vorite package store, where he bought a sausage po-boy.

His stay at the store wasn't long at all; everyone was far too beneath him to deserve any conversation—as he saw it. A minute later, he was back across St. Charles, but unaware of the attention he was drawing. It came from a heavy breathing man on his tail, a man moving just as rapidly as his breaths. John didn't know what to

do, but before he could react, he was in the
man's grasp, his back pinned to the ground behind a holly dwarf bush.

"What the—" John was pressed so flat
against the ground, he could no longer speak.
And when the man's teeth sank deep into his
throat, John felt the force of a vacuum sucking
him dry. Not only was he voiceless, but his body
became paralyzed from his neck to his toes.
Now, feeling himself blacking out, he found the
strength to wheeze: "Please wait… stop…
You're… killing me…"

Flustered beyond his own warped reasoning, John now sat in
his car not far away from Rayna's complex. It didn't take long
for his finger-tapping to turn into a swift punch into his dash,
shattering the car's radio like glass. "*That* fucking night," he
grumbled, "*that* fucking night pisses me off every fucking
time!" No longer did he feel so satisfied. "I'm not done with
you, DuChaine." After a quick breath, John started his car and
screeched away into the night.

Chapter 27

Two Tales of One Day: Tale Number One

Veleta's Day

I felt like crap. It was seven a.m. the morning after attempting to dime-out my former partner and new BFF, and I was still in bed. I knew he was on to me, but I had had no choice; three other agents were in my apartment staring me down like sentinels. Now, I had so much more to tell him, but I knew he would have never called me back, so I texted him: "Tray, sorry about that. i had no choice,,, but what i was trying to tell you before was that a witness came forward in rayna's case. she saw a man exiting her apartment. lean white guy, average height, wearing glasses. hit mw back." *Oops.* "...me back." With my knees nearly to my chin, I waited patiently for his verdict.

More than an hour passed and I'd heard nothing from Tray; all the while, I lay in bed emotionally unraveled, having yet to call into work. That's when my cellphone buzzed—a call from Tray.

"Hey…" I sat up, both ashamed and frightened.

"Hey," he said, "is the coast clear?"

Now, I *knew* I'd been made, but just hearing him ask made me feel even worse. On the other hand, I was at least relieved he called me back. "Yeah, the 'tap.' About that… I'm so sorry. Three fucking agents were in my apartment try-ing to—"

"Yeah, I gathered as much. I heard it in your voice."

"I didn't know what else to do—"

"Hey, listen, no time to dwell on that. You need to get somewhere safe. Now!"

It was the most urgency I'd heard in his voice since … since actually hearing his voice. "Why?" I asked.

"Because the guy you spoke to on my phone is most likely a deadly V, one who may be after you next. You have to get out of there!"

"What!"

"Now!"

I had to take a pause. Did he forget I was an officer of the law? If so, it was time to refresh his memory. "Tray, what are you talking about? I am an agent of the law! I can handle myself, you know!"

"I'm sure you can—to a degree. But did you not hear me say a *Vampyrian* is after you? Woman, what do you not understand?"

I raked my hair back and forth, because the *son of a bitch* had a point. "Okay. Where do I go now?"

Tray paused a few seconds, this part of his plan obviously exhausted. "I don't know... but you'll figure something out. Just call me and let me know once you get there."

I fell back sighing towards the ceiling. "Alright..."

"Cool."

After hanging up, I had a few things to figure out, the most pressing one was still—*Where will I go now?* I had no idea, but being alone seemed like the wrong move, and being around loved ones would have only jeopardized their safety too. Luckily, my Boo, Rob, was out of town on business, but I was sure I would have been protecting him more than the other way around—for *any* dangerous situation. This left me with only one option: I packed a few things and headed to work. If ever I would have been tracked, there would have been a building full of protection and witnesses, or just plain ole assholes to be fed on instead. *What am I saying?* Shameful, was what it was.

"Sleeping late again, Robbins?" Agent Callahan sniped as he passed by my cubicle at work.

"What do you mean, *again*? Never! And how in the hell would you know?"

Callahan, a tall red-headed guy, too freckly for his age, definitely wasn't a superior, nor was he slated for any slot, so I owed him nothing. He continued by without another word, his arrogance evident in every step. In fact, this asshole I had no qualms about booting him into the feeder's path just for the hell of it. Anyway, I'd been recently reassigned to something far on the opposite end from blood-collar duty: white-collar crime. *They*, the bosses, had presented it to me as a promotion, but in a State with one of the lowest white-collar job rates ever, the only cases I saw were miscalculated direct deposits—yawners at best. But today, my lack of focus was on another level. Every pen that dropped, every door that slammed, and every chair that rolled—each contributed to a gasping anxiety attack.

Hours later, my nerves now frayed, I nearly jumped out my chair when my phone vibrated, this time from a text message: "change of plans... do you remember where we found the blood bank thief?" It was from Tray.

I had to think a moment before texting back: "yes."

"wherever you are, leave and meet me there right away... alone."

Now, I *really* started to wonder what was up with Tray and all these cat-and-mouse games. *What in the hell is he up to?* I even wondered if any V was after me at all. Lucky for Tray, I was bored to death; otherwise, I would have never entertained such drama to begin with. "ok," I typed back.

The Marchands' farm, an abandoned property in Zachary, just north of Baton Rouge, was where we'd found the blood-bank thief several months ago. Originally thought to be a V, he ended up being a typical hospital maintenance worker looking to sell discount plasma on the side. Taking advantage of a vacant farm with utilities set on autopay, our thief had managed to maintain his supply in the barn's walk-in freezer. Of course, the V-community was his biggest client.

Close to sunset, as I pulled into the farm's winding dirt driveway, those not-so-distant times now felt like the good ole days. Little had changed on the farm; the Chickweeds and Saint Augustine grass had grown thick and above the ankle, but the barn was practically as rundown as before.

A few clouds had moved in by now, and I didn't know if Tray was driving his own car or not. Either way, there was no other vehicle around. Meanwhile, my car-radio was on low as I rolled to a stop outside the barn, and I was just about to shut it off until hearing the news. I turned it up instead: "This just in: A commotion is brewing around the Vampyrian Council's New Orleans Lakefront Mansion. N.O.P.D. helicopters are currently circling the mansion in search of the suspected mass-murderer, Vampyrian Trémeur DuChaine. Police were called in after receiving a tip that a relative had driven to the mansion to meet DuChaine there and subsequently solicit his surrender. This comes on the heels of a rash of seemingly random murders, including the death of an entire funeral gathering—all in just one night. If all murders are found to be connected, this would make it the most horrendous mass-killing of its kind in Louisiana history. DuChaine was already once accused—"

"Shit!" I slapped my steering wheel. "You've got to be fucking kidding me! What the hell is he doing in New Orleans?"

Now, I was *super* worried. Texting him, I waited five *long* minutes for no response, but I'd come too far; plus, I was armed. So, I eased out of my car and side-stepped into the barn with my pistol drawn. The dimming daylight followed me only enough to dusk the entrance, leaving the rest of the inside shadowy and dark.

"Tray?" I called out. "Tray!" There was no text, no answer. Now, I really felt goddamned duped.

That's when someone's head leaned from the shadows. "What took you so long?"

Just the deep voice alone, out of nowhere, nearly made me drop my weapon. Toggling a nearby wall-switch up and down, it was obvious the Marchands had canceled those auto-paid utilities. "Is that you, Tray?" I looked deeper into the shadows.

"In the flesh." He stepped into the haze towards me. "You can put away the gun. It wouldn't help you even if it wasn't me."

Re-holstering my gun, I followed with a backhand slap against his chest that didn't miss. "What the hell have you been doing, man?"

Painful was how to describe backhanding a V in the chest for the first time, and maybe something I'd never do again.

"Shit," he said, "trying to save you, woman."

"And did you know helicopters are all over the place looking for you?"

"*Helicopters*?" Narrowing his eyes, he aimed his ear towards the roof. "Where? *Here*?"

"No! New Orleans!"

"New Orleans? Really?"

"Anyway, so come again—who exactly are you trying to save me from? What was that story?"

"I don't know his name or who he is yet, but he's a V on a revenge-binge, and somehow, that vengeance is targeted at me and everyone I know and love!"

As much as his concern moved me, I tapped my lips for several seconds. "If you don't know who it is, how do you know he's a V?"

Tray's face went blank before gritting. "We just know a V when we see a V."

"Uh h'unh... and you *saw* him?"

Once again, his face went blank; his eyes rolled. "Anyway, trust me! He's a bloodthirsty V and he's after you!" Then came a look I'd never seen on his face before: worried eyes staring beyond me as if peering through a wall.

"What are you doing?" I looked backwards, then back towards him. "What are you looking at? Hey, wait a minute. Are you wired?" I reached for his ear. "Or are you listening to someone? Tray!"

Fending me off, his eyes returned to me with another look I'd never seen—a look that switched from worry to both harshness and fright at the same time.

"Why are you looking at me like that?" I yelled, but finally figured out what was going on. "Why are you—Oh, shit! You mother fu—"

Those were the last words I remembered screaming before blacking out, only to wake up in the dry musty freezer room with my butt planted in a rickety wooden chair. Gazing around, the door was open and Tray was nowhere in sight. He couldn't have hit me. I even rubbed my jaw to prove it to myself, then picked up where I'd left off: "Tray, you mother fucker!" I thought he said he couldn't hypnotize anyone—but yes, I, Veleta Robbins, had just been "hypno-vamped." And if that wasn't strange enough, sitting in a chair across from me was a patchy haired old man with a fallen face. We would have been staring each other in the eyes if not for *his* drifting towards the floor. He looked to be over one-hundred-years-old and on his last breath. The visual got even weirder when strung around his chest, I saw my very own cellphone.

Wobbling to my feet, I almost fell on the old man to grab it. "Excuse me, Sir," I said, "do you mind if I—yeah—that's all I need, *right* here."

He moaned as I untied it, as if he'd lost something important. He continued his plea with desperate eyes while I silently read the long text message loaded onto my screen. And if what I was reading was true, he was about to lose his freedom. The message opened with: `"Veleta, here sits the one guilty of killing Rayna, the string of women in New Orleans last night, and countless others. I know it's hard to be-`

lieve by the sight of him, but believe me,
you'll understand by the end of this message...."

I read the rest of it, but nearly fainted by the time I reached the end. "Tray, you mother fucker," I grumbled before redrawing my sidearm, this time aiming it at the old man's chest. "Freeze! You are under arrest!"

Chapter 28

Two Tales of One Day
Tale Number Two

Trémeur's Day

Who was I kidding? My cellphone had eight a.m. the morning after I was ambushed, and there was no way I was going back out into all that mayhem this soon. First of all, I still felt the Vyrotellum pumping through my veins, nailing me to the same floor in the same abandoned house I was sitting last night. I rubbed my head, my hair more tangled than ever. The morning sun was beaming through the curtainless windows, but just like the day before, there was no burning sensation—not one twinge.

In a flash the memories came back all at once: Morrow, Ragori, Rafeal, the ambush and the familiar smell of something past. I wasted no time picking up my phone and calling someone I knew would have answers. "Casio?"

"Tray, where are you?" The worry in his voice sounded as genuine as always. "The news has you as a fugitive on the run. Again! But I'm sure the body in your car was not *your* doing." Yet I sensed a touch of doubt in that voice for the first time, especially him having seen me go through this more than once.

But I understood. "Listen, I'll have to explain it to you later, but do you remember that guy? You know... my first night, umm..." I couldn't even get it out my mouth.

"*What?*"

"Uhh... my first kill. My *only* kill."

There was a brief pause. "Uh, yeah... What about him?"

"You tell me. I mean, you guys never told me much about him back then."

"Well, it's not like you were able to *stomach* it all in those days, nor any time thereafter. Plus, we actually did tell you who he was—a goddamn serial killer, remember? The cops even found his last victim's body parts jammed in a washer/dryer set at his own damn house! Don't you remember that?"

"Um, vaguely." I didn't. "What was his name?"

"Uhh... John something... John Parker, I believe. Something plain and simple. Yeah, John *Wilson* Parker to be exact. You know these serial killers always go by three names and shit."

"But you took care of it, right?"

"Yeah, ashes-to-ashes. Tim and I scattered them, ourselves—all over the place. You know the routine."

Before the Treaty, it was customary for concerned members of the V-community to cremate the remains of a victim and scatter handfuls in different parts of the city. Thus, preventing some unprecedented bodily re-assemblage—

especially for someone suspected to reemerge as an abomination—someone like John Wilson Parker.

"Hey," Casio continued, "are you gonna tell me what's bringing on all these questions?"

"Man…, it's too damn ridiculous to even think it," I said.

"Try me."

What I wasn't ready to disclose was that John Wilson Parker's scent had returned, matching that of last night's attacker. *But how?* "Hmm…" I stroked my chin. *Maybe the unprecedented* has *happened. But if he's really returned from the ashes, why was there an odor at all? Is he really V or not?* Judging by the heavy dose of Vyrotellum in my system, my guess was: *Yes, he damn sure is. And what did he mean by he's not finished with me or the ones*—

"Tray? Tray? Tray!"

"Yeah."

"You're taking too goddamn long! Cut to the chase! What are you trying to tell me? Because if anyone can help you, you know it's your brother."

"I know, but rest assured, I didn't do any of this!"

"I know you didn't. That's not what I was trying to imply, but at some point, Tray, you've got to start trusting someone—starting with your own goddamn brothers!"

I sighed, knowing he was right.

"I know it's been a long time," he said, "and you're still pissed about what happened, but I'm not the one who bit you, man. Hell, I can't stand the bitch either, nor the one who bit me! But here we are!"

What in the hell was I trying to prove? Casio was on point again—the first time I'd put together how similar our circumstances were, and how little I've entrusted in Vs, or anyone, because of it. And now was the time I needed help the most.

"I tell you what," I said, "I will call you back *real* soon, but first, I just have some digging to do."

"Okay," he said, "you do that and call me back. Just remember, I'm here for you. Tim *and* I are here for you. And we love you, bro."

"I know. Me too, bro. I'll hit you back."

As soon as I hung up, I had to shake off the emotions. For one, I needed a clear head to think; secondly, the Demoness was *not* who I'd even wanted to imagine at this moment.

My digging up old skeletons started with a web-search for John Wilson Parker, finding out about his abusive past and a few of his victims' profiles. A man of solitude, older white women seemed to be the only targets in his path. Online was his last most-wanted photo posted before he was never seen again. His face, slightly puffed and unremarkable with gray-stranded hair and beard, wasn't far from the median. The more I thought about it, knowing how *this* serial killer had met his end should have given me some solace. *I guess he got his.* But being the actual executioner still rubbed me the wrong way. And after the last few months, I was certain I was no executioner, although I had tasted live blood beyond my experience with Parker—mostly at many of Casio's "buck-wild" human "sip-n-dip" parties, where no one was killed or seriously maimed—just drained a few pints. But never did anyone's blood taste or smell the same, and I remembered Parker's, the only thing physically distinct about him. Now, his exact words reentered my mind: *I'm not finished with you, DuChaine, or the ones you love. And I believe I've identified my next victim.*

"Veleta," I mumbled. Scrolling for her caller I.D., I no longer cared about her little entrapment attempt. Surely, she had been forced to do it, but now was a different story; her life was in danger. "Wait a minute…" I hung up just before dialing, noticing I had an unchecked text message. It was from Veleta and right on time.

"Tray," it read, "sorry about that. i had no choice... but what i was trying to tell you before was that a witness came forward in rayna's case. she saw a man exiting her apartment. lean white guy, average height, wearing glasses. hit mw back." "...me back."

Strange… If Rayna was killed by a V, why was he wearing glasses? It was just another mystery to add to my long list, and while Veleta's information was crucial, it provided nothing to clear my name from this guy's bloody mess, so I hit the dial button; I didn't have time to bullshit around with another text.

When Veleta picked up, she and I went back and forth over last night's attempted call-trace, but once I emphasized the more pressing danger, she was all ears.

"Okay. Where do I go now?" she asked.

Her tone was the softest I'd ever heard from her. I couldn't believe it; there was finally a shred of humbleness in her voice.

"I don't know," I said, "but you'll figure out somewhere safe. Just notify me once you get there."

"Alright…"

Moments after hanging up, I looked towards the window, where the daylight bounced off every speck of dust, enough to give me a new idea. If this guy was truly a V, sun-screened or not, we had until nightfall to devise a plan, and I knew the next person to call.

"It's about time you fucking called!" Frustration leaped from Tim's mouth when he answered my phone call. "Where the hell are you?"

"In a jam," I said, "but I need your help."

"To say the least."

"I need to get to B.R. Fast!"

"Okay, I'll come get you." He didn't hesitate until a couple of seconds later. "Wait a minute… I'm pretty sure we're all being watched right now. Are you close enough to get here right away? You know… the *other* way in."

I had to dig deep into my memory for that one. "I can *make* it close."

"Then that's the way to go. See you soon."

Living for so long had taught Vampyrians to always have an
exit strategy, and this never applied more than when the original houses were built. With Casio's house handed down from
a long line of DuChaines, their exit-strategy was an abandoned
underground conduit-tunnel leading to a drop-inlet three
blocks from the house. If I was ever to find that inlet now, I
had to race at V-speed from corner-to-corner just to avoid detection in broad daylight. This wasn't an easy task since I was
still a little hungover from the Vyrotellum, and my face must
have been plastered across every media outlet. In the end, it
took me nearly fifteen minutes, but I did find that drop-inlet—
chipped and almost as rank as a sanitary sewer. The infiltra-
tion and mud-buildup over time had done quite a number on it,
reminding me of one more thing I needed to do before making
my descent. Holding my breath and straddling the inlet's
edge, I shot Tim a quick text: "Hey, have a clean set
of clothes waiting for me."

He didn't hesitate with his next response either:
"what do i look like, ur fucking maid? pick
em out ur own damn self."

"Prick," I mumbled, looking up just in time to find
someone staring straight at me.

An old lady, decently dressed in clunky heels, was
paused on the sidewalk, her eyes wider than a spotlight.

I paused too, unable to decipher if she recognized me or not, and I didn't want to take any chances. "Lady, you don't know who I am, do you?"

Her mouth dropped and her eyes stiffened even more. "No," she said flatly, "I don't know who you are."

"Good. Then why don't you just forget you ever saw me here, okay?"

"I don't know."

"You don't know what?"

"I don't know why I won't forget I ever saw you here."

Damn, is she looking for hush-money? "Ma'am, please just forget you ever saw me here. It would be good for you and all involved. Not that that's a threat or anything."

"Okay, I'll just forget I ever saw you here," she said before walking away with her eyes now glued ahead, at a sturdy pace, almost trance-like.

"Wow, that was weird," I muttered, followed by returning to my mission down the inlet.

Old tunnels didn't fare too well underneath New Orleans, most of them sheared at the joints with collapsed crowns. This one took me from crouching, to hands-and-knees, to army-crawling until reaching the hatch to our hidden room behind the stairs. Once inside, Tim was already there motioning me forward from the door.

"Coast is clear," he said.

With all lights off, I crept up the stairs to my room. Behind me, Tim had followed and now stood against my doorway with his arms folded, while I scrounged around for clean clothes.

"By the way," he said, "your other brother did you a solid."

I was almost too busy dusting myself off to hear him. "What's that?"

"*Ohh*... he just took a little trip to create a diversion."

"A diversion? Diversion for what?"

"Two guys in a car parked down the street were sitting there for too goddamn long. So, Cas made sure they saw him driving away."

"Oh, yeah? Did it work?"

"It must have. They took off after him without even trying to hide. Shit, all the ins and outs Casio has planned, those sons of bitches'll be driving until they reach retirement. It wouldn't surprise me if a few helicopters join in."

"*Helicopters*?" I couldn't see it. "Get real."

By the time Tim finished his update, I was walking by him with a roll of fresh clothes in my hand. "Let's go," I said.

But Tim threw his arms in the air. "What! Aren't you gonna at least wash the stinkin' mud off? You're smothered in it!"

I was halfway down the stairs when I answered. "Can't. No time!"

Trailing behind me again, he was still grumbling. "You're gonna funk up my motha' fucking car!"

"Then shit, buy a new one."

Changing clothes still had to wait for another "coast" to clear. Attributing enhanced bone and joint strength to our modified DNA, all six-feet-plus of me lay folded in Tim's mini-SUV's trunk—a clown-trick, to say the least. This all may have seemed like a bit much, but I was sure more than just human law enforcement was on the lookout. The V-Council must have surely been aroused, especially Marques.

As soon as the backseat's rest-latch clicked, I climbed into it and slumped below sight—finally changing clothes while peeking over the rear-dash every now and then. Meanwhile, Tim couldn't help glancing back from all the noise I was making, especially when I boot-jabbed his door; I almost knocked it off.

"Damn, man, watch the door, will you?" he yelled. "And *army* boots?"

"Yeah," I said while putting on the other. "I figured we'd be going back to war someday, so I saved them."

"I guess now is as good a time as any," he mumbled.

As much as my brother had my back, him risking it all and driving no less than ninety-miles-per-hour, I still found a reason to gripe: "Slow down, will you? You're gonna draw too much damn attention!" Several more times followed until approaching Baton Rouge.

Plastered in V-Screen, Tim finally let me have it. "Okay, first you have me playing chauffeur during inferno hours, now you ask me to slow down after asking me to speed up five minutes ago! And five minutes before that! And five minutes before that! Look, why don't you just chill and keep laying low? I got this."

He was right; my nerves were up and down like South Louisiana's weather, but I was only thinking about Veleta. I knew she was tough-willed, but no match for the character she'd be facing. My first thought had been to find her and keep her secure, obviously a wise move. But I had another idea, one that would kill several birds with one stone. Texting her a new set of instructions, I prayed she wouldn't be one of those birds.

Afterwards, I looked towards Tim. "Change of plans," I said.

"What?"

"Change of plans. We're heading to Zachary."

Baton Rouge's late afternoon traffic had felt like a wrestling match, landing us in Zachary close to sunset. With no address in hand, it was a miracle I remembered our destination's turn, a seemingly random gravel road off Highway 19. At its end was the Marchands' farm, a twenty-acre lot centered by a patched-up barn with very few other structures remaining. However, parking near the barn seemed too easy.

"Let's park farther down," I told Tim, "out of the way. You know—hidden."

"You got it," Tim said, eventually pulling to a stop at the end of a bend.

We circled back around by foot, both of us wired for espionage. While Tim assumed a lookout point completely across the road from the farm, I veered off into the barn, the same barn where Veleta and I had found the blood-bank thief and his freezer full of stolen plasma several months ago.

Once inside, I backed into the shadows and waited. Now with time to think, the guilt of the entire scenario was beginning to weigh on me. Part of me wanted to secure Veleta, and even devise a better plan. It didn't matter that she had tried to set me up earlier, because I knew her hand was forced. But there was the other part, the cold V side I thought I'd squashed a long time ago, the side that saw a prime opportunity to draw a killer into the open. In other words, I had a feeling this V would be following her, and I would be waiting. By my own doing, my dear friend was now nothing but human bait.

I could have handled things much differently, I thought. *I could have guarded Veleta from a distance; I could have done so much more; I could have—*

"Tray! You read me?" Tim's voice was in my earpiece.

"Yeah."

"Shit, man, I must have called your name about five times now. A car just turned up the road. I think it's Agent Robbins."

"What's she driving?"

"Looks like a blue Camry."

"That should be her. Stay alert."

"More than you. Over and out."

Tim had never been police or military, which made his "read-me's" and "over-and-outs" odd compared to me; I'd recently decided to quit using any of that damn nomenclature. He'd actually given me a chuckle before those next few excruciating minutes waiting for Veleta, but when the barn door creaked open, I tensed as tight as a cable.

"Tray?" Veleta called out with her weapon drawn. Her tension, which I sensed by normal means, was higher than the rafters. "Tray!"

I took a step forward. "What took you so long?"

"Tray, is that you?"

"Yes, it's me—in the flesh." I stepped out farther with one hand up. "You can put away the gun. It wouldn't help you even if it wasn't me."

Punching me in the gut, she ranted. "What the fuck have you been doing, man?"

"Trying to save you!"

"And goddamn helicopters are all over the place looking for you!"

"*Helicopters*?" I looked up through a few holes in the roof, but saw and heard nothing. "Where? *Here*?"

"No! New Orleans!"

"New Orleans? Really?" I couldn't believe it; *Casio really did draw a crowd.*

"Anyway… so, come again—who exactly are you trying to save me from? What was your story?"

"I don't know his name or who he is yet, but he's a V on a revenge-binge, and somehow, that vengeance is targeted at me and everyone I know!"

She tapped her lips. "If you don't know who he is, how do you know he's a V?"

Shit! She's so damn sharp. But I still couldn't say anything about the Vyrotellum. "Damn it, we just know a V when we see a V!"

"Uh h'unh... And you *saw* him?"

She's got an even bigger point. "Anyway, trust me. He's a bloodthirsty V and he's after *you*!"

That's when Tim's voice entered my ear again. "Tray, I see another car parked way outside on the entrance road near the main highway—a gray, mid-sized Accord. I just noticed it. Don't know how long it's been there, but I don't see anyone inside. What do you want me to do?"

Now *he wants my advice.* I needed a few seconds to think, but I didn't have many. *Hmm... no one inside the car ... oh, oh, something's about to go down—*

"What the hell are you doing?" Veleta's glare was somewhere between confusion and hatred—closer to the latter. "What are you looking at?" she shouted.

The truth was, for a second, I'd forgotten she was there, and would have told her about Tim if it wasn't for this eerie-ass feeling I was having. The time to get Veleta out of the way had come sooner than expected. *But how?*

"Hey, wait a minute," she said, reaching for my ear. "Are you wearing a wire?"

As kindly as I could, I swatted her hand away, intent on hearing Tim out.

But Veleta was determined for more. "Or are you listening to someone? Tray!"

She reached again, but I couldn't let her destroy the connection. One more hand-block and the answer became clear; I had no choice but to stare her down.

When our eyes met, she leaned back, placing her hand on her chest. "Why are you looking at me like that?"

I wanted to tell her so badly to—*Just shut the hell up and don't move until I tell you to move*—but I couldn't get it out. All I did was just stare.

"Oh, no!" She gasped. "You mother fuck—errrr," she slurred as her eyelids grew heavy.

Her torso swaying back and forth, I thought she was going to pass-out, so I grabbed her shoulders and yelled, "Veleta, are you okay?"

When she straightened up and her eyes flared, I was relieved, until she just stood there with absolutely nothing else to say.

"Veleta, are you okay?" I shook her gently, but the ordinarily boisterous one still had nothing to say. "You know what," I said, "it doesn't matter. Just go into the freezer and don't come out until I come and get you."

Finally, she huffed. "Okay… I'll just go into the freezer until you come and get me."

I may have needed to guide her, but her pace was as entranced as the woman near the drop-inlet earlier. Even so, I was amazed at how compliant Veleta was in this moment, which worried me even more.

The freezer may have been defunct and musty, but I noticed something different about it since the blood bank thief: it had a keyed lock with a latch on the other side. So, I decided to test my limits once Veleta was inside. "Now, lock the door after I leave," I told her.

Just outside the freezer door, I heard the latch click inside. "Great," I mumbled, now with time to return to Tim. "Tim, what do you see now?"

Tim said nothing.

"Tim, what do you see? Copy?" I figured throwing in a "copy" would get his attention, but still hearing nothing, I readjusted my earpiece. "Tim? Tim? Tim!"

Chapter 29
Of National Concerns

Washington D.C. was abuzz whenever Senator Danvers Stroy's limousine passed by. Draped by its legally-exempt extra heavy window-tint, he and Koncadia, now his chief of staff, sat in the backseat, both deep into their browsers as always. A senator's duties were both nation- and statewide, but Danvers often failed to detach himself from even the most remote local ongoings. Pounding his armrest, he raged. "Damn it! What the hell is he doing down there?"

Koncadia, a bleach-blonde on this day, happened to be on the same site. "I'm not sure, but this kind of behavior definitely does not fit Detective DuChaine's profile."

Danvers's tone dampened as he stroked his chin. "Hmm… losing a lover, losing his career, nearly frying to death in a plane crash. There's no telling how he's been processing it all. This would actually be the perfect scenario for an addiction to arise. Then once you start… get a sweet sip… feel that pulsating, quivering resistance… you just can't stop." He exhaled softly, pausing to stretch his own collar. "You know, we've all been there—before the Treaty, that is."

"Barely. You turned me *after* the Treaty, remember? But *I* was prepared."

"Yes, you practically begged for it. Of course, you *were* more of a monster at heart. Especially before."

Koncadia continued to browse, her silence first deflecting his remarks like a shield, but all of them too true to be contested. She gave brief thought to her human years: back then, political party lines were no more than cobwebs whenever she was solicited for campaign management. From Republican to Democrat, to back and forth, her membership had always flowed to the highest bidder. Many opponents fell into obscurity due to her cunning, and after Danvers had finally given in to her so-called "begging," she'd automatically become a member of the Vampyrian Party, now the nation's largest independent one. Vampyrians and humans, Republicans and Democrats—it didn't matter; they were all joining the V-Party in droves because of Danvers. Better yet, because of Koncadia's soft-spoken influence. And being turned after the Treaty, Koncadia had felt no pressing need to be family-adopted or to alter her own name. It remained, Koncadia Wessler.

All of this now considered, she offered one of those soft-spoken responses: *"Begging?* I wouldn't call pointing out, 'the longer I live, the longer you win,' *begging."*

Danvers paused. "Yes, you possessed quite a unique style of compulsion. W-W-Well anyway, whatever he's doing," he stammered his way back to Trémeur, "he's fucking up my plans for the future! He's got to be stopped and he's got to be stopped now, damn it!"

Unfazed, Koncadia muttered, "You got it."

Chapter 30

Valleys Through the Mind of Evil

Narrated by Trémeur DuChaine

The place was the Marchands' abandoned farm in Zachary, and things were getting pretty tense in the main barn. In the defunct freezer room was Veleta in some kind of trance, while Tim was outside having gone dead in my ear comm. I didn't know what to expect next, but when the barn door started to creak, my senses were telling me—it wasn't Tim. Having returned to the shadows, I braced myself for an intruder of the worst kind. L.B.I. agent or not, I'd never relinquished my private V-gun, which was now in the small of my back with my hand on the handle. My guess was, whoever was opening that door was hyped up on natural blood, so landing a shot of Vyrotellum would most likely only stagger him. The rest I'd have to finish on my own; I knew this much.

When the door swung wide open, my suspense ended with a blast from the not-so-distant past. Dressed in dingy clothes under a wrinkled windbreaker, Landon Levy was standing in the doorway, the last of daylight against his back.

"How?" I mumbled.

Levy saw me clearly in the darkness. "What's that, Detective DuChaine? What? I can't hear you. Cat got your tongue?"

Landon Levy—not the most original guy. "How did you—I mean—how is this possible? I saw you reduced to ashes."

"None of that matters now, DuChaine. What matters is, I came here to try things a little differently. To feast on your friend for a long while before mailing her to you—piece-by-piece." Withdrawing a Samurai sword from behind his back, he stepped all the way inside. "Now, your little trap has definitely succeeded, but seeing you here actually provides a bit of a bonus. Watching you burn to ashes will be like ... dining by fireside."

With his rambling picking up just where he had left off in L.A., I was even more confused, unable to understand this guy's unyielding need for revenge. And dismembering a human was hard to figure since it didn't fit Levy's M.O. Strictly feeding was his thing, but when that human target was my friend, defending her with my life was now *my* thing.

Just as Levy took another step, I was ready to introduce him to a change of plans. I drew my V-gun; that's when that police training of mine returned like a reflex. "Freeze, Levy!"

But Levy simply inhaled with a blissful look on his face. "Ahh, I can smell the Vyrotellum... a heavy dose too. But you will need a lot more than you think, so hit me with what you got!" He challenged with a sinister roar, his chest high and his sword extended to the side.

I accepted that dare with a burst of Vyrotellum bullets into his chest, but that round failed to even buckle his knees.

He advanced towards me without hesitation, his chest stretching his front collar enough for me to see the reason why. Underneath his shirt was something a V had never needed.

"Kevlar?" I said.

"That's right, both bullet- and dart-proof. Finally, something produced by H-Bloods that serves a goddamn real purpose!"

"Yeah, those things have been around awhile," I said, but couldn't believe I'd never thought of it before. *Would have come in handy last night.*

With my weapon now useless, Levy lunged and swung his blade wildly several times, me dodging left and right away from every swing. It was obvious he was no master when it came to sword-play, like he'd just picked it up from the internet. As awkwardly as he was swinging, I barely needed V-speed to avoid him. He swung again and again; I dodged again and again, connecting on a few punches in between, some into his face and a few into his gut.

But Levy kept swinging, absorbing my every punch like a block-wall—a true sign of a naturally-fed V versus one nursed by the bag. He even held back once, gritting, practically joyfully, while I battered away at his ribs. "C'mon!" he goaded. "Is that all you got?"

Our exchange resumed until I withdrew my gun one more time, only to watch Levy slap it right out of my hand. It bounced off a far column like a pinball just as he kicked-pressed me into another one. *That was shifty.* But there was no bouncing back from this one; I went straight through it, falling to the floor before being buried by wooden beams and trash from the loft above.

On my back after swiping away the rubble, I witnessed a most menacing scene. Levy was airborne, grimacing with his sword cocked behind his head, both hands on the hilt. It was a scene I never expected when I'd changed into my army boots back in the car. But Levy felt my full sole into that grimace—jolting him back in the opposite direction. And when he hit the ground, so did the sword, now free from his grip.

I'd played a little basketball back in my young human days, so I knew a loose ball was anybody's, and that sword was suddenly just as loose. I rolled over and dove for it, but even with my head-start, Levy was back on his feet, beating me to it by a split second. With me laid flat and exposed, he swung again and chopped the dirt right before my eyes. Afterwards, there was a long stare between us, a sure sign I still had my head, but when I tried to lift myself, I fell face-first to the dirt-covered floor. Something was missing, and I couldn't believe what it was: one of my arms was a few feet away, detached and smoldering on the floor.

Oh, my God! It was my left arm, and watching it fizzle into ashes I wanted to scream, but there was no time. Levy was re-cocked and aimed at my neck. Even with one arm, I rolled away, leaving him chopping nothing but dirt for sure this time. But he tried again, and again, and again, with me rolling away every time until we both recessed from exhaustion. Somehow, I scooted back on my ass until propping myself against something solid, maybe something from the fallen loft—I wasn't sure.

Meanwhile, Levy was strutting around and twirling his blade as if victory was near. "You know, DuChaine," he said, "I suppose I should thank you for what you've done for me— for what you've given me. I've been able to be my true self ever since. I've been able to enjoy satisfying the thirst that's been deep inside me since before my immortal years. It's been a joy. But you know what? I'm just not that kind o' guy. You see, I made a promise to myself after I was turned. I vowed that if I were to ever see you again, I would make you suffer. Slowly. Methodically. Surgically—without any V-anesthesia. After which, I'd watch you die!"

Since the beginning of his little soliloquy, I'd been wondering the whole time: *What in the hell is he talking about? All of this animosity from just our one meeting in Los Angeles?* And I couldn't hold it back any longer: "Dude, I have no idea what the *fuck* you're talking about! Plus—isn't my missing arm enough of a damn punishment for whatever it is, *you son of a bitch!*"

"Uhh, is it enough? No. Am I a son of a bitch? Yes! The bitch-ass mother is where it all begins, isn't it? And now for you, it all ends."

On that note, Levy approached me with another grimace on his face, but I was too exhausted to move. He reached down and grabbed a fistful of my hair, tilted my head to the side, and exposed my neck while cocking his sword back for one final swing.

I may have been facing the end, but I wasn't ready to give up; I *had* to know the source of this guy's frustration. As that sword slowly reached its apex, Levy in my face was my chance to figure it out. Getting a closer look, his eyes reminded me of a human I'd once seen, while his faint residual aroma also reminded me of that same human, one whose blood I'd tasted before. Instincts alone led me to my next move: I grabbed Levy's forehead with my remaining hand. Gripping it like a handle was the only thing keeping me from falling flat, while the energy transmitted between us halted his sword in mid-swing. I felt a charge flowing from Levy through my hand, through my body, and finally into my head. Just like what I'd experienced with Casio on our grand-room floor, I was experiencing the same thing with Levy, but what I saw in Landon Levy's soul was so disturbing, I had to close my eyes:

When I reopened them, I was staring into a kitchen from a dining room's edge. Inside the kitchen was a man and a woman arguing with one another, the woman ending her point with a plate crashing against the wall.

The man ducked and yelled, "What the fuck are you doin,' you crazy bitch!"

"Stoppin' you from doin' somethin' to me first, you sick-ass bastard!" the woman shouted.

"Oh, yeah? Oh, yeah?" The man retaliated by punching her in the jaw, bouncing her off the stove before she smacked the floor. "Get up, you lazy-ass whore of a wife!" But he didn't wait; he lifted her by the throat and spat in her face. "I'm gonna do somethin' to you alright, you crazy bitch! Now, turn around, you fuckin' whore!"

But he still refused to wait. As much as she resisted, he turned her around, raised her dress and yanked down her panties. And when he pulled down his boxers, he inserted himself in a spot that not only made the woman cringe, but me also all the way from the doorway. In the midst of his violent thrusts, he looked me in the eye and said, "John Wilson, this is how you treat a slut-ass whore like your momma. Now get your ass back to your room and close the god-damn door! Go on, Son! Show some getup about it! Get!" During the man's entire command, the thrusting never ceased.

Somehow my eyes opened again, but I felt trapped in a nightmare, until reality struck—I was just in one of serial killer John Wilson Parker's memories. *But how?* There were still some things I had to figure out, so I closed my eyes again and squeezed Levy's head harder—hard enough until he trembled:

Being inside that frightened little boy again, I turned away and ran, but my next step landed me

somewhere other than I was commanded. I ended up in another home, where a woman was bent
over and quivering in front of me. Gripped
around her waist were my grown "white" hands,
this time me being the one thrusting from behind.
I was now the adult version of John Wilson Parker. Meanwhile, the woman's pain seemed so
great, I desperately tried to withdraw, but I
couldn't; John wouldn't let me. Next he grabbed
the woman by the hair and yanked her upright,
where he slit her throat with a boxcutter. At this
point, I fought with all I had to escape, but John
held me hostage until we both felt a release. All-
in-all, it was worse than a V-feeding.

Immediately after, the experience transferred to another scene, another home, another
room, and to another woman. It even happened
again a few times after that. Sometimes John
climaxed with a boxcutter; other times, he got
there with a simple steak-knife, but each occur-
rence always led to a deadly ending. And how
he pre-disposed of the bodies—the sawing, the
breaking, the gutting—was even more sickening.
John wasn't just a killer—John Wilson Parker
was a *monster*!

Then one night after another of his trans-
gressions, John's fate was sealed—attacked by
another monster that drained every drop of his

blood.   That monster was *me*, and my crazed bloodthirsty eyes were far more frightening when headed in my own direction.

When the barn came back into view, both Levy and I were thoroughly drained, as if every gruesome rape and murder had happened again. The sword had even fallen back to the floor, laying there waiting for me to pick it up, but I couldn't let go of Levy's forehead. I *had* to find out how John had survived our encounter. So I held on, gripping it tighter until Levy moaned in anguish—gripping it tighter until submerging even deeper into his psyche. Again, my eyes closed tightly, reopening inside another precarious situation:

As frigid as my insides felt, I also felt what must have been the heat of the sun approaching my head, but quickly realized, *I* was the one approaching the heat. Startled, naked and on my back, it was actually John who was slowly being inserted into a cremating retort like an injection—the assurance strategy Casio had mentioned.

When John looked up at the last second, the crematory attendant had her back turned, giving John the opportunity to roll over the edge onto his bare feet. Not only did I feel every ripple of his wobbly landing, but I felt his stomach already rumbling to feed, and the attendant becom-

ing his prey. Before knowing his own strength
and speed, John was buried into the attendant's
neck, his new fangs sucking the life right out of
her. And if the kill wasn't complete, the heat
from the furnace had given him a novel idea.
Seconds later, he tossed the attendant into it like
a sack—listening to her body snap and crackle
into ashes. At this moment I knew, it was an innocent young woman's ashes, not John's, that
were later scattered all over New Orleans.

With my grip still firm, I raised Levy's brow, now seeing the
true picture. His face may have been much leaner due to his
transition, but it was now obvious. I was staring into the eyes
of both Landon Levy *and* John Wilson Parker. But I still had
to see more. I dove back in and journeyed through the years
afterwards, those with the Levys, John's adoptive V-family:

Now as Landon Levy, like me, he'd been trained
to avoid detection, encouraged to feed by artifi-
cial means, and re-educated and cultured beyond
his crude upbringing. But with an infatuation for
blood far too innate to overcome, Levy could be
none other than what he was: still a monster.

Just like inside John, I suffered through
Levy's many more deadly excursions, before *and*
after his escape from prison. I even witnessed
the secret deals he, himself, had brokered with

the new white supremacist groups for his DNA.
I also witnessed his deal with Zandamoor &
Company to do the same, but with lower concen-
trations added to their high-end immuno-
boosters, compounds only the wealthy could af-
ford. Through Levy's eyes, I saw it brokered by
Koncadia Wessler in her own limousine, her hair
now dyed fiery red:

"Do not think this freedom you've been
granted comes without strings attached." I heard
her say while face-to-face with her imposing
stare.

"Freedom!" Levy and I blasted. "You
call *this* freedom? I'm living on the fucking
run!"

"You've always been living on the run,
Mr. Levy. We thought you might prefer it this
way. Do you not?"

"Well…" I actually felt his embarrass-
ment, his first time having to face such logic. "It
does match my craving for a pounding heartbeat." I felt his joy bubbling inside.

"Wonderful. Then you are to meet with
Mr. Ivander Oxley of Zandamoor & Company.
He will provide you with further details. And by
the way," she said with a piercing look and a
waving forefinger, "no feeding on the money."

Levy huffed. "Not even a little sip?"

"No." Koncadia didn't flinch.

"Why can't I just turn them? That would at least be a tad bit exhilarating, and it's what they want, isn't it?"

"No. It's the longevity they want, not the complete transformation. And you're not capable. There's only one being on this planet who is, but she's not on our side."

Artreaux, I figured.

"Anyway, afterwards," Koncadia continued, "we will need you to stay away from Louisiana. Forever. Is this understood?"

He huffed again, louder.

But Koncadia's brow crunched as she gritted. "Is this understood?"

Koncadia, one who consistently sipped from live familiar donors like glasses of wine, was still of a breed strong enough for Levy to fear. In turn, he offered one slow head-bob. "Understood... But where will I go?"

"You will be provided a one-way ticket to Los Angeles for starters. From there, we'll just have to see, but never back to Louisiana."

"Oh... what a pity." He may have been shaking his head, but I definitely felt the hint of a facetious smirk.

Levy exited the vehicle with his mood a little lighter. And me, I had no doubt one Danvers Stroy was at the root of Koncadia Wessler's scheme.

As I clinched Levy's forehead even tighter, his moans grew louder and his face began to wither. Without a blink, I was back in his mind to a moment after the Lakers' game, the night of our standoff in a Los Angeles parking garage. It was before Detective Flores and I had entered the garage, where Levy, now with "this me" inside, was already waiting behind a support column:

"Hiding from someone, Levy?" A deep voice rose from the shadows.

Levy looked up in shock, surprised by a lean, casually clothed man approaching, someone I recognized. Madhav Sahib, one of the New Orleans V-Council's security officers, one of Marques's men, approached carrying a Samurai sword, similar to the one now on the barn's floor. Watching him cock it behind his head, it became apparent—not all in the Council had shared in Levy's efforts.

"The Council has a message for you and your mission to sabotage the Treaty," Sahib explained just before his downswing towards Levy's neck.

I felt Levy's nerves quiver at the potential outcome, but he ducked just in time to watch it shear a concrete wedge from the column. Now cement-covered, Levy took advantage by plugging Sahib with a round of Vyrotellum—straight from the bottom of a cookie bag.

Sahib, a strong V, no matter his choice of blood, was only stifled a bit, but his sword was now on the deck within Levy's reach. When Sahib made another charge, Levy was waiting with the sword awkwardly in hand, but steady enough to pierce straight through Sahib's neck.

Seconds later, Sahib did manage to pull himself off the blade's surface, but not without severe consequences. Both the Vyrotellum and the critical wound staggered him only one step back before timbering forward at Levy's feet.

Meanwhile, Levy was just about to finish off his adversary when he heard footsteps. Those steps happened to be from my past-self approaching from the distance, while Levy wasted no time making his presence known. Just like before, he fired a round of Vyrotellum in my direction.

As our encounter was coming to its second ending, Levy removed his shirt and threw it over Sahib's back, followed by a swift chop with Sahib's own sword. The ensuing sparks sprayed off the deck like fireworks, leaving Levy amazed by how easy the blade had sliced off his attacker's head. In fact, he admired it with nothing less than morbid curiosity: *Like butter.*

The sword's clank was what I had heard that night, but time was fleeting for Levy, leaving him with none of it to watch the body smolder, and none of it to worship his own accomplishment. Grabbing Sahib's head, Levy was off in a flash. *At least I have his head to watch disintegrate. It's so damn interesting... and... so serendipitous.*

One more victim followed in Los Angeles, but Levy couldn't deny something was amiss: *The blood running through the veins of Louisianians is so much sweeter to my taste buds.* There in Louisiana flowed the blood he was weaned on. Thus ignoring Koncadia's mandate, he flew back home under an alias and returned to old habits. Through his memories, I watched him drain helpless souls from Baton Rouge to New Orleans, most of them he'd slurped behind bushes as I had done to him, except for one beautiful young woman, one he'd murdered in her own apartment. Then came the string of murders just to pin on me, followed by the funeral home massacre just to give himself a rush. And now—*wait a minute...*

I paused, backtracking through his maze of memories until returning to the young woman murdered in her apartment. She had looked extremely familiar, but faded by Levy's clouded recollection:

> Rayna was standing before me as beautiful as the morning I had last seen her, except now in a sexy slip, not terrycloth, leaving little to the imagination. Yet when she looked into my eyes, the fear in hers was even more frightening to me. At that moment, I felt Levy lunge and snatch her by the throat, followed by jabbing his fully elongated fangs into her neck.

It was the most horrible feeling of every last one I'd just experienced, forcing me to shut down all thought, but not before hearing Levy say: "Don't bail out on me now, detective. Things are about to get extremely... *tasty*..." His tone was tauntingly sinister and definitely directed towards me. Levy was now in my head as much as I was in his.

That and the myriad of memories finally got to me. I couldn't let him drag me in any further. *I have to clear him out!* "Enough!" I roared while releasing his forehead, then grabbed my own in anguish, desperate to erase every God-forsaken image. But it was too late; I was consumed.

Eventually I lifted my head, unsure exactly how long we'd been under. It must have been a pretty long time, because on his back underneath me was a fossil of a man trembling on the floor. I couldn't recognize him, but his head was bald with long strands of gray hair, and he was wearing Levy's clothes, now a size too large. But Levy was nowhere around, having left his sword behind on the floor next to the old man. With all the strangeness around me, I was now abusing what seemed to be a frail human, but this one with no distinct scent. Nonetheless, I had to get off of him, but not until leaning over to take another close look, seeing one thing Levy *did* leave behind—his eyes, both embedded in the old man's sockets. It may have been inexplicable, but when I realized who he was, I picked up the sword, recognizing it as the same blade I'd just seen in Levy's memory, the blade that once belonged to Madhav Sahib.

As I rose to my feet, I realized one more thing: I wasn't a master swordsman either. But on this night, I was determined to finally remove someone's head. That someone was going to be Landon Levy, soon to be released from his miserable existence—decrepit old man or not.

When I lifted Sahib's blade, Levy still wasn't finished; his trembling ceased just long enough for one last taunting grin as his final word.

"Wait!" A familiar voice blurted from behind. When I looked around, Tim was staggering through the barndoor. "You can't do that!" he shouted. "We need him alive… to prove your innocence!"

I wrestled with God and all of Heaven to hold back my swing, but in the end, I couldn't dispute Tim's logic. It appeared that Levy would live to see another day, or at least another hour by the looks of things.

Tim dragged himself over while rubbing the back of his own neck, though his eyes widened when seeing the complete picture. "Shit! What happened to your arm?"

"It got smoked." It was strange; I'd almost forgotten all about it.

"Damn... how does it feel?"

"Like it's not there." In fact, there was absolutely no more pain or feeling, not even the slightest of a phantom limb. "What, hasn't this ever happened to you before?"

"No, bro. I've been lucky. I never get in as much fucking trouble as you—'till now." He looked at the near-death candidate lying on the floor and stroked his own chin. "Hey, you know... when I just said all that back there, I was thinking that was our perp you were about to chop up, but who the fuck is this old guy?"

"That—is Landon Levy."

"*Landon Levy*? I thought he was dead?"

"So did I. Wait—you mean he wasn't the reason you just went dark out there?"

"I guess so. I never saw him coming. But why does he look as old as Methuselah?"

I would have been scratching my head if it wasn't for the sword in my only hand. "I... uhh... think it was something I did. Like the day when Casio went delirious."

But Tim did scratch his. "Whoa... that's deep. You
have to tell me all about it later, but right now, where's Agent
Robbins?"

"She should be in the freezer."

"In the freezer? Why is she in the—oh, never mind."
He had apparently heard enough. Hurrying over to the freezer,
Tim's body went stiff when he looked through the door-
window. "Why is she just standing there like the... like the...
the 'standing' damn dead? I can't say 'walking.'" He
knocked on the door. "Agent Robbins? Agent Robbins?" After no response, he tugged on the locked door, then yanked it
until breaking it open. "Agent Robbins! Are you okay?"
Still, there was no response, so he turned back to me. "She
ain't budgin.' What in the shit did you do to her?"

I thought again about the woman near the drop-inlet,
my last words to her and how she'd reacted. And now, my last
words to Veleta began to make sense. "Maybe...," I mumbled.
Whatever was going on with her, I had a feeling I could fix it,
but first, Tim and I had a job to do. I had Tim drag Levy's
feeble body into the freezer, where he propped him up in a
chair in front of Veleta, who remained totally adrift. From
there, I stepped in front of her and asked, "Veleta?"

"Yes?" She stood there like a swaying tree, her eyes
straight ahead with not one flinch in my direction, giving me
time to find the only other chair in the room.

"Here. Sit down," I said.

Just as before, she obeyed. "Okay."

"Now, take out your phone and access your document processor."

As she continued to obey without question, Tim's face faded into a stupor of disbelief.

"Now type this message," I commanded her before dictating all the relevant facts, enough to place Levy back behind bars for good.

Veleta went on to take dictations like a pro, and when all was said and done, and her phone was strapped to Levy's torso, I left her with one final order: "Oh, and by the way, please snap out of this in five minutes."

Chapter 31

An "I" to the Sky

Narrated by Trémeur DuChaine

"What, are you kidding me?" This was just *one* of my reactions when I read the line on my prescription sheet: *A long ass vacation!!!* It was written by Dr. Hailu, the very same doctor who was on the private jet after the crash, and today, much out of her character. By the number of certificates on her office wall, she actually was both surgeon and psychiatrist, a feat consistent with multiple lifespans. And while she was easy on the eyes, I had to seriously challenge her judgement. "You've got to be kidding me!"

"Nope." Her stare was as stiff as her chair.

This is why I avoid got-damn shrinks! I was expecting something along the lines of prescription V-drugs, word-association, electrodes to the skull—*hell, hypnosis for God's sake!* Anything to reduce the grind from days-on-end would have been enough; anything to wipe away the pain from two lost lovers would have worked; or *anything* to remove the stench of rapist/serial killer from my veins would have been appreciated. But the doctor's posture remained rigid, her stare unequivocally decisive.

It had been two weeks since capturing Landon Levy in the barn, and there were many things that happened afterwards.

One being Levy's subsequent plight. Veleta had left a message in my voicemail not long after we'd departed the scene: "Goddamn it, Tray! Where in the hell are you, and how am I supposed to explain this old-ass mother fucker in front of me to the Bureau?" Well, I didn't have an answer at the time, but she didn't have to wait long. John Wilson Parker, a.k.a. Landon Levy, ended up dying in police custody before ever reaching the hospital. Veleta, with her full wits back intact, went on to touch up her story as Levy's last confession. Yet my note and Levy's return to humanity, she'd kept to herself—per one of my requests. This, she'd explained as "a viral abnormality unique to Levy's strand."

And later, in front of a private gathering of thankful V-Council members, Levy's cremation was re-executed to perfection, followed by his ashes being scattered in different countries altogether.

Meanwhile, I'd found no way to explain Rafael's situation to Mrs. Etienne and her crew. Proving compulsion in a human court would have been impossible at best, while incarcerating an Old-Worlder by human means would have been more dangerous than trying to hold Levy—especially for the humans. This all led to a clearer solution: after reporting my findings to the V-Council, who was more interested in Stroy's involvement than Rafael's innocence, Ragori had become theirs to deal with. Arraigning an Old-Worlder was surely going to be a long, arduous process. *And thank God, no longer my problem.*

Self-therapy was the only thing I had left in order to give flying another shot. Equipped with a shoulder bag under one arm
and an articulated prosthetic on the other, I trailed several pas-
sengers down the airplane's aisle until reaching my seat. With
a sling over the prosthetic, I was able to avoid proving how it
worked, as well as getting a little extra attention from the flight
attendant, who'd slid through the line just to help me load my
bag.

        "Don't worry, Sir," she said with a charming smile,
"let me get that for you."

It took me a few minutes after taking my aisle seat, but I finally noticed something out of the ordinary: someone was sitting
right next to me, and someone else in the window seat.   I
couldn't believe it. It was like being human all over again—
also something I greatly needed at this point.

Hours later, I was back in a taxicab on my way to East Hampton. Since becoming a V, I hadn't had much need for drugs
until now. Weed, which I couldn't believe people still called a
drug, had little effect, casually smoked by some Vs as only a
fashion-statement. I did, however, succeed at soliciting a low-
dosage Vyrotellum pill from Dr. Hailu before I'd left. It was
just what I'd needed to sleep nearly the entire flight. Now riding in the back of the taxicab, the only thing I felt was my arm-
cells tingling and growing. Sliced by the highest bond of steel,
this regeneration was taking a little longer than before.

I could have called this trip a vacation, one which I finally had a chance to see the Hamptons under daylight hours, but my plan was to make it a bit more. I had the cabby drop me off at Phoebe Artreaux's front door with unfinished business to settle.

"Can you wait here, please?" I asked the cabby on the way out.

"Sure," he said with a shrug and a heavy New York accent. "You paying,' I'm staying."

"Great."

"Hey! Same rate by the way!"

"Great." I slammed the door.

Artreaux still had the most casual approach to home-security I'd ever seen. Again, I eased open her already slightly opened front door, this time at least knocking. When I heard no response, I simply followed the sound of televised field reporters, leading me all the way through the house to the back-porch, where Artreaux sat staring beyond the television and out into the ocean. Wearing bright island garments, she was swinging in a Caribbean rope hammock like a pendulum on its last tick. Normally, I would have been angry by now, but seeing her there reminded me of something Casio had once touched on, and something I'd never asked about: *How did she end up with the smoothest brown human skin I've ever seen?* It had to be a tie-in to her comfort in sunlight, and I may have even considered her "stunning," if not for the "demon" hiding underneath.

With me now standing as stiff as Lady Liberty, my arm now out of its sling, Artreaux's eyes remained cast beyond her hanging widescreen. "I had a feeling you'd be showing up *ri-ight* about now," she said. "Have a seat."

But having a seat wasn't on my mind at the moment. "I can tell by your open-door policy, but exactly how did you know I'd be showing up at all?"

"Ahh, mon amie, a little voodoo and an old-world virus can reach brave new heights when married together."

Her tone was sagely, something I had never expected, and still, she never broke her gaze from beyond a lone jetty. The sublime moment was the perfect time for me to pull out a surprise she would never see coming. With V-swiftness, I reached into my back-pocket with my live hand and flicked it towards her, but to my surprise, she caught it without a single glance in my direction.

"What's this?" she asked, staring at it and gasping. "Oh, my goodness!" In a matter of seconds, she was barely able to hold back the tears from the Polaroid of her, Tasha and me.

"I remembered from the last time I was here, you had no pictures of her," I said while taking a seat in a wooden chair not far away. The television screen was now in full view between us.

Artreaux shook her head in awe for every second she held the photo. "Simply beautiful… But I don't need a picture to remember her by." She laid it on her lap before gazing back over the water's horizon. "Her essence is always with me."

In this particular case I didn't know whether she was speaking metaphorically or realistically. With her, anything was more possible than with anyone else. Regardless, now was another perfect moment to broach the subject that brought me here, if it wasn't for her beating me to the point.

"I suppose the photograph is your attempt at some kind of quid pro quo, is it not?" she asked.

"No, but actually, I *was* hoping you'd explain exactly what's going on with me right now. Considering..."

"Considering *what*?" She finally turned and looked me in the eyes, but with the sternness of a school principal.

"Do I really need to say it?"

"Negro, please. You still don't get it, do you? In fact, you don't *need* to be offering me a photograph. What you *need* to be offering me is something else!"

"Like?"

Her eyes expanded. "Like... a *thank you*!"

"A *thank you*?"

"You're welcome."

I jittered both hands in the air—even my prosthetic. "Oh, no! That was *not* what I meant! Hell no!"

"That's okay. You wouldn't be here if you weren't thankful."

"Oh, *yes*... I would."

"Anyway, what *exactly* is going on with you?"

It was easy to tell, *this* was Phoebe Artreaux, able to shrug off any losing debate at a second's notice.

"Hmm... let's see... where should I start?" I asked. "Perhaps you can call it a case of enhanced metaphysical perception with a touch of hypnotic suggestion." I may have phrased it as a supposition, but I was *certain* of what it was.

While I stroked my chin, she shrugged hers. "Hmph. Fancy."

"Along with the ability to detect the essence of fellow Vampyrians and sensational remnants of their past humanity."

"Ooh, just as fancy! Sounds like someone has had a date with Dr. Hailu, *hmm*? And I suppose you've been paid a little visit by the Realm Walkers as well, haven't you?"

She knew the answer just by my silence, I could tell. Dr. Hailu didn't mention the Realm Walkers in our latest meeting, but I was still embarrassed having forgotten such a thing.

"Yes, you do have a lot to learn," Artreaux concluded. "Anyway, your friend is about to make an announcement." Her hand opened towards the television.

"Friend?"

On the widescreen emerged Senator Danvers Stroy, momentarily back in Southwest Louisiana among his favorite Cajun crowd, the only folks loco enough to feed his boundless ego. Artreaux *had* to have known he and I were never friends, but it was amazing how tapped-in she was to Louisiana's ongoings.

Meanwhile, Stroy's speech was already in progress: "....listen, listen!" He beckoned the crowd to silence. "We're almost there! We are almost there! And people... *my* people! You have nothing to fear! *I* delivered the monster, Landon

Levy, to the Louisiana Bureau of Investigation!" Turning away from the mic, he looked at the filled seats behind him. "Of course, with some help from my capable staff," he said before turning back to the mic. "No longer will *anyone*! I mean, *anyone*—be victimized by another of his *ilk*!" Stepping back, he paused to absorb the crowd's feverish pitch.

"What a load o' shit," I said, knowing exactly who was responsible for unleashing the same monster. "And do they even know what 'ilk' means?"

"Shh," was Artreaux's response.

And the speech continued: "That is my pledge to you, Louisiana! And *this* is my pledge to the rest of this great nation, the nation I love so dearly: only someone like *me*—can protect *you*—from any other like Landon Levy!"

"You tell 'em, Danvers!" someone from the crowd shouted.

"And that's why I, Danvers Stroy, am announcing in front of my beloved sisters and brothers of my home State— my candidacy for President—of the United States of America!"

The crowd's pitch went from feverish to raucous, while reporters squirmed through to follow-up. Meanwhile, the cameras strobed for signs, some reading: **Stroy for President!**; others reading even bolder: **DANVERS FOREVER!**— already a first name idol, with "forever" closer to the truth.

"We're in trouble," I mumbled.

"Huh!" Artreaux scoffed. "*I'm* not in trouble. You and *the world* may be in trouble, but *I'm* not in trouble! I mean, he's one shit-stain of a leader, but his entertainment value—out the fucking roof!"

"He's barely a U.S. senator, and now this!"

"Hmm… it makes sense, you know."

"How's that?"

"Making his move on the heels of a fellow Vampyrian's demise—on the back of someone else's hard work!" She raised a brow in my direction. "Shows impartiality, don't you think?" But she didn't wait for an answer. "It's brilliant when you think about it."

She was right; mixing in Levy's demise with a presidential announcement was a crafty-ass move, especially announcing it in the State of Louisiana. At this point, I rose from the chair totally disgusted as the crowd lifted his name in unison: "Danvers! Danvers! Danvers!"

But Artreaux wasted no time asking, "Where're you goin'?"

"Maybe another country, but right now, the cab's outside waiting for me."

"Well, send him on his way. Stay a while. You need fare?"

"No, I don't think that'll be a good idea."

"Yes, it would be a *great* idea! I insist! As another condition of your training, I insist! Shit, I've got guestrooms out my ass. Only my part-time maid has seen *all* of them."

Hearing her offer was shocking at first, but it shouldn't have been. A woman of Artreaux's natural beauty couldn't have been hurting for company, but as far as her own kind, she was as lonely as a widowed heiress.

"Well, I guess you do owe me at least one night's stay," I said.

"Mm hmm. Plus, if you need to get around, see that garage right there?" She pointed to a detached single-car garage, not nearly as well-dressed as her main house.

I felt my brow furrow as I stared at it. "Yeah…"

"If you really need to get around, and you need to do it in style, there's a classic silver convertible Thunderbird in there. It could use a little work—maybe a good *wax-on, wax-off* moment to *get'cha* started." She threw me a wink, along with waxing the air with her hand.

My eyes fell back on her like a tumbling avalanche; my remaining hand was now crunched into a fist. "You've got to be fucking kidding me."

However, *her* eyes had already fallen back on the television screen, her stare now stoic, but I didn't need any extrasensory gifts to feel her chuckling inside. This *witch* was at times the most insulting person I'd ever met, but her suggestion to stay wasn't a bad one.

I was almost off the back-porch and back in the house, when out the corner of my eye, I noticed Stroy silencing the crowd again. Raising his fists to the sky, he issued his final words: "With me as your president, you will witness heights never experienced by any society. Any culture. Moving forward, yes, we *will* be great! But moving forward together, we will be—*immortal*!"

The crowd roared to a crescendo, one sure to last throughout the evening and beyond. It forced me to give Phoebe Artreaux another look—now needing her more than ever to prepare for the worst to come. All in all, for me, walking the line between V-business and human justice had always been on a tightrope. But like navigating from one side of a jaded family to the next, both were important to my existence, yet each was just as treacherous.

Epilogue

Narrated by A Man Named Dalton

The date was April 2nd, 1968. I was sitting at a table in a Memphis grill a block off from a now well-known building. That building was the Lorraine Motel, and the grill was "Jim's Grill," underscored as a place of "fine foods." Fine foods, *my ass*. I would've been lucky to get a cup of good coffee, but I had to try it out. With my hair already naturally curly, just a light conk and a cap was all I needed to enter as a white boy from out-of-town.

I sat at a small two-chaired table, where I sipped my coffee without a care, as I'd done in many other white-owned establishments. A mixed kid from South Louisiana could blend in on either side of the tracks almost anywhere in those days, especially in Memphis. This highlighted the main reason I was at this particular grill on this particular afternoon. To the folks from the Leadership Conference, I *was* a kid, but I was both old enough and savvy enough to handle their recon detail. Now, I was raised a staunch Catholic, but these Baptist brothers had a mission the Catholic Church wouldn't dare touch. That's why they'd hired me, an independent security contractor, one who would have done this mission for free if asked. A very important man, a reverend, was going to be arriving the next day at that motel around the corner, and his life was dependent on whatever my ears picked up here and there. Now, this grill was actually a random choice, but with the look of a white fly on a white wall, these ears picked up all sorts of stirrings, like the two voices at the table a few feet behind me.

"How's it gonna go down, Lloyd?" The man asking the question carried a distinct rural Italian-American accent.

There was a brief pause before Lloyd, already suspected as the grill's owner, gave his answer. "Well, Frank, I gotta be honest with you—that ole boy I done picked is gettin' cold feet."

"Cold feet?" Frank blasted.

"Shhh … quiet down now."

Frank lowered his tone, but not much. "All this damn money I'm payin' you, and your boy's *'gettin' cold feet'*? You got to be out o' your fuckin' mind."

"Now, now, hold your giddy-up. I got somebody else in his stead."

"Who?"

I practically felt Lloyd looking around before whispering. "A cop buddy o' mine. He'll take that son of a gun out real quick and precise. It'll be above the law—real clean and easy."

"It better be… because if that ni**er preacher gets his way, first the sanitation workers'll get theirs. Then it'll be produce workers next, and then we'll all be fucked. Plus, there's a whole lot o' eyes on this one. This goes way above us. You know what I'm sayin'?"

"Oh yeah, I catch your point, Frank."

"You know what they say—he who controls the workers… controls the world."

Shit! I was hoping my nerves were only shaking on the inside. If not, it would have spelled the end before even finishing my coffee. So, I managed to sit content for a few minutes as Lloyd and Frank drifted on to other matters. That's when a woman's voice almost shot the fear right out of me.

"Can I get you another, hon?" Their scrawny little waitress caught me off-guard.

"No thank you, Ma'am. I'm almost done," I said along with tipping my cap.

My answer may have been polite, calm, cool and smooth, but it failed to keep the suspicious look off her face. And that's when I damned myself, having overlooked one critical rule: most white boys back then didn't address many women as "ma'am," especially those under sixty, and this one couldn't have been any more than forty-five. It was enough for me to slap all my spare change on the table and make a quick exit.

Once outside, looking over my shoulder, I saw Lloyd and Frank through the window, and the waitress leaning into Lloyd. She and Lloyd both mumbled something to each other, but with their eyes locked on me, followed by Frank turning my way with a grimace. I'd been made; I knew it.

There was another motel off the beaten path that not many others knew about. It was on the outskirts of Memphis off U.S. 61, and for secrecy's sake, I was instructed to deliver my report to members of the S.C.L.C. in person, not over the phone. No matter where these folks stayed, the F.B.I. was hooked into their lines like a third party. I was also told I'd have a room waiting—no plans of returning to any of this week's events. Afterall, why risk exposing their secret weapon to the cameras?

Now with my cohort, Aldrick Dixon, in the passenger's seat, it was going to be a ride straight back to Louisiana afterwards. More things about those days, no route was a safe one for two black men in a car, which was why Aldrick was the spotter on this mission.

"We got company about twenty-car-lengths back, Dalton," he said with his sights over our Chevy Impala's rear dash.

Glancing out the rearview, I saw the headlights of a pickup truck gaining on us. Just as I pressed the accelerator, Aldrick was patting air like it was a bus horn.

"Hold on now," he said. "Slow your roll. We don't want the cops on our asses too!"

"I don't know, Rick," I said, "we might just be better off with me sweettalking the cops than these other crazy-ass crackers!"

A few seconds later, as advised, I lifted off the pedal. "This is a bad idea, Rick."

But Aldrick had gone both deaf and mute, his eyes wide and straight ahead as that pickup caught up to just a touch from our rear bumper. Its high beams nearly blinded us both before weaving around and pulling beside us. As expected, two white boys were in the truck-cabin, the passenger staring hard, real hard, until tipping his cap as they sped on by. To this, I tipped mine back.

The sighs of relief that filled our car could have put air in all four tires. I figured they must have been unable to see Aldrick's darker skin, or else there would have surely been trouble. None of it mattered now; we were in the clear. But were we really? One more set of lights emerged over the vertical curve behind us, this time with a single siren spinning.

"Oh, shit," I mumbled.

"'Oh, shit' is right," Aldrick said. "Looks like you just got your wish."

By the time we were pulled over, the siren behind us was still strobing, but it was clear the car was marked neither sheriff, state trooper, nor police squad car. It looked all black with a man stepping out wearing a police uniform, his tag labeled, Lieutenant Clark, as he approached my open window.

I took the lead, banking on my manners to soften his mood. "Good evening, Officer! Was I doing something wrong?"

But manners didn't stop him from blinding me with his flashlight. "You in a hurry, son?"

I tried my best to hide my fear. "No, Sir, Officer. I'm pretty sure I was driving the speed limit."

Meanwhile, Aldrick sat as stiff and as silent as a cardboard cutout, enough to make the lieutenant switch off his flashlight with a nod. Again, we were in the clear—that's what I *thought*.

"I reckon you were," he said politely, just before his tone deepened. "But I heard you might've been somewhere you weren't supposed to be a little earlier. Would that be a fair assessment?"

"Sir?" Just as I'd suspected, I *had* been made.

"Why don't you and your buddy there step out o' the vehicle?" He stepped back, resting his hand on his revolver-handle. "*Real* slow."

"Why yes, Sir," I said with a glance towards my passenger.

Seeing Aldrick's head now shaking like a tuning fork, his eyes bulging, I practically read his mind saying not to do it. But I couldn't see why *not* to do "it." He knew we had to get to Johnny and the boys so we could warn them. The good reverend-doctor's life was at stake; the sanitation workers' plight was at stake; I even figured—*hell, the plight of the world as we know it was at stake*! What was one little cop's feelings going to matter in the scheme of it all? My options considered, I decided to do "it." Stomping the gas, I left Lieutenant Clark behind fanning and choking on smoke from burnt rubber.

Aldrick stopped vibrating just enough to look back. "Oh, shit!"

And I saw the same thing in my rearview: the lieutenant had drawn his weapon, firing two shots before running back to his vehicle. Shortly after, he was back in close pursuit.

"Oh, shit!" Aldrick repeated. "You better floor it now!"

Which was exactly what I did, reaching just over eighty miles-per-hour before we started drifting to the right. Along the way, my body was growing numb while my vision started to blur.

"What's happening, Dalton?   Dalton!" my partner yelled just before we went airborne.

By the grace of God, our seatbelts held us in as the Impala flipped, tumbled and disassembled until landing upright in a clearing surrounded by pine trees. It had to have been divine intervention that prevented us from smacking a tree dead-on. In the end, both of Lieutenant Clark's bullets had landed true—one in my shoulder and one in my neck. And still, I was alive. Aldrick, however, I wasn't so sure, not until he finally started moving. Fortunately, only his forehead was bloodied from the dashboard.

"Dalton…, you alright?" he asked.

He sounded groggy, but *I* was barely able to speak. "Quiet…"

There were multiple trees between us and the highway, yet I was still able to see Clark's vehicle rolling along its shoulder. Although, my timing must have been jumbled, because as soon as it stopped, it looked like he was standing in front of it at the same time—shining that bright-ass flashlight from afar. Then, inside the blur of lights, he was back in his vehicle and off to his next destination—a man obviously satisfied by his efforts.

When I looked back towards Aldrick, his face wasn't nearly as clear as before. Again, I felt my vision getting blurry, and my time coming to an end. "Rick," I muttered, "you got to get outta here and get to the reverend-doctor's boys... You gotta get the message to Johnny."

"No, Dalton," he said while grabbing my shoulder. "I can't leave you behind like this."

He even grappled my neck to try to stop the bleeding, but it was far too late.

"Rick, you got to, man. You got to..." I felt myself now wheezing out of control.

My timing must have skipped again, because as soon as I heard a loud raking noise, the passenger's seat was empty; Aldrick was no longer in it. And along with the noise, the entire Impala was shaking from side-to-side. *Damn...* I knew I'd told him to leave, but I didn't think I'd convinced him so quickly. As I focused with all I had left, I saw that empty passenger's seat again, accompanied by a ripped seatbelt and a missing door. Seconds later, someone was standing outside *my* door, but it wasn't Aldrick.

It was a chilly night for April in the South, but now breathing in my face was a creature whose breaths were almost as cool as the air; barely a puff of steam flowed. My vision cleared just enough to see a pale, somewhat human face with wide black veins pulsating, and blood dripping down its chin. And when it opened its mouth, it hissed, all of its teeth razor sharp with both canines longer and blood-stained. At that horrifying moment, I searched every piece of my past, desperately trying to decipher how I'd arrived here. One second, I was an altar boy from years ago; the next, I was here in the presence of Satan, but praying to my God for answers—praying to know what I'd done to deserve such a fate.

Despite surviving the crash, I no longer knew if God was still with me or not, yet when I closed my eyes and braced for a mauling, I heard a hideous piss-draining voice instead.

"Ahh, there's not as much fear in you as you think." The creature had actually spoken, and when I reopened my eyes, the *it*, now a *he*, spoke again while stroking his chin, but still in a piss-draining tone. "Let me see... I have to figure this out. *Hmm...*"

Placing his clawed fingers on my skull, he began to feed, but not from a bite of any kind. It wasn't my blood it sought; it was my memories, seen by him from mere contact. I actually felt the beastly monstrosity lurking around inside.

"Yes," he continued, "you're a loyal one, you are—crafty, even. I like that." He paused, massaging my scalp gently, our metaphysical connection the only thing keeping me alive at this point. "Oh, yes," he said, "you were brought here to protect a king, one whose words are far more powerful than all the human wealth in the world. One whose words may make for a very challenging day tomorrow. Yessss... very noble, you are. But humans can be a tad bit... unappreciative, can't they? For here you lie on the precipice of death for your sacrifice, yet soon to be unknown and forgotten by history. *Hmph.* I see you planned it that way. But you know what they say about plans: man comes up with one, and his maker only laughs. Something like that. But *this* maker has a plan you most definitely will agree with—enjoy even! A plan that will lift you and all our kind to the top of the world! And once it starts, you will no longer care about these piddling human melodramas they call life. You will see things differently. In fact, history will both stop and start at *your* name."

"Our kind? My name?" I wheezed. "What... in the hell... are you talking about, you ghoulish mother fucker?"

"Cute," he said. "You'll see."

He was right. Another raking noise and a ripped seatbelt later, I was suddenly lying on my back in the dirt, the creature fang-deep into my neck, sucking the life right out of me, but infusing it back into my veins, or some malady of it. It had only lasted for a few seconds, but by the end, I was undergoing a new adventure—gripped by my head and dragged deeper into the forest, all the while listening to more of the creature's ramblings.

"My name is Stroy," he said. "Just Stroy. I know *your* name. It's Dalton, Dalton Danvers, isn't it?"

That was my name, something he'd obviously seeped out of my brain while in the car. Meanwhile, his tone was now oddly playful, more like a little girl dragging a new baby doll around. "I don't like the name Dalton," he said. "Do you really like the name *Dalton*? I like Danvers, though. I *love* Danvers! Do you like the name, Danvers? Sure, you do. Who wouldn't? I think I'll name you Danvers! Danvers Stroy! I like that. I *love, love* Danvers Stroy!"

I didn't know what this creep had juiced me with, but it was already starting to sharpen my eyesight, allowing me to see Aldrick fading farther away, his body pale and motionless.

I even heard my own heart beating loudly, a mouse's heart beating in the brush, but nothing beating in Aldrick's chest. "Rick...," I gasped, but Aldrick was dead, now completely out of sight as my helpless body bounced over a hill. And with this moment, died all hopes of saving a "king," and everyone's chance for a brighter future.

ABOUT THE AUTHOR

Jay A. Harris is an award-winning novelist from Baton Rouge, Louisiana. A graduate of Louisiana State University, he also attended Southern University (Baton Rouge) and Xavier University (New Orleans) in route to ultimately achieving a bachelor's degree in civil engineering. His work career was even more varied, including engineering and project management assignments spanning the entire southeastern United States, as well as territories overseas. After an early retirement, Jay has found joy in writing fiction and plans on writing from here on. When not writing, he can be found sightseeing, exploring new restaurants, or attending a nearby film or book festival.

For more stories by Jay A. Harris, visit
jaysbooksite.com

Jay can also be followed on Facebook at:
Jay A. Harris, Novelist

Made in the USA
Columbia, SC
21 February 2024

32088154R00171